The Fairy Books

Andrew Lang

PART I—DETECTIVE STORIES FROM REAL LIFE
PART II—TRUE STORIES OF MODERN MAGIC

ANDREW LANG

PART I—DETECTIVE STORIES FROM REAL LIFE
Arthur Train
A Flight into Texas

The flight and extradition of Charles F. Dodge unquestionably involved one of the most extraordinary battles with justice in the history of the criminal law. The funds at the disposal of those who were interested in procuring the prisoner's escape were unlimited in extent, and the arch conspirator for whose safety Dodge was spirited away was so influential in political and criminal circles that he was all but successful in defying the prosecutor of New York County, even supported as the latter was by the military and judicial arm of the United States Government. For, at the time that Dodge made his escape, a whisper from Hummel was enough to make the dry bones of many a powerful and ostensibly respectable official rattle and the tongue cleave to the roof of his mouth in terror.

(The District Attorney's office in New York City is undoubtedly one of the best watch-towers known from which to observe "Real Life Detective Stories."

Arthur Train, sometime member of this prosecuting staff, has opportunity to record several of these curious and exciting "True Stories of Crime" (copyright, 1908, by Charles Scribners Sons). None yields less to fiction save in the fact that it is true, and not at all in quality of dramatic interest, than "A Flight into Texas," here given.

Readers of the newspapers a few years ago will remember the names of Abraham Hummel and Charles F. Dodge. The latter, a railroad conductor, was alleged to have committed perjury at the dictate of the former, known as one of the brightest, least scrupulous lawyers in this city. It was one of District Attorney Jerome's great ambitions to bring Hummel to justice. Here was an opportunity. If Dodge could only be forced to testify to this perjury before a court, Hummel could undoubtedly be convicted of a crime that would not only disbar him from the legal profession, but would put him in jail.

Dodge had run away and disappeared as the storm seemed about to burst. Where was he? Who could find and bring him back—against Abe Hummel's wish?—EDITOR.)

Who could accomplish that in which the law was powerless?—Hummel. Who could drive to the uttermost ends of the earth persons against whom not a shadow of suspicion had previously rested?—Hummel. Who dictated to the chiefs of police of foreign cities what they should or should not do in certain cases; and who could, at the beckoning of his little finger, summon to his dungeon-like offices in the New York Life Building, whither his firm had removed from Centre Street, the most prominent of lawyers, the most eminent of citizens?—Surely none but Hummel. And now Hummel was fighting for his own life. The only man that stood between him and the iron bars of Blackwell's Island was Charles F. Dodge—the man whom he had patted on the knee in his office and called a "Mascot," when quite in the nature of business he needed a little perjury to assist a wealthy client.

Hummel in terror called into play every resource upon which, during forty years of practice, his tiny tentacles had fastened. Who shall say that while he made a show of enjoying himself

1

nightly with his accustomed lightheartedness in the Tenderloin, he did not feel confident that in the end this peril would disappear like the others which had from time to time threatened him during his criminal career? But Hummel was fully aware of the tenacity of the man who had resolved to rid New York of his malign influence. His Nemesis was following him. In his dreams, if he ever dreamed, it probably took the shape of the square-shouldered District Attorney in the shadow of whose office building the little shyster practiced his profession. Had he been told that this Nemesis was in reality a jovial little man with a round, ruddy face and twinkling blue eyes he would have laughed as heartily as it was in his power to laugh. Yet such was the fact. A little man who looked less like a detective than a commercial traveler selling St. Peter's Oil or some other cheerful concoction, with manners as gentle and a voice as soft as a spring zephyr, who always took off his hat when he came into a business office, seemingly bashful to the point of self-effacement, was the one who snatched Charles F. Dodge from the borders of Mexico and held him in an iron grip when every influence upon which Hummel could call for aid, from crooked police officials, corrupt judges, and a gang of cutthroats under the guise of a sheriff's posse, were fighting for his release.

Jesse Blocher is not employed in New York County, and for business reasons he does not wish his present address known. When he comes to New York he occasionally drops into the writer's office for a cigar and a friendly chat about old times. And as he sits there and talks so modestly and with such quiet humor about his adventures with the Texas Rangers among the cactus-studded plains of the Lone Star State, it is hard, even for one who knows the truth, to realize that this man is one of the greatest of detectives, or rather one of the most capable, resourceful, adroit, and quick-witted knights of adventure who ever set forth upon a seemingly impossible errand.

It is unnecessary to state just how the District Attorney discovered the existence of "Jesse," as we knew him. It is enough to say that on Saturday morning, July 23, 1904, he was furnished with the proper credentials and given instructions to proceed at once to New Orleans, Louisiana, and "locate," if it were humanly possible to do so, Charles F. Dodge, under indictment for perjury, and potentially the chief witness against Abraham H. Hummel, on a charge of conspiracy. He was told briefly and to the point that, in spite of the official reports from the police headquarters of both New York City and New Orleans to the contrary, there was reason to believe that Dodge was living, although not registered, as a guest at the St. Charles Hotel in the latter city. A partial and inaccurate description of Dodge was given him and he was warned to use extreme caution to prevent any knowledge of his mission from being made known. Once Dodge had been discovered, he was to keep him under surveillance and wire New York immediately.

Accordingly, Jesse left the city upon the same day at 4.45 P. M. and arrived two days later, at 9.15 on Monday morning, at New Orleans, where he went directly to the St. Charles Hotel, registered, and was assigned to room Number 547 on the fifth floor. Somewhere in the hotel Dodge was secreted. The question was how to find him. For an hour Jesse sat in the hotel foyer and meditatively watched the visitors come and go, but saw no sign of his quarry. Then he arose, put on his hat, and hunted out a stationery store where for two cents he bought a bright-red envelope. He then visited a ticket-scalper's office, secured the owner's business card, and wrote a note on its back to Dodge, offering him cheap transportation to any point that he might desire. Armed with this he returned to the hotel, walked to the desk, glanced casually over a number of telegrams exposed in a rack and, when the clerk turned his back, placed the note, addressed to

2

Charles F. Dodge, unobserved, upon the counter. The office was a busy one, guests were constantly depositing their keys and receiving their mail, and, even as Jesse stood there watching developments, the clerk turned round, found the note, and promptly placed it in box Number 420. The very simple scheme had worked, and quite unconsciously the clerk had indicated the number of the room occupied by Dodge.

Jesse lost no time in ascending to the fourth floor, viewed room Number 420, returned to the desk, told the clerk that he was dissatisfied with the room assigned him, and requested that he be given either room Number 421, 423, or 425, one of which he stated that he had occupied on a previous visit. After some discussion the clerk allotted him room Number 423, which was almost directly opposite that occupied by Dodge, and the detective at once took up his task of watching for the fugitive to appear.

Within the hour the door opened and Dodge and a companion, who subsequently proved to be E. M. Bracken, alias "Bradley," an agent employed by Howe and Hummel, left the room, went to the elevator, and descended to the dining-room upon the second floor. Jesse watched until they were safely ensconced at breakfast and then returned to the fourth floor where he tipped the chambermaid, told her that he had left his key at the office, and induced her to unlock the door of room Number 420, which she did under the supposition that Jesse was the person who had left the chamber in Dodge's company. The contents of the room convinced Jesse that he had found Dodge, for he discovered there two grips bearing Dodge's name as well as several letters on the table addressed to him. The detective returned to the hall and had a little talk with the maid.

"The old gentleman with you has been quite sick," she said. "How is he to-day?"

"He is some better," answered Jesse.

"Yes, he does look better to-day," she added, "but he sho'ly was powerful sick yesterday. Why, he hasn't been out of his room befo' fo' five or six days."

This statement was corroborated by Dodge's physical appearance, for he looked haggard and worn.

Jesse was now confident that he had found Dodge, in spite of the reports of the New Orleans police to the contrary, and he was also reasonably sure that the fugitive was too sick to leave the hotel immediately. He therefore telegraphed his superiors that he had discovered Dodge and that the latter was ill at the St. Charles Hotel.

At three o'clock in the afternoon Jesse received a wire from New

York as follows:

"New Orleans police department claims party not there. Left for Mexico three weeks ago. Ascertain correct destination and wire at once."

Jesse at once replied:

"No question as to identity and presence here at this time."

He now took up the task of keeping his quarry under absolute surveillance day and night, which duty from that moment he continued for a period of nearly ten months.

During the remainder of the afternoon and throughout the night Dodge and Bracken remained in room Number 420, and during the evening were visited by several strangers, including a plain- clothes officer from the New Orleans Police Headquarters. Little Hummel, dining in Long Acre Square in the glare of Broadway, was pressing some invisible button that transmitted the power of his influence even to the police government of a city two thousand miles away.

3

The following day, January 26th, at about 8.40 in the morning, Dodge and Bracken descended to the lobby. Bracken departed from the hotel, leaving Dodge to pay the bill at the cashier's window and Jesse heard him order a cab for the 11.30 A. M. Sunset Limited on the Southern Pacific Railroad and direct that his baggage be removed from his room. Jesse did the same.

In the meantime Bracken returned and promptly at 11 A. M. left for the railroad station in a cab with Dodge. Jesse followed in another. As the two passed through the gates the detective caught a glimpse of Dodge's ticket and saw that it had been issued by the Mexican National Railway. Retiring to the telegraph office in the station he wired New York as follows:

"Bird flying.—Sunset Limited. Destination not known. I am with him."

He then hastily purchased a ticket to Houston, Texas, and boarded the train. Dodge's companion had bidden him good-by as the engine started, and Jesse's task now became that of ferreting out Dodge's destination. After some difficulty he managed to get a glimpse of the whole of the fugitive's ticket and thus discovered that he was on his way to the City of Mexico, via Eagle Pass, Texas, while from the Pullman conductor he learned that Dodge had secured sleeping- car accommodation as far as San Antonio, Texas, only.

So far all was well. He knew Dodge but Dodge did not know him, and later on in the afternoon he had the satisfaction of a long talk with his quarry in the observation car where they amiably discussed together current events and argued politics with the same vehemence as if they had been commercial travellers thrown fortuitously into each other's company. Dodge, however, cleverly evaded any reference to his destination.

When the train reached Morgan City, Louisiana, at 3 P. M., which was the first stop, Jesse wired New York as follows:

"On Sunset Limited with friend. He has transportation to the City of Mexico, via Eagle Pass, where I am now journeying with him. Answer to Beaumont, Texas."

Later in the afternoon he sent an additional message from

Lafayette, Louisiana:

"Have seen transportation of friend and am positive of destination."

Dodge was occupying Section 3 of the sleeping car "Capitola," and, as became an invalid, retired early.

At Beaumont Jesse failed to receive any reply to his various messages, and when the train arrived at Houston no word came from New York until it was almost the time of departure. Waiting until practically the last moment Jesse hurried through the gates of the Union Station at Houston and bought a ticket to San Antonio. As he was leaving the ticket window Night Chief of Police John Howard and two officers came hurrying up inquiring anxiously for "Mr. Jesse." The reenforcements had arrived.

Outside on the track "The Sunset Limited" was just getting under way. The first frantic puffs were being vomited from the funnel. Inside Dodge was sleeping peacefully in his berth. Jesse, accompanied by Chief Howard, hurried up to the conductor who was about to swing on to the steps of the sleeper, and ordered him to hold the train till the fugitive could be removed. After some argument the conductor grumblingly complied and Dodge was aroused from pleasant dreams of the "Creole Quarter" to the cold reality of being dragged out of bed by a policeman. He was unceremoniously hustled out of the sleeping car into a carriage and taken to Headquarters where he admitted his identity and remarked:

"I know what I am wanted for, but I will never return to New York."

In his grip was found the sum of $1,563.15, as well as numerous letters from the law firm of Howe and Hummel, and a quantity of newspaper clippings relative to his case.

Dodge pleaded with Chief Howard not to lock him up, urging that he was a sick man and offering a goodly sum if he might be taken to a hotel and guarded for the remainder of the night. But what "went" in New Orleans did not "go" in Houston, and the best that Dodge could get for himself was a cot in the "Ladies' Detention Room" on the second floor of the jail.

Early the following morning Jesse visited Police Headquarters and for the first time met George Ellis, Chief of Police of Houston, for whom he will always have a feeling of deep gratitude for his enthusiastic cooperation and loyalty in the many stirring events that followed. Dodge now received a telegram from New York, which was submitted to Jesse before reaching the prisoner, to the effect that Howe and Hummel were sending on an attorney to aid the fugitive in resisting extradition, and informing him that they had employed Messrs. Hunt and Meyers as attorneys to look out for his welfare. These last immediately jumped in medias res and on the afternoon of the same day secured a writ of habeas corpus from Norman J. Kitrell, District Judge of Harris County, Texas, returnable the following morning.

The next day, January 28th, Kitrell released Dodge from custody.

Jesse had anticipated this and immediately swore out another warrant with the result that the prisoner was rearrested before he left the courtroom.

Meantime the Dodge interests retained another firm of lawyers, Messrs. Andrews and Ball, who, on the following day, secured a second writ of habeas corpus from Judge Ashe.

The result of the first engagement thus being a draw, counsel on both sides agreed that this writ should not be returnable for six days. During this period District Attorney Jerome employed Messrs. Baker, Botts, Parker and Garwood to represent him and secured from Governor Odell at Albany a requisition on Governor Lanham of Texas for the extradition of the prisoner, which he entrusted to Detective Sergeant Herlihy of the New York Police. Herlihy reached Houston with the papers on the evening of January 30th, and on the same train with him came Abraham Kaffenburgh, a member of the law firm of Howe and Hummel and a nephew of the latter. Likewise also came Bracken, still styling himself "E. M. Bradley," and from now on Bracken was the inseparable companion, guide, philosopher, and friend (?) of the unfortunate Dodge, whose continued existence upon this earth had become such a menace to the little lawyer in New York.

Herlihy, accompanied by Judge Garwood, proceeded direct to Austin where they found Dodge already represented by Messrs. Andrews and Ball who, at the hearing before Governor Lanham, made a strong effort to induce that executive to refuse to honor the requisition of the Governor of New York. This effort failed and Governor Lanham issued his warrant, but Herlihy had no sooner returned to Houston for the purpose of taking possession of the prisoner than he was served with an injunction enjoining him, together with Chief of Police Ellis, from taking Dodge into custody, pending a hearing upon a new habeas corpus which had been issued by Judge Waller T. Burns of the United States District Court for the Southern District of Texas. This new writ was returnable February 9th.

After exhaustive but futile argument by the counsel for Dodge, Judge Burns remanded the prisoner to Herlihy's custody to be returned to the State of New York, but this decision had no sooner been rendered than an appeal was taken therefrom by Dodge's lawyers, and the prisoner released upon bail fixed at twenty thousand dollars.

During this period Dodge was quartered under guard at the Rice Hotel in Houston, and the day following the argument the twenty- thousand-dollars bail was put up in cash and Dodge released from custody.

In the meantime, however, Jesse, knowing that no sum, however large, would deter Hummel from spiriting Dodge out of the country, had made his arrangements to secure a new extradition warrant from the Governor of Texas, so that if the prisoner did succeed in getting beyond the Southern District of the Federal Court of Texas, he could be seized and conveyed to New York.

Of course someone had to keep watch over Dodge while Jesse hurried to Austin to see the Governor, and it was decided to leave Sergeant Herlihy, re-enforced by a number of local detectives for that purpose. But while the watchful Jesse was away, Bracken proceeded to get busy in the good old Howe and Hummel fashion. Lots of people that Herlihy had never seen before turned up and protested that he was the finest fellow they had ever met. And as Herlihy was, in fact, a good fellow, he made them welcome and dined and wined at their expense until he woke up in the Menger Hotel in San Antonio and inquired where he was.

Jesse meantime had returned from Austin to discover that Dodge with his companions, Kaffenburgh and Bracken, had slipped out of Houston early in the morning of February 11th, after disposing of Herlihy and eluding the watchfulness of Herlihy's assistants. Hummel was leading and by ten o'clock the next morning Dodge and his comrades were on board an English merchantman lying in the harbor of Galveston. Later in the same day the Hummel interests chartered from the Southern Pacific Railroad for the sum of three thousand dollars the sea-going tug Hughes, to which Dodge was now transferred for the purpose of being conveyed to the port of Tampico in the Republic of Mexico.

But here Hummel's wires became crossed with Jerome's, and unfortunately for the little lawyer, the persons from whom the tug had been leased turned out to be closely allied with the prosecution's interests, with the result that the captain of the tug was instructed by his superiors under no consideration to put into any Mexican port, but on the contrary, to delay his departure from the harbor of Galveston for a period of two days and then to proceed only as far as Brownsville, Texas, where he should compel the debarkation of the fugitive. The captain, who was a good sport as well as a good officer, promptly threw himself into the part and told Bracken and Kaffenburgh that it was evident from the barometer that a severe storm was approaching (which must have had a sinister implication to these two unfortunate gentlemen), and that he could not think of putting to sea. Once the "storm" had blown over, the tug started out across the blue waters of the Gulf of Mexico. But now Bracken and Kaffenburgh were informed for the first time it was impossible to consider putting into any port of the Republic of Mexico, since to do so would cause international complications and compel the revocation of the captain's license. In desperation the Hummel interests offered the captain five thousand dollars in cash to disregard his instructions and put into Tampico, but the worthy sea-dog was adamant. It was probably worth five thousand dollars to him to see three gentry of this pattern so much put about.

While Dodge and his accomplices were dallying in the harbor of Galveston, Jesse was taking advantage of his opportunity to proceed at once by railroad to Alice, Texas, which at that time was the furthermost southern point reached by any railway in the direction of Brownsville. On his arrival, he at once applied to Captain John R. Hughes, commanding Company D of the Texas Rangers, who received him with great joy and ordered a detachment of the Rangers to meet the tug at Point Isabelle at the mouth of the Rio Grande River on the border of Mexico. In the meantime, Jesse started on a toilsome stage journey to Brownsville, across one hundred and seventy miles of desert, which occupied two days and nights, and necessitated his going without sleep for that period. During the trip Jesse heard no word of English and had as his associates only Mexican cattlemen. Every fifteen miles a fresh relay of broncos was hitched to the stage and after a few moments' rest the misery began again.

Jesse had been hurrying toward Brownsville by stage while Dodge, Kaffenburgh, and Bracken were landing at Point Isabelle, where they were kept under close surveillance by Sergeant Tom Ross of the Rangers. Thence they took the train to Brownsville, registering at the Miller House under the assumed names of C. F. Dougherty, A. Koontzman, and E. M. Barker, all of Oklahoma. But, although they knew it not, Sergeant Tom was at their elbow, and had Dodge attempted to cross the border into Mexico he would instantly have been placed under arrest.

As Brownsville was within the Southern District of the Federal Court of Texas, Jesse decided not to arrest Dodge until he should actually attempt flight, and when Dodge and his companions, on the following morning, February 15th, entered the stage (the same upon which Jesse had arrived) and started for Alice, Jesse and Tom Ross procured the best horses they could find and started after them, keeping just in sight of the stage. Dodge's intention in making this move was to take the Mexican International Railway at Alice and cross over to Mexico via Laredo.

Jesse and Ross covered the seventy-four miles from Brownsville to Santa La Cruz Ranch by four in the afternoon, which was fairly strenuous work for a New York detective, and here found themselves so sore and exhausted from their ride that they were glad to hire a pair of horses and buggy with which to complete the journey to Alice. Luckily they were able to get into telephonic communication with various ranch owners along the road and arrange to have fresh relays of horses supplied to them every twenty miles, and here also Jesse called up Captain Hughes at Alice, and suggested that he substitute for the regular night clerk at the City Hotel one of the privates of the Rangers by the name of Harrod.

Dodge and his companions arrived in Alice on February 17th, and, as Jesse had anticipated, repaired at once to the City Hotel, where, inasmuch as they were dry from the dust of their trip and depressed by lack of society, they entered at once into an enthusiastic and confidential friendship with the man behind the counter in the hotel office, sublimely ignorant that they were unfolding to a member of the Texas Rangers all their most secret intentions. Harrod was just as glad to see Dodge as Dodge apparently was to see Harrod, and kindly offered to assist the fugitive to get into Mexico in any way that the latter desired. Dodge, for his part, took advantage of his usefulness to the extent of requesting him to purchase them railroad tickets, the plan being to leave Alice the following morning for Monterey, Mexico. Three hours after the stage bearing Dodge and his party pulled up at the City Hotel, Tom Ross and Jesse drove in behind a pair of fagged-out broncos at two in the morning. Jesse had had no sleep of any sort and no proper nourishment for five days, and had just strength enough left to drag himself up one flight of stairs and tumble into bed, from which he did not emerge for many hours.

In the meantime day broke and Dodge, Kaffenburgh, and Bracken, having breakfasted, drove comfortably down to the International Railway Station and settled themselves in the smoker, but they had no sooner given this direct evidence of their intention before Captain Hughes entered and placed Dodge under arrest. The latter's surprise may be appreciated when it is stated that from the time the three had left Houston, they had no idea that they were being followed and believed that they had completely foiled Jesse and his assistants.

While Jesse had been chasing Dodge across the desert, his lawyers had not been idle and had secured at Austin another extradition warrant from Governor Lanham, who, on receiving news of the arrest, promptly instructed Captain Hughes by wire to assume charge of the prisoner and to deliver him into the hands of the New York officer to be conveyed to New York.

There now began such a legal battle as the State of Texas had never known. Hummel had been forced into his last ditch and was fighting desperately for life. Through Kaffenburgh he at once applied for a new writ of habeas corpus in Nueces County and engaged counsel at Corpus Christi to assist in fighting for the release of the prisoner. Precisely as Hummel had intended, Chief Wright of Nueces rode into Alice and demanded the prisoner from Captain Hughes. As Hummel had NOT intended, Captain Hughes refused to surrender the prisoner and told Chief Wright to go to—well, he told him that he intended to obey his commander-in-chief, the Governor of Texas.

On February 20th, Hummel, through Kaffenburgh, attempted to get another writ of habeas corpus in Bee County, and promptly the Bee chief came buzzing over and demanded Dodge, but to him Hughes replied even as he had spoken to Wright.

Excitement in Alice had now reached such a pitch that Judge Burns, of the Federal Court, in Houston, ordered United States Marshal John W. Vann, of Alice, to assume charge of the prisoner. The indomitable Hughes, however, paid no more attention to the United States Marshal than he had to the local chiefs. But the situation was so delicate and the clash of authority might so easily have resulted in bloodshed that it was finally agreed by all parties that the best thing to do was to have the prisoner returned to Houston in the JOINT custody of Captain Hughes of the Rangers and the United States Marshal.

Jesse, through his counsel, in proper course, made application to forfeit Dodge's bond and remand him to jail, but the Hummel attorneys finally induced the Court, on the plea that to confine Dodge in jail would be detrimental to his already badly impaired health, to permit the prisoner to go free on a greatly increased bond, nevertheless restricting his movements to Harris County, Texas.

While Jesse had fought a winning battle up to this point he was at the end of his resources so far as the extradition of the prisoner was concerned, for Dodge was now at liberty, pending the decisions upon the habeas corpus proceedings of the United States Circuit Court of Appeals at Fort Worth, and the United States Supreme Court at Washington. But his orders were to BRING DODGE BACK TO New York. Hence, with the aid of some new men sent him from the North, he commenced an even closer surveillance of the prisoner than ever before by both day and night.

Meantime Kaffenburgh departed for New York, fleeing from the wrath of Judge Burns, who had issued a summons for him for contempt of the Federal Court on the ground that he had induced Dodge to attempt to jump his bond. In place of the blustering Kaffenburgh was sent another member of the famous law firm of Howe and Hummel, David May, an entirely different type of man. May was as mild as a day in June—as urbane as Kaffenburgh had been insolent. He fluttered into Houston like a white dove of peace with the proverbial olive branch in his mouth. From now on the tactics employed by the representatives of Hummel were conciliatory in the extreme. Mr. May, however, did not long remain in Houston, as it was apparent that there was nothing to be done by either side pending the action of the courts, and in any event Dodge was abundantly supplied with local counsel. The time had now come when Hummel must have begun to feel that the fates were against him and that a twenty-year term in state prison was a concrete possibility even for him.

In the meantime, Dodge and Bracken had taken up their headquarters at the Rice Hotel in the most expensive suite of rooms in the house, a new scheme for getting the prisoner beyond the reach of the New York courts apparently having been concocted. Dodge was now indulged in every conceivable luxury and vice. He was plunged into every sort of excess, there was no debauchery which Bracken could supply that was not his and their rapid method of existence was soon the talk of the county and continued to be so for ten long months. There is more than one way to kill a cat and more than one method of wiping out the only existing witness against a desperate man striving to escape the consequences of crime.

Dodge's daily routine was somewhat as follows: He never slept at his own hotel, but arose in the morning between ten and eleven o'clock, when he was at once visited by Bracken and supplied with numerous drinks in lieu of the breakfast for which he never had any desire. At noon the two would have luncheon with more drinks. In the afternoon they would retire to the poolrooms and play the races, and, when the races were over, they would then visit the faro banks and gamble until midnight or later. Later on they would proceed to another resort on Louisiana Street where Dodge really lived. Here his day may be said to have begun and here he spent most of his money, frequently paying out as much as fifty dollars a night for wine and invariably ending in a beastly state of intoxication. It is quite probable that never in the history of debauchery has any one man ever been so indulged in excesses of every sort for the same period of time as Dodge was during the summer and fall of 1904. The fugitive never placed his foot on mother earth. If they were going only a block, Bracken called for a cab, and the two seemed to take a special delight in making Jesse, as Jerome's representative, spend as much money in cab hire as possible. The Houston jehus never again experienced so profitable a time as they did during Dodge's wet season; and the life of dissipation was continued until, from time to time, the prisoner became so weak from its effects that he was forced to go under the care of a physician. A few days of abstinence always restored his vitality and he would then start out upon another round of pleasure.

During this period Jesse maintained a close and vigilant personal espionage over the prisoner. For over ten months he slept less than four hours each day, his fatigue being increased by the constant apprehension of treachery among his own men, and the necessity of being ever on the alert to prevent some move on the part of the defense to spirit the prisoner away. During the summer attempts were repeatedly made to evade the vigilance of Jesse and his men and several desperate dashes were frustrated by them, including one occasion when Bracken succeeded in rushing Dodge as far as Galveston, where they were forced to abandon their design.

From time to time Bracken would disappear from Houston for a week or ten days, stating on his return that he had been to New York, after which there was invariably some new move to get the prisoner away. Time and space prevent giving a detailed account of all the marches and counter-marches that took place in this battle of wit against wit.

In August, 1904, Bracken made one of his periodical visits to New York, and when he returned sought out Jesse and said: "Blocher, you might as well be a good fellow and get yours while you can. I mean that Dodge is not going back to New York, even if it cost a million dollars to prevent it." A few days later Bracken sent a gambler named Warner to Jesse, who offered the latter thirty-five hundred dollars to get "lost" long enough for the prisoner to slip over to Mexico. Acting upon the advice of his attorney, Jesse encouraged this attempt, under the belief that if he could get the Hummel forces in the position of having attempted to bribe him the prisoner's bail

9

could then be forfeited and Dodge himself taken into custody. Hummel became wary, however, and apparently abandoned for the time the idea of bribery. Later on Bracken again disappeared. On his return a marked change was noticeable in his demeanor and Jesse observed that he was in constant consultation with Dodge, from which the detective drew the inference that some last desperate move was to be made towards the escape of the prisoner.

On one occasion Jesse saw Bracken showing Dodge a map and some drawings on paper, which so excited his suspicions that he followed the two with unremitting assiduity, and within a day or two was rewarded through Bracken's carelessness with an opportunity for going through the latter's coat pockets in the billiard room. Here he found a complete set of plans worked out in every detail for spiriting the prisoner from San Antonio into Mexico during the State Fair. These plans were very elaborate, every item having been planned out from the purchase of tickets, and passing of baggage through the customs, to hotel accommodation in the City of Mexico and Tampico, and steamship tickets from Tampico to Europe.

The plan had been to secure permission from the Court for Dodge to leave Houston long enough ostensibly to attend the fair at San Antonio and to "lose" him during the excitement and crowded condition of the city at that time.

It is, of course, needless to say that these plans were abandoned when Bracken discovered that Jesse had been forewarned.

Almost immediately thereafter the Circuit Court of Appeals at Fort Worth, Texas, decided one of the habeas corpus cases adversely to Dodge, but it still permitted him to retain his liberty pending the final determination of the questions involved by the Supreme Court at Washington.

The Hummel forces were apparently losing hope, however, for early in October another attempt was made to bribe Jesse. Bracken entered his room one evening and informed him that he could get his own price if he would only be a good fellow, and even went so far as to exhibit a quantity of money which he stated was twenty-five thousand dollars. The only result of this offer was to lead Jesse to redouble his precautions, for he argued that the situation must indeed be acute when such an offer could be deemed worth while. Thereafter it was obvious that the revelry of Dodge and his companions was on the increase. Accordingly Jesse added to his force of assistants.

On December 2, 1904, Nathaniel Cohen, another member of the firm of Howe and Hummel, arrived at Houston, and the next day the Supreme Court at Washington decided the appeal in the habeas corpus against the prisoner, who was at once ordered by Judge Burns into the custody of United States Marshall William M. Hansen.

Things looked black indeed for Dodge and blacker still for Hummel. How the little attorney, eating his midday lunch four thousand miles away, at Pontin's restaurant on Franklin Street, must have trembled in his patent leather boots! His last emissary, Cohen, at once procured an assistant by the name of Brookman and with him proceeded to Wharton County, Texas, where they secured a new writ of habeas corpus and induced the local sheriff, one Rich, to swear in a posse comitatus of one hundred men for the purpose of coming to Houston to take the prisoner by force of arms out of the hands of the United States Marshal.

This was one of the most daring and desperate attempts made in recent years to frustrate the law. Jesse believes that the real object of this posse was to precipitate a fight between themselves and the Federal authorities. It is not inconceivable that in such an event Dodge might either have escaped or been killed. The men composing the posse were of the most desperate character, and consisted largely of the so-called "feud factions" of Wharton County, known as "The Wood

Peckers" and "The Jay Birds." Jesse has been informed, on what he regards as reliable authority, that this move cost the Hummel forces fifteen thousand dollars and that each member of the posse received one hundred dollars for his contemplated services in the "rescue" of the prisoner. But civil war, even on a small scale, cannot be indulged in without some inkling of the facts becoming known to the authorities, and prior to the receipt of the mandate of the Supreme Court, Judge Burns ordered the prisoner removed to Galveston for safe keeping.

Thus the long, expensive, and arduous struggle came finally to an end, for Judge Burns in due course ordered that Charles F. Dodge should be conveyed to New York in the personal custody of the United States Marshal and delivered by him to the New York authorities "within the borders of that State." Such an order was, of course, exceedingly unusual, if not almost unheard of, but it was rendered absolutely necessary by the powerful influence and resources, as well as the unscrupulous character, of those interested in securing Dodge's disappearance.

In order to thwart any plans for releasing the prisoner by violence or otherwise, and to prevent delay through the invoking of legal technicalities, Hansen and Jesse decided to convey Dodge to New York by water, and on the 16th of December the marshal and his five deputies boarded a Mallory Line steamer at Galveston and arrived in New York with their prisoner on the evening of December 23d.

Dodge reached New York a physical wreck. How he was induced to tell the whole truth after he had pleaded guilty to the charge against him is a story in itself. A complete reaction from his dissipation now occurred and for days his life was despaired of. Jesse, too, was, as the expression is, "all in," and the only persons who were still able to appreciate the delights of New York were the stalwart marshal and his boys, who for some time were objects of interest as they strolled along Broadway and drank "deep and hearty" in the cafes. To the assistants in the District Attorney's office they were heroes and were treated as such.

How Dodge finally testified against Hummel on the witness stand has already been told. As they say downtown, if Jerome had never done anything else, he would have "made good" by locking up Abe Hummel. No one ever believed he would do it. But Jerome never would have locked up Hummel without Jesse. And, as Jesse says with a laugh, leaning back in his chair and taking a long pull on his cigar, "I guess I would not do it again—no, I WOULD not do it again for all the money you could give me. The wonder is that I came out of it alive." When the reader comes to think about it he will probably agree with him.

P. H. Woodward

Adventures in the Secret Service of the Post-Office Department*

* The author of the pages that follow was chief special agent of the Secret Service of the United States Post-Office Department during pioneer and romantic days. The curious adventures related are partly from his own observation, and partly from the notebooks of fellow officers, operating in many sections of the Country.

The stories are true, although, of course, justice demands that in some cases persons and places be usually disguised under fictitious names.

The stories have interest not only for their exciting play of honest wits against dishonest, but also for the cautions they sound against believing things "too good to be true" from the pen of strangers.

There is a class of post-office thieves who make a specialty of rifling the registered letters that pass through their hands in transit on journeys of greater or less length. Some of them have managed operations very shrewdly, in the evident belief that they had discovered an infallible method for doing the work and at the same time escaping detection. Too late they generally learn by sad experience that no patents can be taken out for the protection of crime.

In this class of cases something tangible always remains to exhibit the peculiar style of workmanship belonging to each; and it would often surprise the uninitiated to learn how many traits of character, what indexes of habit and vocation, can be picked up by careful study of the minute points presented for inspection. Unless, however, an agent cultivates a taste for thoroughness even to details and trifles that might at first view appear utterly insignificant, he will never succeed in interpreting the hieroglyphics.

At intervals of two or three weeks, beginning in the summer of 1871, registered packages passing to and fro from Chicago to a town in the interior of Dakota Territory, which for convenience will be called Wellington,—though that was not its name,—were reported to the department as rifled. As the season wore on, the complaints increased in frequency. Under the old method of doing business at headquarters, which often amounted practically to a distribution of the cases about equally "among the boys," the agent stationed at Chicago received most of them at first; then a part were sent to an agent in Iowa; and as the number multiplied, Furay, at Omaha, was favored with an occasional sprinkling. Under the present more perfect system, great care is taken to group together all the complaints growing out of each series of depredations, to locate the seat of trouble by comparisons carefully made in the department itself, and to give everything bearing on the subject to the officer specifically charged with the investigation.

March came around before Mr. Furay found time to give personal attention to this particular thief. He then passed over the route to Wellington, eighty miles by stagecoach from the nearest railroad station, with ten intermediate offices. All the packages remained over night at Sioux City, Iowa, a fact sufficiently important to invite close scrutiny; but the detective soon became satisfied that he must look elsewhere for the robber. His suspicions were next directed to another office, where also the mails lay over night; but the postmaster bore a countenance so open and honest that he too was eliminated from the problem.

He continued on to Wellington, skirmishing along the line, and observing the faces of the postmasters; but these studies in physiognomy threw no light on the mystery, as the officials of the department on the route, though far removed from central supervision, seemed to be all that their affectionate uncle at Washington could wish. On the return trip the detective was equally observant and equally perplexed. At that season the stage stopped for the night at Hannibal; but there, likewise, the postmaster shared the honest looks that seemed to prevail through eastern Dakota.

Proceeding on, the passengers dined at Raven's Nest, where one Michael Mahoney, Sr., kept a small store and the post-office, running also—with the aid of a young son and a son-in-law—a farm. The store was managed by Michael Mahoney, Jr., a married son, who happened to be absent both when the special agent went up and when he returned. The face of the old man indicated that he was vicious, ignorant, and unscrupulous; but clearly he was not sharp enough to execute nice work like that under investigation.

With the exception of a general knowledge of the offices, the special agent returned but little wiser for the trip, and concluded, as the best that could be done under the circumstances, to allow the bird to flutter a little longer before renewing the hunt. Meanwhile the thief grew more reckless, and the papers that came to Mr. Furay, though covering a fraction only of the depredations, located the thief on the lower end of the route, within fifty miles of the terminus.

During the summer one or two other agents took up the matter cursorily, but made no discoveries. In the meantime Mr. Furay was kept too busily occupied with a succession of important cases in Nebraska to give much thought to the outlying territory of Dakota. At length, in September, he went carefully over the papers that had accumulated during his late prolonged absences, and soon knew exactly where to look for the chap who had so long plundered the public with impunity.

For some time Chicago had been closing registered package envelopes with wax, which, on this route at least, effectually secured them against molestation. Imitating the example, Camden, Dakota, began to do the same; but, having no seal suitable for the purpose, improvised a substitute by using the flat surface of a rasp.

Camden placed the wax near each end of the envelope, which materially interfered with the game of the thief, because it was just here that he operated. Evidently piqued that a rural postmaster should presume to outwit him, he studied hard to devise some means for opening these particular packages without leaving such traces of his handiwork as would attract the notice of other officials through whose hands they might subsequently pass. The effort was crowned with a measurable degree of success, for Mr. Furay, at the general overhauling referred to, was the first to discover that the seal had been tampered with.

As it was necessary to break one of the seals, the object of the robber was to restore it as nearly as possible to its original appearance; and to effect this he used a dampened thimble, rolling it over the wax while the latter was hot. There was but one envelope of the kind in the lot, but it told the whole story to the eye that could penetrate its meaning. As the thimble passed along the edge, it left the mark of the rim, then a smooth, narrow band, followed by pointed elevations closely resembling continuous lines, thus:

========= ——————— …….. ……..

On the opposite side of the same seal the wax flattened out so as to cover a good deal of surface; and, to give it the desired appearance, the manipulator resorted to the thimble again, but this time USED A DIFFERENT ONE, the indentations on the surface being perceptibly finer and more shallow.

The violation of that single seal betrayed the thief, for the detective at once inferred that the job was done in a store where the operator had access to a variety of thimbles. Only one was required; and no person but a merchant would be likely to have more than one within convenient reach. In a store, however, it would be natural to take down a boxful, and place it on the counter, to be selected from at random. One is picked up, used, and thrown back. The operator now finds another spot that requires attention, and without waiting to hunt for the thimble that has already served as a seal,—for the wax is cooling and no time must be lost,—grasps the first that comes to hand, too absorbed in the main issue to give a thought to what would pass as an insignificant subsidiary trifle. No rascal is sharp enough to guard every point,—a general fact that illustrates over and over again, in the experience of man, the seminal truth that in a mercenary and physical as well as in a high and spiritual, sense there is neither wisdom nor profit outside of the limits of absolute integrity and unflinching uprightness.

The detective laid aside the papers with a light heart, knowing that at last he was complete master of the situation. Below Camden on the infested route the post-office was kept in a store at two points only, and in one of those no thimbles were sold. The clew pointed unerringly to

Raven's Nest as the spot where alone the requisite conditions to account for the imprint on the violated seal were to be found. Thither the officer accordingly went; and the moment his eye rested on Michael Mahoney, Jr., he recognized the heaven-branded features of a thief.

Returning to Sioux City, he telegraphed to another agent, who had a large number of the cases growing out of the robberies, to come on at once. The two men took stations, one on each side of Raven's Nest, and in thirty hours they arrested the youthful criminal, who in the interval stole four decoy letters, and paid a portion of the contents to one of the officers who was testing him.

Mr. Furay collected from the thief and his relatives the full amount stolen from the mails during the entire continuance of the depredations, restoring the money to the rightful owners dollar for dollar. Young Mahoney made a written confession, supplemented by three or four codicils relating to items which, to use his own language, "at first did not to me occur." He was tried the following February, and sentenced to the penitentiary for the term of three years.

Within fifteen days from the time when the doors of the prison were closed upon the son, the villainous old father, acting perhaps on the theory that no two shots ever strike in exactly the same place, began also to rob the mails. In due time Mr. Furay again appeared on the scene and took the old reprobate away a prisoner. When the trial came on, a material witness for the prosecution happened to be absent, the lack of whose testimony proved fatal to the case, for after hanging a day and a night, the jury brought in a verdict of acquittal.

AN ERRING SHEPHERD

The ingenuity and perseverance of the fraternity of swindlers is only equaled by the gullibility and patience of their dupes. During the flush times that followed the war, immense fortunes were suddenly acquired by a class of cheats who operated on the credulity of the public through gift enterprises, lotteries, and other kindred schemes. Most of the large concerns established their headquarters in New York City, flooding the entire country, particularly the South and West, with lithographic circulars, written apparently with the pen for the exclusive benefit of the recipient, and showing how fortunes could be securely made by remitting specified sums to the houses in question. Some of the bogus firms simply pocketed the cash of correspondents without pretending to render any equivalent whatever; while others, no more honest, but a little more politic, sent forth worthless jewelry and other stuff by the bushel.

One of the most villainous and at the same time successful devices was built up on the offer of counterfeit currency at a heavy discount. In substance, the circulars, emanating from different parties, and from the same parties under different names, were all alike. They usually began with an insidious compliment to the person addressed, to the effect that from trustworthy sources the writer had heard of him as a man of more than ordinary capacity and shrewdness, and, emboldened by the high estimate placed upon his abilities by persons well qualified to judge, had selected him as the very individual to aid in securing a fortune for both with "absolute safety." The circular usually goes on to state that the writer is a first-class engraver,—indeed "one of the most expert in the United States,"—while his partner is a first-class printer. Hence the firm possess unrivaled facilities for imitating the national currency. The recipient is particularly cautioned to beware of a class of miscreants who infest the city of New York and advertise throughout the country the goods that he manufactures, but send nothing except rubbish. The "original Doctor Jacobs" excoriates unmercifully the whole tribe of swindlers whose rascalities debauch and bring

14

odium upon the trade. He exhorts the gentleman of great reputed "shrewdness and sagacity" to observe the utmost caution in conducting operations, and gives him explicit directions how to forward the purchase-money.

Several years ago a preacher of the gospel, stationed not far from the northern frontier of the republic, received by mail one of the seductive missives of Ragem & Co., of New York City. The douceur opened with the usual complimentary references to the peculiar personal fitness of the clergyman for the proposed enterprise, and went on to state that, in exchange for genuine greenbacks, Ragem & Co. would furnish in the proportion of fifty to one imitations so absolutely perfect that the most experienced bank officers could not distinguish the difference. Rev. Zachariah Sapp,—for such was the euphonious name of the preacher,—after an attentive perusal of the flattering proposal, deposited the document in his coat-pocket for convenience of reference. Having pondered the subject for a day or two, he decided to write to Ragem & Co. for more explicit information.

Divining with the peculiar instinct of the guild the character of the fish now nibbling at the naked hook, the cheat resolved to risk a little bait, and accordingly sent by return mail a genuine one- dollar note, with a written invitation both for a reply and a personal conference.

Never before did the Rev. Zachariah Sapp subject a piece of paper to such scrutiny. Both with the naked eye and with a microscope,— a relic of collegiate days,—he studied the engravings and filigree work. Detail by detail he compared the supposed imitation with bills of known genuineness without being able to discover the slightest point of variation between them. Paper, printing, and engraving seemed to be absolutely perfect. While the study was progressing, the imagination of the clergyman soared through the empyrean of dazzling expectations. Why continue to toil hard for a small pittance when the golden apples were hanging within easy reach? Why drag out an existence in penury when wealth and its joys were thrust upon him?

Zachariah, however, was prudent and thrifty—indeed rather more thrifty in the estimation of parishioners than befitted one who held by right of faith a title-deed to mansions in the skies. Almost as soon would he risk his future inheritance as peril on a doubtful venture the few hundred dollars snugly saved up for a wet day by prudence and economy.

Not willing to rely entirely on his own judgment, he rather reluctantly decided to call on a banker in an adjacent town, with whom he enjoyed a slight acquaintance. In thinking the matter over he was greatly perplexed to determine how to introduce the subject. Of course it would not answer to allow the cashier to fathom his secret purpose, and yet he was oppressed with a vague consciousness that only a translucent film hid his thought from the world. Once or twice, in driving over on the unfamiliar errand, weak and irresolute he half resolved to turn back, but greed finally prevailed, and he kept on to the village.

With a strong but unsatisfactory effort to appear at ease, he sauntered into the bank. After the usual interchange of greetings, he nervously remarked, "Brother Hyde, as I was coming this way to- day to call on Brother Tompkins, I have taken the liberty to drop in to ask you a question on a matter in your line."

"Very well," replied the banker, "I shall be happy to serve you."

"I had a transaction a few days ago," resumed the clergyman, "with a peddler,—an entire stranger to me,—who, in making change, gave me a number of bills which I have reason to suspect are counterfeits. I desire your opinion."

"Please let me see them," said Mr. Hyde.

He took the one-dollar note from the hand of the unfaithful pastor, and after scanning it a moment, inquired, "What is the matter with it?"

"Is it good?" queried the anxious owner.

"I wish I had my safe full of the same sort," answered the banker.

"There is nothing bad about the bill. What makes you think so?

Perhaps you have shown me the wrong one. Let me see the others."

"I must have left the rest at home," replied the preacher, fumbling among the compartments of the pocket-book.

Having accomplished the object of his mission without perpetrating, as he thought, any disastrous blunder, Mr. Sapp brought the interview to a close with a few commonplace remarks, and hurried away to enjoy in solitary self-communion the thick-crowding visions of future affluence.

With the last doubt satisfactorily overcome, the plans of the prospective millionaire rapidly took shape. He could raise five hundred dollars, which at the proposed rate of interchange would purchase twenty-five thousand of the "absolutely perfect imitations." The sum seemed vast— incalculable. His imagination, hitherto bound down by the narrow circumstances of remote rural life, staggered while trying to grasp the conception of so much wealth. Like the mysteries of time and space, it appeared too grand for comprehension. Then his reveries strayed into another channel. What noble fellows were Ragem & Co. Why, among forty millions of people, did they pick out him, an unknown clergyman, living in an obscure place hundreds of miles from the metropolis, to be the favored recipient of untold wealth? Surely, this is a special Providence. Not a sparrow falleth to the ground without His knowledge. He watches over his own. Suddenly the erring clergyman feels a terrible pull at his heart-strings. What right has he, about to betray a sacred trust, and engage in operations branded as infamous by the laws of the land, to claim the watchful care of Providence? Will not the all-seeing eye follow him? Will not the omnipotent hand strike him heavily in wrath? The poor man wipes the cold perspiration from his forehead, and wonders if it will pay.

But he has paltered too long, and now the devil claims him for his own.

Returning home, Sapp wrote to Ragem & Co., stating the amount of his available resources, and saying that upon a given day and hour he would meet them at the appointed rendezvous. On the following Sunday the congregation were startled at the close of the afternoon services by an extraordinary announcement from the pulpit.

Before pronouncing the benediction the pastor said: "I take this opportunity to communicate to you collectively a piece of personal intelligence which I have hitherto kept secret. Under the will of a relative who recently died in the State of Michigan, I inherit a large sum—to me, with my humble wants, a very large sum. By appointment, I am to meet the executor of the estate this week in New York City to receive the first installment of the legacy. I do not propose to leave you, my dear parishioners, but to remain among you and toil with you as I have done for so many years. A goodly portion at least of my inheritance I intend to invest in this community, that neighbors and friends may share jointly in my prosperity. I trust I may be guided to make a wise use of the talents thus unexpectedly, and I may say providentially, committed to my keeping. We know from the teachings of Scripture that wealth brings great responsibilities, and that we shall be held to a strict account for the manner in which we employ it. May your prayers go with me."

The congregation crowded around the pastor with congratulations. Particularly demonstrative were the ebullitions of two or three brothers who saw a chance of exchanging sundry unsalable possessions for slices in the inheritance.

Mr. Sapp reached New York City in the evening, and the momentous interview was to take place at an early hour the next day. Sleep came in brief and fitful snatches. But the stars roll on in their majestic spheres, regardless of mortal hopes and fears. At length day broke, when the preacher rose from bed anxious and unrefreshed. A little before the appointed time he proceeded to a certain building, and having mounted two flights of stairs, saw the magic number on the door in front of him. As the clock struck he entered. Agreeably to a preconcerted plan, he wiped the right corner of his mouth with a white handkerchief, and nodded three times. The only person in the room, a well-dressed and apparently affable gentleman, responded by wiping the left corner of his mouth with a red silk handkerchief, and nodding three times. The signal is correctly answered: it is he! So far all works beautifully, with every promise kept. The bill was a perfect imitation, the engraver is on hand to a second.

> "Two truths are told,
>
> As happy prologues to the swelling act
>
> Of the imperial theme."

The fellow passing under the name of Ragem & Co. welcomed the new arrival cordially. "Ah," said he "your promptness and circumspection show that I am not disappointed in my man. I see that you come up to the full measure of my expectations. Do you know I am a remarkable judge of character? In fact, I seldom or never make a mistake. We are both in luck."

"I was trained to punctuality from early youth," replied the preacher; and proceeding directly to business, without further circumlocution, continued, "I succeeded in raising five hundred dollars, which entitles me under the agreement to twenty-five thousand."

From an inner pocket, after removing a number of pins, he produced six one hundred dollar notes, saying, by way of explanation, "For greater security I converted my funds into bills of large denomination. One I reserve for contingencies; the other five are for you."

"Your money is here in the safe," said Ragem, taking the five notes, and turning toward the safe as if to unlock it. But the scoundrel evidently reasoned that it would be silly to remain content with the five when he could just as easily capture the sixth.

Walking back, he remarked, "I want to show you that my large bills are just as perfect as the small ones"; and, as if for purposes of comparison, he took the remaining note from the hand of the clergyman.

At this moment began a fearful knocking on a side door, that threatened the speedy demolition of the frail barrier. "Run, run," whispered Ragem, as if in the extremity of terror, "the police are on us."

The preacher needed no second invitation, fear of exposure giving wings to his feet. Almost at a bound he cleared the two flights of stairs and emerged into the street, walking several blocks, and turning a number of corners before he dared to look back.

The bona fide occupant of the room where these parties met had no share whatever in the nefarious transactions carried on there. Through the treachery of the janitor, Ragem was permitted at certain hours to make use of the apartment for the purpose of keeping appointments with his victims. A confederate stationed on the outside delivered the knocks as soon as customers were plucked and it became desirable to get rid of their company. Occasional hints of improper practices reached the ear of the real lessee, but these had never yet taken such shape as

17

to give a decisive clew to the trouble, dupes for the most part pocketing their losses in silence.

After an interval of two or three hours Mr. Sapp plucked up courage to return. Having mounted the stairs, he entered the room warily. His late partner was not there. A stalwart gentleman, who seemed to be the proprietor, looked up inquiringly, and was not a little puzzled when the visitor supplemented the performance of wiping the right corner of his mouth by three deliberate nods. "What can I do for you to-day?" inquired the gentleman, rising.

"You are, I presume, a partner of Mr. Ragem," answered Sapp. "I see he is out. Our business this morning was unfortunately interrupted by the police, and I have returned to complete it."

"What business?" asked the proprietor, in undisguised astonishment.

Now the preacher made the very natural mistake of supposing that the surprise manifested by his interlocutor was a mere matter of policy and caution. Hence he proceeded to explain. "Ragem must have told you. I am the gentleman who gave him the five hundred dollars, and he said that my twenty-five thousand were locked up in the safe."

The proprietor did not wait to hear more, but seizing the affrighted creature by the collar, thundered forth, "I have heard of you before. You are the villain, are you, who has been turning my office into a den of thieves? I have caught you at last!"

Awaking to a partial comprehension of the situation, the poor wretch stammered forth, "There must be some mistake. My name is a— is a—is a Smith—Smith—John Smith."

"John Smith, is it?" growled the proprietor. "Well, all I have to say is, John Smith, if not the biggest is the most numerous rascal in the city. John, come along to the police station."

And John went, billows of trouble rolling over him as the waters of the Red Sea closed over Pharaoh. Vain the effort to recall consolatory texts pertinent to the occasion! He was sorely chastened indeed, but the stripes were inflicted not in love but in wrath. He mourned, yet whence could he look for comfort?

To avoid a worse fate, the prisoner revealed his identity, exhibited the correspondence from "Ragem & Co.," and made a full statement of the facts. The painful news reached the church shortly after the return of the pastor, when his pulpit career came to an ignominious end. He soon removed to the far West, hoping to bury his disgrace in the shades of the primeval forest.

The fall of Rev. Zachariah Sapp sounds a note of warning not without its lessons. The only safety in dealing with temptation is to repel its insidious approaches from the outset. Whoever listens in patience to the siren whisper is half lost already. Human experience abundantly confirms the divine wisdom of the command, "Get thee behind me, Satan," as the one sole safe way of meeting evil advances. At the close of well-spent, useful lives, myriads can thank a kind Providence, not that they have been stronger than others who have turned out differently, but that they have been tried less. Walking among unseen perils, none can without danger of ruin discard even for a moment the armor of honesty and truth.

AN ASPIRANT FOR CONGRESS

A few years ago, the "Hon." John Whimpery Brass, of Georgia, one of the "thoughtful patriots" of the period, who now and then found time to lay aside the cares of statecraft to nurse little private jobs of his own, allured by the seductive offers of "Wogan & Co." of New York City, wrote to that somewhat mythical concern proposing to become their agent for the circulation of the "queer." Even after receiving the first installment of their wares, the honorable gentleman did not comprehend that the firm dealt exclusively in sawdust, not in currency. He wrote again, complaining that, after a journey of sixty miles over a rough road to the nearest reliable express office, he found nothing but a worthless package, marked "C. O. D.," awaiting him. Did Wogan & Co. distrust either his parts or fidelity? He ventured to assert that no man in the State could serve them so effectually. He had just run for Congress, and though beaten at the polls by "fraud," intended to contest the seat with the chances of success in his favor. The mountaineers among whom he lived did not care whether the money in their pockets was good or bad so long as it circulated. He could put thousands of counterfeits afloat without the slightest fear of detection. His constituency believed in him and would stand by him. Currency was very scarce in that congressional district, and it would really be doing his people a great favor to give them more. After setting forth the mutual benefits to accrue from trusting him, he appealed to Wogan & Co. with the vehemence and energy of the sewing-machine man, or life-insurance agent, to send on the goods without further delay. They should never regret dealing with him, his character and standing being a sufficient guaranty that he could not play false. He was acting in good faith, and expected like treatment in return.

Unfortunately for the political aspirations of "Hon." John Whimpery Brass, the authorities not long after made a descent upon the den of Wogan & Co., finding a great many letters from credulous fools, and a large supply of sawdust—their only stock in trade. The missives of the prospective congressman were published, thus gaining much more extensive currency than he proposed to give to the imitation greenbacks. It was supposed that the noisy fellow would slink away to some cave in his native mountains, and never show his brazen face among honest people again. But the impudence of "Hon." John Whimpery Brass rose to the level of the emergency. Instead of hiding or hanging himself, he published a card representing that he embarked in the scheme for the purpose of entrapping Wogan & Co. and bringing them to justice.

Pathetic was the spectacle, showing the confidence of an ingenuous soul in its own prowess, of the volunteer detective, digging parallels on the southern spurs of the Blue Ridge for the capture of the wily swindler a thousand miles away! Armed with a kernel of corn, the doughty gosling sets forth to catch the wicked fox that is preying on the flock! If the bold mountaineers, the constituency of "Hon." John Whimpery Brass, cannot commend the discretion displayed by the projector of the enterprise, they must certainly admire his pluck. In face of the odds, few goslings would volunteer.

Perhaps the card might have been accepted by the more trustful class of adherents as a satisfactory explanation of the letters, had not the aspiring statesman in course of time fallen under the ban of the law for defrauding widows of their pensions, the campaign against Wogan & Co. having so completely exhausted the virtue of the amateur who planned it as to leave no residue to fructify in subsequent operations.

THE FORTUNE OF SETH SAVAGE

At one time the bogus-lottery men drove a thrifty business, but the efforts, virtually cooperative, of the post-office department and of the legislatures of the older states, have latterly pretty effectually forced them into the wilderness. The managers forage on the same class of people as the sawdust swindlers, procuring lists of names in the same way. A common method of procedure is to inclose with advertisements announcing the prizes, together with the place and date of drawing, one or more tickets duly numbered. Great confidence is expressed in the personal fitness of the party addressed, who is requested to act as agent for the sale of the tickets. A few weeks later another letter is sent to the intended victim, informing him that the ticket of a given number forwarded to him at such a date had drawn a prize, the value of which is variously stated from a few hundred to many thousand dollars. He is then requested to send immediately ten dollars—more or less— for the ticket, perhaps ten or twenty more for additional charges, when the full face value of the prize will be forwarded promptly by express, check on New York, or in any other way the recipient may direct. He is also told to antedate the letter, the intermediary promising to blur the postmark to correspond, so that the remittance may appear to have been made prior to the drawing. In conclusion the writer adroitly suggests that he desires the fortunate man to exhibit the money to his neighbors, stating how he obtained it, and mentioning particularly the address of the agent from whom the ticket was purchased, the object being to create an excitement in the place with a view to large sales for the next drawing.

Even of a trick as transparent as this the victims are counted by thousands, exposures and warnings being alike disregarded. The infatuation of a certain class of ignorant and credulous people is well illustrated by the case of Seth Savage, a poor man possessed of a few acres in the vicinity of a small village in Vermont. One day, when a special agent of wide experience happened to be visiting the post-office, Seth received a letter, the perusal of which threw him into a frenzy of excitement.

"What is the matter?" inquired the postmaster. "You seem to have good news."

"Look a-here," replied Seth, holding forth the missive in his shriveled and bony fingers, "for nigh on to sixty-five year, Mr. Martin, I've fit and work'd and work'd and fit jest for my vittles and drink. Neow when I'm tew old tew 'joy it, a fortin comes to me."

"Is that so?" answered Mr. Martin. "I am very glad; but tell me, what is it? Your neighbors will all be glad to hear of your good luck."

"Read that," said Seth, handing him the letter triumphantly.

The postmaster read the manuscript. One Dewitt of New York City assured Mr. Savage that a certain ticket sent to him a month before had drawn a prize of three thousand dollars; that on receipt of thirty-five dollars in a letter antedated according to directions, the full amount would be forwarded to him.

"Surely, Seth," expostulated the postmaster, "you are not going to be fooled in this way. Dewitt is a humbug, a swindler."

"Neow, heow dew yeou know that?" inquired Seth. "Has he ever fool'd yeou?"

"I don't deal with that sort of people," replied Mr. Martin mildly. "I dislike to see anyone wronged, especially a neighbor. Here is a gentleman who knows all about such matters." And Seth was formally introduced to the special agent, who took pains to explain the character of the swindle fully.

The officer left the village with the pleasant assurance that his brief visit had contributed at least toward the rescue of one poor object from the jaws of the devourer.

After all, however, Seth was not convinced. By selling his only cow he managed to swell his scanty stock of cash to the requisite sum, which he sent to Dewitt, fully expecting to be able in a few days to confound the postmaster by the actual display of his newly gotten wealth. The dupe, who had invested a goodly portion of his scanty means in the venture, waited long if not patiently. At length, after the expiration of the last hope, Mr. Martin inquired, "How did it happen, Seth, that you threw away your money on that lottery scamp, when we showed you that the whole thing was a cheat?"

"Wall, neow, arter it's all lost," replied Seth, "I'll tell yeou jest heow 'twas. Human natur' is naturally suspectin'. I tho't yeou and that ar' t'other postoffis fellah want'd to git the prize for

20

yeourselfs; an' I didn't mean to be beat so."

A WISH UNEXPECTEDLY GRATIFIED

When the bogus-lottery men were driven out of the large cities by the vigor of the postal authorities, they tried for a while to operate from small country towns by collusion with dishonest postmasters. As the delinquencies of the offenders were successively brought to light, their heads rolled into the basket at the foot of the official guillotine. The swindlers, however, succeeded in bribing fresh victims, and for a time cunning and duplicity managed with tolerable success to maintain a foothold against the power of the department.

Among other similar swindles, sealed circulars were at one time scattered broadcast over the more remote states, announcing that on a given date the drawing for a series of magnificent prizes would take place at Livingston Hall, No. 42 Elm Avenue, Wington Junction, Connecticut. Patrons were urged to remit the purchase-money for tickets promptly, as there would be no postponement of the grand event under any circumstances. "Fortune," continued the glittering advertisement, "knocks once at every one's door, and she is now knocking at yours."

As usual, multitudes swallowed the bait, but some, instead of sending the greenbacks to Highfalutin & Co., forwarded the circulars to the department. Thereupon special agent Sharretts was instructed to visit Wington Junction, with the view of learning whether the postmaster was properly discharging his duties. Taking an early opportunity to perform the mission, he alighted at the station one morning, and proceeded to survey the town, which consisted of four or five houses scattered along the highway for a distance of half a mile. "Livingston Hall" and "Elm Avenue" were nowhere visible. It was apparent that "No. 42" on any avenue was a remote contingency not likely to arise in the present generation.

Having previously ascertained that the postmaster was also switch- tender at the junction, and that the cares of the office devolved on his wife, the officer walked up to a keen-looking man in front of the little round switch-house, whose energies were devoted exclusively at that moment to the mastication of a huge quid of tobacco, and who, after a prolonged scrutiny of the stranger, answered his salutation in an attenuated drawl,' "Meornin', sir."

"Will you be kind enough to tell me, sir, where Mr. Morris, the postmaster, can be found?" asked the agent.

"Wall, I guess my name's Morris. What kin I do fur yeou?"

"Mr. Morris, I should like a few minutes' private conversation on business of great importance, which can be so managed as to turn out advantageously to us both. I do not wish to be overheard or interrupted. In these times even blank walls have ears, you know."

The last suggestion seemed to serve as a passport to the confidence of the postmaster. Leading the way into the switch-house, he remarked, "Come in heear. Neow, what is it?"

"The fact is, Mr. Morris, some friends of mine propose to go into a little speculation, which will involve a large correspondence; and for reasons that I need not specify to a man like you, they do not wish to have every ragtag, bobtail post-office clerk poring over their letters, and asking impertinent questions at the delivery- window. If they can find a shrewd, square man, who knows how to keep his mouth shut, and who can't be fooled, that for a handsome consideration will put the letters away in a safe place till called for, they are willing to make an arrangement that will be profitable all around. You have been recommended as just the person. I am told that you generally know which side your bread is buttered, and have called to see if we can't arrange to pull together."

21

"'Nuff said," ejaculated Morris, with a sly wink. "I know what yeou want, but my wife is the one to fix things. I don't have nuthin' to dew with the letters. Sue 'tends to everything. The folks as we'se a-workin' for said we must be plaguey keerful about the deetecters. I'll bet nun on 'em can't play it on my wife tho'. If they dew, they'll have to git up arly in the mornin'."

With that he thrust his head out of the window, and yelled: "Sue,
Sue!"

As the sound died away, a tall, raw-boned female, from whose cheeks the bloom of youth had faded a number of years before, emerged from the side door of a two-story cottage, about eighty rods distant, and walked briskly to the switch-house, where she was introduced to the stranger as "my wife."

After a little preliminary skirmishing, she invited the agent to go over to the cottage. Having been duly ushered into the "best room," he embellished for her benefit the story already told to the husband.

"I think I kin 'commodate yeou," she broke forth, "but yeou'll have to pay putty well for't. Laws me, I'm told—and I've ways o' heerin' 'bout these things—that the deetecters are jest as likely as not to come a-swoopin' deown enny minnit. Yeou know, if they feound it out, we'd be smash'd."

Her terms were ten dollars a week. Highfalutin & Co. paid six, but she understood the business a great deal better now than when she made the bargain with them. The agent thought the price rather high, but finally consented to contract at that figure.

Then, as if troubled by an after-thought, he said, "Madam, how do I know but some of these 'deetecters' may come around, and, seeing my letters, get me into difficulty?"

"Why, laws a' mercy," said she, "don't be skeer'd. Yeou jest leave that to me. The minnit them air letters gits here, I hides 'em in that bewro-draw'r," pointing to an article of furniture in the corner.

"Is it a safe place?" queried the agent.

"Yas, it is," answered the woman. "Got it half full neow. Carry the key in my pocket."

She gave a grin, intended for a knowing smile, in admiration of her own cleverness.

"I believe the hiding-place is tolerably secure," replied the officer, with the air of one who desired to be convinced, but had not yet reached the point of full assurance.

"You seem to be very particl'r and diffikilt to satisfy," continued Mrs. Morris; "but, if yeou don't believe it, jest come and see for you'sef."

She led the way to the bureau, opened the drawer, and, raising a plaid cotton handkerchief, displayed the contraband letters by the score. All were directed to the lottery firm, and were turned over to the knave from time to time as it suited his convenience to call for them. As no such firm did business at Wington Junction, it was the duty of the postmaster to forward to the department, as fictitious and undeliverable, all letters bearing the address of the swindlers. In similar cases neglect to obey the regulation was treated as sufficient ground for instant removal.

More fully pleased with the result of the examination than the woman surmised, the officer resumed: "I see you are very particular about your methods of doing business, and do not mean to be caught napping. The arrangement we are about to enter into is a very important one, and, as you are not postmaster, your husband will have to be present to witness and ratify the bargain."

"Bless yeour soul," replied she, "it's all right. I 'tend to all the biznis. My husband doesn't bother hissef abeout it in the least."

"Madam," answered the officer, "pardon me. I had my training in a large city, and am accustomed to pay minute attention to every detail. Your husband is the principal in this case, and must ratify the agreement to make it binding. Of course you will derive all the benefit, but his presence is essential as a matter of form."

Apparently satisfied, she called for "John," who replied promptly to the summons.

"Mr. Morris," said the officer, "your wife has agreed to keep my letters for me—"

"Yaas," broke in the postmaster. "I know'd she would. Yeou'll find she'll dew it right, tew. Nobody can't come enny tricks on her—can they, Sue? I wish one o' 'em durn'd deetecters would come around, jest tew see heow she'd pull the wool over 'im. I wudn't ax enny better fun;" and he indulged in a fit of loud cachinnation at the absurdity of supposing that anyone could match in sharpness his own beloved Sue.

"The letters will come to that address," said the agent, pulling out his commission from the postmaster-general, and exhibiting it to the pair.

Taking in the purport of it at a glance, Morris jumped several inches into the air, slapped his sides, and exclaimed, "A deetecter, arter all; sold, by jingo!"

"We're bust'd then," chimed in Sue, with a melancholy grin.

It was even so. The letters for Highfalutin & Co. went to Washington, and Morris went out of the post-office; but the fact that Sue was overmatched hurt him more than the loss of the place.

June 8, 1872, a law was approved making it a penal offense to use the mails for the purpose of defrauding others, whether residing within or outside of the United States. The postmaster-general was also authorized to forbid the payment of postal money orders to persons engaged in fraudulent lotteries, gift enterprises, and other schemes for swindling the public, and to instruct postmasters to return to the writers, with the word "fraudulent" written or stamped on the outside, all registered letters directed to such persons or firms. Prior to the enactment of this law, the most wholesale and barefaced operations were conducted by professional cheats, mainly through the facilities afforded by the mails, with almost absolute impunity. Letters addressed to bogus firms were indeed forwarded from the offices of delivery to the department as "fictitious" and "undeliverable," and many colluding postmasters were decapitated. Such petty measures of warfare served merely to annoy the vampires and to whet their diabolical ingenuity for the contrivance of new devices. Since the law of 1872 went into effect, however, the scoundrels have been compelled to travel a thorny road. Scores of arrests have been made, and in many cases the criminals have been sentenced to the penitentiary.

It would exceed our limits even to enumerate the devices which have been tried by different swindlers with greater or less success. Gift enterprises of various kinds are the most common and notorious, constituting a distinct branch of the business; but the pretenses on which human credulity is invited to part with actual cash for imaginary benefits are innumerable. A few specimens are given as illustrations.

AN OLD GAME REVIVED

On the 18th of September, 1875, a fellow was arrested in West Virginia who sent the victims whom he proposed to bleed letters whereof the following is a copy:—

"A lady who boarded with me died on last Saturday of apoplexy. She left a trunk containing the following property: One very fine ladies' gold watch and chain, one ladies' gold necklace, six ladies' finger rings, earrings, and a great deal of ladies' clothing. Among other things was a letter addressed to you. I suppose you to be a relative of the deceased, and want to send you the trunk.

23

When Miss Thompson died she left a board bill unpaid amounting to $20.50. You will please send this amount by return mail, and the trunk will be forwarded to you immediately."

Instead of remitting the money as modestly requested, the recipient of one of these choice douceurs, a lady residing in the interior of Pennsylvania, sent the letter to the mayor of the town where it was dated and postmarked, who in turn handed it over to special agent T. P. Shallcross; and he in the course of a day or two succeeded in capturing the miscreant.

This particular form of the confidence game is very old; yet in the year of our Lord eighteen hundred and seventy-five a swindler by means of it succeeds not only in maintaining himself in dashing style, but also in sporting a flashy traveling companion of the female persuasion!

Where the letters are addressed to men, the articles reported to be found in the imaginary trunk are changed to correspond to masculine habits and wants. The operators receive many singular and some entertaining replies. The following, dated long ago from a small town at the South, may serve as a sample, the orthography of the original being preserved:—

"COL. SNOWDEN,

"Dear Sir,—Yours received, and you say John is dead. Poor fellow! I always expected it. Death runs in the family. Dyed suddenly of appleplexy—eat too many apples. Well, I always thought John would hurt himself eating apples. I s'pose you had him buried. You said nothing about funeral expenses. He had a trunk—gold watch in it, &c. Well, well, what an unexpected legacy! but strange things happen sometimes. Never thought I should get a gold watch so. And he had the watch in his trunk, did he? Poor fellow! was always so particular 'bout his watch and fixings. Had two revolvers. What is them? I never heard John say anything about them. Well, you have been so kind as to write to me; just keep all the balance of the things, you can have them; but the gold watch, send that to me by express. Send immediately if not sooner."

"Very truly,

"GEO. STREAM.

"P. S. My mother in law says, if you come this way, call. She likes to know all such good, kind folks."

It is safe to conclude that "Col. Snowden" never accepted the invitation to call from the hospitable mother-in-law.

A FORMIDABLE WEAPON

In the summer and fall of 1875 circulars were scattered broadcast over the country, and advertisements appeared in the weekly editions of several leading papers of New York City and other large towns, setting forth the rare merits of a weapon of destruction called "Allan's New Low-Priced Seven-Shooter." As a specimen of ingenious description, the more salient parts of the circular are herewith reproduced:—

"In introducing this triumph of mechanical genius to the American public, it is proper to say that it is not an entirely new article, but that it has lately been improved in appearance, simplicity of construction, and accuracy, having new points of excellence, making it superior in many respects to those first made. The manufacturers having improved facilities for making them cheaply and rapidly, have reduced the price to one dollar and fifty cents; and while the profits on a single one are necessarily small, this price places them within the reach of all.

"We wish it distinctly understood that this is no cheap, good-for- nothing 'pop-gun'; and while none can expect it to be 'silver- mounted' for $1.50, they have a right to expect the worth of their money, and in this new improved seven-shooter a want is supplied.

"Great care is taken in the adjustment of EACH, so that ALL are equally good and reliable. In their production no trouble or expense has been spared. An elaborate and complete set of machinery and gauges has been made, by means of which all the parts are produced exactly alike, thus insuring great uniformity in the character of the work produced."

This remarkable implement, equally useful for peace or war, is offered to an eager public at the low price of $1.50 each, or $13 per dozen. On the score of cheapness, the inventor greatly prefers the mails to the express as a vehicle for the transport of his wares. In fact, he declines to patronize the express companies at all, unless a prepayment of twenty-five per cent, accompanies each order as a guaranty of the "purchaser's good faith."

At first the enterprise succeeded even beyond the most sanguine expectations of its projector, letters with the cash inclosed pouring in by the hundred. For several months, however, after the first publication of the advertisement, "this triumph of mechanical genius," though "not an entirely new article," existed only in the comprehensive brain of the gentleman who had the greatness to discern in the imperfect work of predecessors the germs of ideal perfection. Having no seven-shooters to send, he was compelled to dishonor the requisitions of the expectant "traveler, sailor, hunter, fisherman, etc." While careful to lay aside the inclosures, he entirely forgot even to so far remember his patrons as to make a record of their names.

In due time, however, the "factory" went into operation, and the seven-shooters were actually produced. The mechanical "triumph," rudely made of a cheap metal composition, is a duplicate of a toy long used by boys to the delight of each other, and to the annoyance of their elders. The propulsive power resides in a steel spring, which has force enough to send a bird-shot across a good- sized room. The outfit would cost perhaps six or eight cents to the manufacturer. A portion of the orders were now filled, the greater part being still thrown unhonored into the waste-basket as before.

Curses both loud and deep began to be showered on the head of the swindler. Complaints having reached the department, special agent C. E. Henry started to hunt for "Wilcox & Co.," of Windsor, Ohio, for such was the direction in the advertisements and on the circular. Proceeding several miles from the nearest railroad, he found the rural settlement where the factory was supposed to be located.

Guided by various inquiries, he finally drove up to the small farm- house where the parents of Wilcox & Co. resided. On entering, the officer said, "I am in search of Mr. Wilcox, of the firm of Wilcox & Co."

"I am your man," remarked a youth, perhaps twenty-two years of age, whose countenance at once suggested acuteness and cunning. "What will you have?"

"I would like to take a look about the arsenal and gun-factory located here," replied the detective, leisurely surveying the landscape.

"The works are in Cleveland," answered the great inventor. "You can see them by calling there."

"But where is the arsenal? I understand it was situated here."

"Your information is correct," replied the young man. "That is it, across the road."

Casting his eye in the direction indicated, the officer saw a rickety woodshed about seven feet by nine in size.

Observing the smile of amused incredulity that played upon the features of his questioner, Wilcox reiterated, with an air of half offended dignity,—

"That's it. We keep our seven-shooters there. But look here; before this thing goes any further, I want to know who you are."

"Oh, certainly, sir," answered the stranger. "You will find nothing about me that I care to keep concealed. I am a special agent of the post-office department, and my business here is to arrest you."

"Why, what have I done to warrant such a visit?" queried youthful innocence.

"I shall be happy to make that point clear to you," replied the detective, "though I am afraid the enlightenment will come too late to prove of much service to you. In using the mails for the purpose of swindling, you have violated the laws of the country, and must suffer the penalty."

"But where does the swindling come in?" expostulated Wilcox. "I advertised a seven-shooter. I didn't say anything about a revolver. It will shoot seven shot, or twice that number, if you only put them in. If anybody is green enough to suppose I meant a revolver, that's his lookout, not mine."

"We are not called upon to decide the point," said the special agent. "The question is one for the court and the jury. But you must go with me to Cleveland. So get ready."

Finding persuasion, argument, and remonstrance alike useless, the great mechanical genius packed his satchel in preparation for the journey. Once fairly on the road, he became communicative, and explained the reasons which led him to embark in the enterprise. "In the first place," said he, "I read Barnum's Life, and accepted the doctrine that the American people like to be humbugged. I planned the shooter myself, and, in wording the circular, aimed to cover the points and keep within the law. I think I have succeeded."

"I beg leave to differ," argued the special agent. "Aside from the general falsity of the description, there are specific claims which you cannot make good."

"I don't see the matter in that light," replied the champion of the seven-shooter. "I say, 'Wherever introduced, they advertise themselves.' Well, don't they? Whoever gets one will be apt to tell his neighbors. Isn't that advertising itself? I also say, 'The sale of one opens the market for a dozen in any neighborhood;' but observe, I don't claim that any more will be sold in that neighborhood, even if the market is opened. So far as my guaranty is concerned, I only warrant them to be as good after three years' use as when first purchased. Will you, or will any court, call that in question?"

"It is charged," said the officer, changing the subject, "that you neglected to fill a good many orders. How do you explain that?"

"Why, to furnish the shooter and pay the postage cuts down the profits terribly," was the unique and characteristic reply.

Orders began to arrive in response to the circular nearly five months before the first shooter came from the hands of the manufacturer; and as none of them were ever filled, or even recorded, it is impossible to estimate how many dupes long watched the mails in anxious expectancy, and perhaps attributed their disappointment to dishonesty among the employees of the department.

Of course the papers which printed the advertisement would have spurned the impostor and exposed the fraud, had they discovered the facts. The most scrupulous and careful publishers are often deceived in the character of advertisements that come through the regular channels of business, and appear plausible on their face. In fact, the religious journals are the favorite vehicles of the swindlers. The solicitude felt by the newspapers, not only for their own reputation, but for the interests of their patrons, was illustrated in the correspondence found on the person of

Wilcox. An influential western journal had addressed him two notes which ran thus:—

GENTS: We receive frequent letters from subscribers, saying they receive no answers to letters they send you containing money for '7-Shooters.' How is it? Are you swindlers?"

Wilcox, though fully able to answer the conundrum, did not see fit to do so; and hence, on the 3d of November, the same parties deployed their forces to renew the charge.

"—, Nov. 3, 1875.

"WILCOX & CO.:

"We have written you once before, that our patrons complain to us that you do not fill their cash orders, and will not answer their letters of inquiry as to why you don't. We have received so many such that we suspect there is something wrong, and, unless you explain satisfactorily, we will have to expose you."

As the special agent arrived on the same day with the inquiry, the young man had no opportunity to make the desired explanation. Indeed it is doubtful if one so modest and reticent on matters of personal merit, would have answered the question even if permitted to take all winter to do it in.

The United States commissioner, while fully recognizing the ingenuity of the circular, differed somewhat from its author in interpreting its legal construction, and accordingly placed him under a bond of fifteen hundred dollars to appear for trial.

Andrew Lang

Saint-Germain the Deathless

Among the best brief masterpieces of fiction are Lytton's The Haunters and the Haunted, and Thackeray's Notch on the Axe in Roundabout Papers.* Both deal with a mysterious being who passes through the ages, rich, powerful, always behind the scenes, coming no man knows whence, and dying, or pretending to die, obscurely— you never find authentic evidence of his disease. In other later times, at other courts, such an one reappears and runs the same course of luxury, marvel, and hidden potency.

* Both given in the accompanying volume containing "Old Time English" Stories. See also the first story in the "North Europe" volume.—Editor.

Lytton returned to and elaborated his idea in the Margrave of A Strange Story, who has no "soul," and prolongs his physical and intellectual life by means of an elixir. Margrave is not bad, but he is inferior to the hero, less elaborately designed, of The Haunters and the Haunted. Thackeray's tale is written in a tone of mock mysticism, but he confesses that he likes his own story, in which the strange hero through all his many lives or reappearances, and through all the countless loves on which he fatuously plumes himself, retains a slight German-Jewish accent.

It appears to me that the historic original of these romantic characters is no other than the mysterious Comte de Saint-Germain— not, of course, the contemporary and normal French soldier and minister, of 1707-1778, who bore the same name. I have found the name, with dim allusions, in the unpublished letters and MSS. of Prince Charles Edward Stuart, and have not always been certain whether the reference was to the man of action or to the man of mystery. On the secret of the latter, the deathless one, I have no new light to throw, and only speak of him for a single reason. Aristotle assures us, in his Poetics, that the best-known myths dramatized on the Athenian stage were known to very few of the Athenian audience. It is not impossible that the story of Saint- Germain, though it seems as familiar as the myth of Oedipus or Thyestes, may, after all, not be vividly present to the memory of every reader. The omniscient Larousse, of the

Dictionnaire Universel, certainly did not know one very accessible fact about Saint-Germain, nor have I seen it mentioned in other versions of his legend. We read, in Larousse, "Saint-Germain is not heard of in France before 1750, when he established himself in Paris. No adventure had called attention to his existence; it was only known that he had moved about Europe, lived in Italy, Holland, and in England, and had borne the names of Marquis de Monteferrat, and of Comte de Bellamye, which he used at Venice."

Lascelles Wraxall, again, in Remarkable Adventures (1863), says: "Whatever truth there may be in Saint-Germain's travels in England and the East Indies, it is undubitable that, for from 1745 to 1755, he was a man of high position in Vienna," while in Paris he does not appear, according to Wraxall, till 1757, having been brought from Germany by the Marechal de Belle-Isle, whose "old boots," says Macallester the spy, Prince Charles freely damned, "because they were always stuffed with projects." Now we hear of Saint-Germain, by that name, as resident, not in Vienna, but in London, at the very moment when Prince Charles, evading Cumberland, who lay with his army at Stone, in Staffordshire, marched to Derby. Horace Walpole writes to Mann in Florence (December 9, 1745):

"We begin to take up people . . . the other day they seized an odd man who goes by the name of Count Saint-Germain. He has been here these two years, and will not tell who he is, or whence, but professes that he does not go by his right name. He sings, plays on the violin wonderfully, composes, is mad, and not very sensible. He is called an Italian, a Spaniard, a Pole; a somebody that married a great fortune in Mexico, and ran away with her jewels to Constantinople; a priest, a fiddler, a vast nobleman. The Prince of Wales has had unsatiated curiosity about him, but in vain. However, nothing has been made out against him; he is released, and, what convinces me he is not a gentleman, stays here, and talks of his being taken up for a spy."

Here is our earliest authentic note on Saint-Germain; a note omitted by his French students. He was in London from 1743 to 1745, under a name not his own, but that which he later bore at the Court of France. From the allusion to his jewels (those of a deserted Mexican bride), it appears that he was already as rich in these treasures as he was afterwards, when his French acquaintances marveled at them. (As to his being "mad," Walpole may refer to Saint-Germain's way of talking as if he had lived in remote ages, and known famous people of the past).

Having caught this daylight glimpse of Saint-Germain in Walpole, having learned that in December, 1745, he was arrested and examined as a possible Jacobite agent, we naturally expect to find our contemporary official documents about his examination by the Government. Scores of such records exist, containing the questions put to, and the answers given by, suspected persons. But we vainly hunt through the Newcastle MSS., and the State Papers, Domestic, in the Record Office, for a trace of the examination of Saint-Germain. I am not aware that he was anywhere left his trail in official documents; he lives in more or less legendary memoirs, alone.

At what precise date Saint-Germain became an intimate of Louis XV., the Duc de Choiseul, Madame de Pompadour, and the Marechal de Belle-Isle, one cannot ascertain. The writers of memoirs are the vaguest of mortals about dates; only one discerns that Saint-Germain was much about the French Court, and high in the favor of the King, having rooms at Chambord, during the Seven Years' War, and just before the time of the peace negotiations of 1762-1763. The art of compiling false or forged memoirs of that period was widely practiced; but the memoirs of Madame du Hausset, who speaks of Saint-Germain, are authentic. She was the widow of a poor man of noble family, and was one of two femmes de chambre of Madame de Pompadour. Her manuscript was written, she explains, by aid of a brief diary which she kept during her term of service. One day M. Senac de Meilhan found Madame de Pompadour's brother, M. de Marigny, about to burn a packet of papers. "It is the journal," he said, "of a femme de chambre of my sister, a good, kind woman." De Meilhan asked for the manuscript, which he later gave to Mr. Crawford, one of the Kilwinning family, in Ayrshire, who later helped in the escape of Louis XVI. and Marie Antoinette to Varennes, where they were captured. With the journal of Madame du Hausset were several letters to Marigny on points of historical anecdote.[1]

[1] One of these gives Madame de Vieux-Maison as the author of a roman a clef, Secret Memoirs of the Court of Persia, which contains an early reference to the Man in the Iron Mask (died 1703). The letter-writer avers that D'Argenson, the famous minister of Louis XV., said that the Man in the Iron Mask was really a person fort peu de chose, 'of very little account,' and that the Regent d'Orleans was of the same opinion. This corroborates my theory, that the Mask was merely the valet of a Huguenot conspirator, Roux de Marsilly, captured in England, and imprisoned because he was supposed to know some terrible secret—which he knew nothing about. See The Valet's Tragedy, Longmans, 1903.

Crawford published the manuscript of Madame du Hausset, which he was given by de Meilhan, and the memoirs are thus from an authentic source. The author says that Louis XV. was always kind to her, but spoke little to her, whereas Madame de Pompadour remarked, "The King and I trust you so much that we treat you like a cat or a dog, and talk freely before you."

As to Saint-Germain, Madame du Hausset writes: "A man who was as amazing as a witch came often to see Madame de Pompadour. This was the Comte de Saint-Germain, who wished to make people believe that he had lived for several centuries. One day Madame said to him, while at her toilet, "What sort of man was Francis I., a king whom I could have loved?" "A good sort of fellow," said Saint-Germain; "too fiery—I could have given him a useful piece of advice, but he would not have listened." He then described, in very general terms, the beauty of Mary Stuart and La Reine Margot. "You seem to have seen them all," said Madame de Pompadour, laughing. "Sometimes," said Saint-Germain, "I amuse myself, not by making people believe, but by letting them believe, that I have lived from time immemorial." "But you do not tell us your age, and you give yourself out as very old. Madame de Gergy, who was wife of the French ambassador at Venice fifty years ago, I think, says that she knew you there, and that you are not changed in the least." "It is true, Madame, that I knew Madame de Gergy long ago." "But according to her story you must now be over a century old." "It may be so, but I admit that even more possibly the respected lady is in her dotage."

At this time Saint-Germain, says Madame du Hausset, looked about fifty, was neither thin nor stout, seemed clever, and dressed simply, as a rule, but in good taste. Say that the date was 1760, Saint-Germain looked fifty; but he had looked the same age, according to Madame de Gergy, at Venice, fifty years earlier, in 1710. We see how pleasantly he left Madame de Pompadour in doubt on that point.

He pretended to have the secret of removing flaws from diamonds. The King showed him a stone valued at 6,000 francs—without a flaw it would have been worth 10,000. Saint-Germain said that he could remove the flaw in a month, and in a month he brought back the diamond— flawless. The King sent it, without any comment, to his jeweler, who gave 9,600 francs for the stone, but the King returned the money, and kept the gem as a curiosity. Probably it was not the original stone, but another cut in the same fashion, Saint- Germain sacrificing 3,000 or 4,000 francs to his practical joke. He also said that he could increase the size of pearls, which he could have proved very easily—in the same manner. He would not oblige Madame de Pompadour by giving the King an elixir of life: "I should be mad if I gave the King a drug." There seems to be a reference to this desire of Madame de Pompadour in an unlikely place, a letter of Pickle the Spy to Mr. Vaughan (1754)! This conversation Madame du Hausset wrote down on the day of its occurrence.

Both Louis XV. and Madame de Pompadour treated Saint-Germain as a person of consequence. "He is a quack, for he says he has an elixir," said Dr. Quesnay, with medical skepticism. "Moreover, our master, the King, is obstinate; he sometimes speaks of Saint- Germain as a person of illustrious birth."

The age was skeptical, unscientific, and, by reaction, credulous. The philosophes, Hume, Voltaire, and others, were exposing, like an ingenious American gentleman, "the mistakes of Moses." The Earl of Marischal told Hume that life had been chemically produced in a laboratory, so what becomes of Creation? Prince Charles, hidden in a convent, was being tutored by Mlle. Luci in the sensational philosophy of Locke, "nothing in the intellect which does not come through the senses"—a queer theme for a man of the sword to study. But, thirty years earlier, the Regent d'Orleans had made crystal- gazing fashionable, and stories of ghosts and second-sight in the highest circles were popular. Mesmer had not yet appeared, to give a fresh start to the old savage practice of hypnotism; Cagliostro was not yet on the scene with his free-masonry of the ancient Egyptian school. But people were already in extremes of doubt and of belief; there might be something in the elixir of life and in the philosopher's stone; it might be possible to make precious stones chemically, and Saint-Germain, who seemed to be over a century old at least, might have all these secrets.

Whence came his wealth in precious stones, people asked, unless from some mysterious knowledge, or some equally mysterious and illustrious birth?

He showed Madame de Pompadour a little box full of rubies, topazes, and diamonds. Madame de Pompadour called Madame du Hausset to look at them; she was dazzled, but skeptical, and made a sign to show that she thought them paste. The Count then exhibited a superb ruby, tossing aside contemptuously a cross covered with gems. "That is not so contemptible," said Madame du Hausset, hanging it round her neck. The Count begged her to keep the jewel; she refused, and Madame de Pompadour backed her refusal. But Saint- Germain insisted, and Madame de Pompadour, thinking that the cross might be worth forty louis, made a sign to Madame du Hausset that she accept. She did, and the jewel was valued at 1,500 francs—which hardly proves that the other large jewels were genuine, though Von Gleichen believed they were, and thought the Count's cabinet of old masters very valuable.

The fingers, the watch, the snuffbox, the shoe-buckles, the garter studs, the solitaires of the Count, on high days, all burned with diamonds and rubies, which were estimated, one day, at 200,000 francs. His wealth did not come from cards or swindling—no such charges are ever hinted at; he did not sell elixirs, nor prophecies, nor initiations. His habits do not seem to have been extravagant. One might regard him as a clever eccentric person, the unacknowledged child, perhaps, of some noble, who had put his capital mainly into precious stones. But Louis XV. treated him as a serious personage, and probably knew, or thought he knew, the secret of his birth. People held that he was a bastard of a king of Portugal, says Madame du Hausset. Perhaps the most ingenious and plausible theory of the birth of Saint-Germain makes him the natural son, not of a king of Portugal, but of a queen of Spain. The evidence is not evidence, but a series of surmises. Saint- Germain, on this theory, 'wrop his buth up in a mistry' (like that of Charles James Fitzjames de la Pluche), out of regard for the character of his royal mamma. I believe this about as much as I believe that a certain Rev. Mr. Douglas, an obstreperous Covenanting minister, was a descendant of the captive Mary Stuart. However, Saint-Germain is said, like Kaspar Hauser, to have murmured of dim memories of his infancy, of diversions on magnificent terraces, and of palaces glowing beneath an azure sky. This is reported by Von Gleichen, who knew him very well, but thought him rather a quack. Possibly he meant to convey the idea that he was Moses, and that he had dwelt in the palaces of the Ramessids. The grave of the prophet was never known, and Saint- Germain may have insinuated that he began a new avatar in a cleft of Mount Pisgah; he was capable of it.

However, a less wild surmise avers that, in 1763, the secrets of his birth and the source of his opulence were known in Holland. The authority is the Memoirs of Grosley (1813). Grosley was an archaeologist of Troyes; he had traveled in Italy, and written an account of his travels; he also visited Holland and England, and later, from a Dutchman, he picked up his information about Saint- Germain. Grosley was a Fellow of our Royal Society, and I greatly revere the authority of a F.R.S. His later years were occupied in the compilation of his Memoirs, including an account of what he did and heard in Holland, and he died in 1785. According to Grosley's account of what the Dutchman knew, Saint-Germain was the son of a princess who fled (obviously from Spain) to Bayonne, and of a Portuguese Jew dwelling in Bordeaux.

What fairy and fugitive princess can this be, whom not in vain the ardent Hebrew wooed? She was, she must have been, as Grosley saw, the heroine of Victor Hugo's Ruy Blas. The unhappy Charles II. of Spain, a kind of "mammet" (as the English called the Richard II. who appeared up in Islay, having escaped from Pomfret Castle), had for his first wife a daughter of Henrietta, the favorite sister of our Charles II. This childless bride, after some ghostly years of matrimony, after being exorcised in disgusting circumstances, died in February, 1689. In May, 1690 a new bride, Marie de Neuborg, was brought to the grisly side of the crowned mammet of Spain. She, too, failed to prevent the wars of the Spanish Succession by giving an heir to the Crown of Spain. Scandalous chronicles aver that Marie was chosen as Queen of Spain for the levity of her character, and that the Crown was expected, as in the Pictish monarchy, to descend on the female side; the father of the prince might be anybody. What was needed was simply a son of the QUEEN of Spain. She had, while Queen, no son, as far as is ascertained, but she had a favorite, a Count Andanero, whom she made minister of finance. "He was not a born Count," he was a financier, this favorite of the Queen of Spain. That lady did go to live in Bayonne in 1706, six years after the death of Charles II., her husband. The hypothesis is, then, that Saint-Germain was the son of this ex-Queen of Spain, and of the financial Count, Andanero, a man, "not born in the sphere of Counts," and easily transformed by tradition into a Jewish banker of Bordeaux. The Duc de Choiseul, who disliked the intimacy of Louis XV. and of the Court with Saint-Germain, said that the Count was "the son of a Portuguese Jew, WHO DECEIVES THE COURT. It is strange that the King is so often allowed to be almost alone with this man, though, when he goes out, he is surrounded by guards, as if he feared assassins everywhere." This anecdote is from the Memoirs of Gleichen, who had seen a great deal of the world. He died in 1807.

It seems a fair inference that the Duc de Choiseul knew what the Dutch bankers knew, the story of the Count's being a child of a princess retired to Bayonne—namely, the ex-Queen of

Spain—and of a Portuguese-Hebrew financier. De Choiseul was ready to accept the Jewish father, but thought that, in the matter of the royal mother, Saint-Germain "deceived the Court."

A queen of Spain might have carried off any quantity of the diamonds of Brazil. The presents of diamonds from her almost idiotic lord must have been among the few comforts of her situation in a Court overridden by etiquette. The reader of Madame d'Aulnoy's contemporary account of the Court of Spain knows what a dreadful dungeon it was. Again, if born at Bayonne about 1706, the Count would naturally seem to be about fifty in 1760. The purity with which he spoke German, and his familiarity with German princely Courts—where I do not remember that Barry Lyndon ever met him—are easily accounted for if he had a royal German to his mother. But, alas! if he was the son of a Hebrew financier, Portuguese or Alsatian (as some said), he was likely, whoever his mother may have been, to know German, and to be fond of precious stones. That Oriental taste notoriously abides in the hearts of the Chosen People.[1]

[1] Voyage en Angleterre, 1770.

"Nay, nefer shague your gory locks at me,
Dou canst not say I did it,"

quotes Pinto, the hero of Thackeray's Notch on the Axe. "He pronounced it, by the way, I DIT it, by which I KNOW that Pinto was a German," says Thackeray. I make little doubt but that Saint- Germain, too, was a German, whether by the mother's side, and of princely blood, or quite the reverse.

Grosley mixes Saint-Germain up with a lady as mysterious as himself, who also lived in Holland, on wealth of an unknown source, and Grosley inclines to think that the Count found his way into a French prison, where he was treated with extraordinary respect.

Von Gleichen, on the other hand, shows the Count making love to a daughter of Madame Lambert, and lodging in the house of the mother. Here Von Gleichen met the man of mystery and became rather intimate with him. Von Gleichen deemed him very much older than he looked, but did not believe in his elixir.

In any case, he was not a cardsharper, a swindler, a professional medium, or a spy. He passed many evenings almost alone with Louis XV., who, where men were concerned, liked them to be of good family (about ladies he was much less exclusive). The Count had a grand manner; he treated some great personages in a cavalier way, as if he were at least their equal. On the whole, if not really the son of a princess, he probably persuaded Louis XV. that he did come of that blue blood, and the King would have every access to authentic information. Horace Walpole's reasons for thinking Saint-Germain "not a gentleman" scarcely seem convincing.

The Duc de Choiseul did not like the fashionable Saint-Germain. He thought him a humbug, even when the doings of the deathless one were perfectly harmless. As far as is known, his recipe for health consisted in drinking a horrible mixture called "senna tea"—which was administered to small boys when I was a small boy—and in not drinking anything at his meals. Many people still observe this regimen, in the interest, it is said, of their figures. Saint- Germain used to come to the house of de Choiseul, but one day, when Von Gleichen was present, the minister lost his temper with his wife. He observed that she took no wine at dinner, and told her that she had learned that habit of abstinence from Saint-Germain; that HE might do as he pleased, "but you, madame, whose health is precious to me, I forbid to imitate the regimen of such a dubious character." Gleichen, who tells the anecdote, says that he was present when de Choiseul thus lost his temper with his wife. The dislike of de Choiseul had a mournful effect on the career of Saint-Germain.

In discussing the strange story of the Chevalier d'Eon, one has seen that Louis XV. amused himself by carrying on a secret scheme of fantastic diplomacy through subordinate agents, behind the backs and without the knowledge of his responsible ministers. The Duc de Choiseul, as Minister of Foreign Affairs, was excluded, it seems, from all knowledge of these double intrigues, and the Marechal de Belle-Isle, Minister of War, was obviously kept in the dark, as was Madame de Pompadour. Now it is stated by Von Gleichen that the Marechal de Belle-Isle, from the War Office, started a NEW secret diplomacy behind the back of de Choiseul, at the Foreign Office. The King and Madame de Pompadour (who was not initiated into the general scheme of the King's secret) were both acquainted with what de Choiseul was not to know—namely, Belle-Isle's plan for secretly making peace through the mediation, or management, at all events, of Holland. All this must have been prior to the death of the Marechal de Belle-Isle in 1761; and probably de Broglie, who managed the regular old secret policy of Louis XV., knew nothing about this new clandestine adventure; at all events, the late Duc de Broglie says nothing about it in his book The King's Secret.[1]

[1] The Duc de Broglie, I am privately informed, could find no clue to the mystery of Saint-Germain.

The story, as given by Von Gleichen, goes on to say that Saint- Germain offered to conduct the intrigue at the Hague. As Louis XV. certainly allowed that maidenly captain of dragoons, d'Eon, to manage his hidden policy in London, it is not at all improbable that he really intrusted this fresh cabal in Holland to Saint- Germain, whom he admitted to great intimacy. To The Hague went Saint-Germain, diamonds, rubies, senna tea, and all, and began to diplomatize with the Dutch. But the regular French minister at The Hague, d'Affry, found out what was going on behind his back—found it out either because he was sharper than other ambassadors, or because a personage so extraordinary as Saint-Germain was certain to be very closely watched, or because the Dutch did not take to the Undying One, and told d'Affry what he was doing. D'Affry wrote to de Choiseul. An immortal but dubious personage, he said, was treating in the interests of France, for peace, which it was d'Affry's business to do if the thing was to be done at all. Choiseul replied in a rage by the same courier. Saint-Germain, he said, must be extradited, bound hand and foot, and sent to the Bastille. Choiseul thought that he might practice his regimen and drink his senna tea, to the advantage of public affairs, within those venerable walls. Then the angry minister went to the King, told him what orders he had given, and said that, of course, in a case of this kind it was superfluous to inquire as to the royal pleasure. Louis XV. was caught; so was the Marechal de Belle-Isle. They blushed and were silent.

It must be remembered that this report of a private incident could only come to the narrator, Von Gleichen, from de Choiseul, with whom he professes to have been intimate. The King and the Marechal de Belle-Isle would not tell the story of their own discomfiture. It is not very likely that de Choiseul himself would blab. However, the anecdote avers that the King and the Minister for War thought it best to say nothing, and the demand for Saint-Germain's extradition was presented at The Hague. But the Dutch were not fond of giving up political offenders. They let Saint-Germain have a hint; he slipped over to London, and a London paper published a kind of veiled interview with him in June 1760.

His name, we read, when announced after his death, will astonish the world more than all the marvels of his life. He has been in England already (1743-17—?); he is a great unknown. Nobody can accuse him of anything dishonest or dishonorable. When he was here before we were all mad about music, and so he enchanted us with his violin. But Italy knows him as an expert in the plastic arts, and Germany admires in him a master in chemical science. In France, where he was supposed to possess the secret of the transmutation of metals, the police for two years sought and failed to find any normal source of his opulence. A lady of forty-five once swallowed a whole bottle of his elixir. Nobody recognized her, for she had become a girl of sixteen without observing the transformation!

Saint-Germain is said to have remained in London but for a short period. Horace Walpole does not speak of him again, which is odd, but probably the Count did not again go into society. Our information, mainly from Von Gleichen, becomes very misty, a thing of surmises, really worthless. The Count is credited with a great part in the palace conspiracies of St. Petersburg; he lived at Berlin, and, under the name of Tzarogy, at the Court of the Margrave of Anspach. Then he went, they say, to Italy, and then north to the Landgrave Charles of Hesse, who dabbled in alchemy. Here he is said to have died about 1780-85, leaving his papers to the Landgrave but all is very vague after he disappeared from Paris in 1760. When next I meet Saint-Germain he is again at Paris, again mysteriously rich, again he rather disappears than dies, he calls himself Major Fraser, and the date is in the last years of Louis Philippe. My authority may be caviled at; it is that of the late ingenious Mr. Van Damme, who describes Major Fraser in a book on the characters of the Second Empire. He does not seem to have heard of Saint-Germain, whom he does not mention.

Major Fraser, "in spite of his English (sic) name, was decidedly not English, though he spoke the language." He was (like Saint-Germain) "one of the best dressed men of the period. . . . He lived alone, and never alluded to his parentage. He was always flush of money, though the sources of his income were a mystery to everyone." The French police vainly sought to detect the origin of Saint-Germain's supplies, opening his letters at the post-office. Major Fraser's knowledge of every civilized country at every period was marvelous, though he had very few books. "His memory was something prodigious. . . . Strange to say, he used often to hint that his was no mere book knowledge. "'Of course, it is perfectly ridiculous,'" he remarked, with a strange smile, "'but every now and then I feel as if this did not come to me from reading, but from personal experience. At times I become almost convinced that I lived with Nero, that I knew Dante personally, and so forth.'"[1] At the major's death not a letter was found giving a clew to his antecedents, and no money was discovered. DID he die? As in the case of Saint-Germain, no date is given. The author had an idea that the major was "an illegitimate son of some exalted person" of the period of Charles IV. and Ferdinand VII. of Spain.

[1] An Englishman in Paris, vol. i., pp. 130-133. London, 1892.

The author does not mention Saint-Germain, and may never have heard of him. If his account of Major Fraser is not mere romance, in that warrior we have the undying friend of Louis XV. and Madame de Pompadour. He had drunk at Medmenham with Jack Wilkes; as Riccio he had sung duets with the fairest of unhappy queens; he had extracted from Blanche de Bechamel the secret of Goby de Mouchy. As Pinto, he told much of his secret history to Mr. Thackeray, who says: "I am rather sorry to lose him after three little bits of Roundabout Papers."

Did Saint-Germain really die in a palace of Prince Charles of Hesse about 1780-85? Did he, on the other hand, escape from the French prison where Grosley thought he saw him, during the French Revolution? Was he known to Lord Lytton about 1860? Was he then Major Fraser? Is he the mysterious Muscovite adviser of the Dalai Lama? Who knows? He is a will-o'-the-wisp of the memoir-writers of the eighteenth century. Whenever you think you have a chance of finding him in good authentic State papers, he gives you the slip; and if his existence were not vouched for by Horace Walpole, I should incline to deem him as Betsy Prig thought of Mrs. Harris.

The Man in the Iron Mask

I

THE LEGEND

The Mystery of the Man in the Iron Mask is, despite a pleasant saying of Lord Beaconsfield's, one of the most fascinating in history. By a curious coincidence the wildest legend on the subject, and the correct explanation of the problem, were offered to the world in the same year, 1801. According to this form of the legend, the Man in the Iron Mask was the genuine Louis XIV., deprived of his rights in favor of a child of Anne of Austria and of Mazarin. Immured in the Isles Sainte-Marguerite, in the bay of Cannes (where you are shown his cell, looking north to the sunny town), he married, and begot a son. That son was carried to Corsica, was named de Buona Parte, and was the ancestor of Napoleon. The Emperor was thus the legitimate representative of the House of Bourbon.

This legend was circulated in 1801, and is referred to in a proclamation of the Royalists of La Vendee. In the same year, 1801, Roux Fazaillac, a Citoyen and a revolutionary legislator, published a work in which he asserted that the Man in the Iron Mask (as known in rumor) was not one man, but a myth, in which the actual facts concerning at least two men were blended. It is certain that Roux Fazaillac was right; or that, if he was wrong, the Man in the Iron Mask was an obscure valet, of French birth, residing in England, whose real name was Martin.

Before we enter on the topic of this poor menial's tragic history, it may be as well to trace the progress of the romantic legend, as it blossomed after the death of the Man, whose Mask was not of iron, but of black velvet. Later we shall show how the legend struck root and flowered, from the moment when the poor valet, Martin (by his prison pseudonym "Eustache Dauger"), was immured in the French fortress of Pignerol, in Piedmont (August, 1669).

The Man, in connection with the Mask, is first known to us from a kind of notebook kept by du Junca, Lieutenant of the Bastille. On September 18, 1698, he records the arrival of the new Governor of the Bastille, M. de Saint-Mars, bringing with him, from his last place, the Isles Sainte-Marguerite, in the bay of Camnes, "an old prisoner whom he had at Pignerol. He keeps the prisoner always masked, his name is not spoken . . . and I have put him alone, in the third chamber of the Bertaudiere tower, having furnished it some days before with everything, by order of M. de Saint-Mars. The prisoner is to be served and cared for by M. de Rosarges," the officer next in command under Saint-Mars.[1]

[1] Funck-Brentano, Legendes et Archives de la Bastille, pp. 86, 87. Paris, 1898, p. 277, a facsimile of this entry.

The prisoner's death is entered by du Junca on November 19, 1703.

To that entry we return later.

The existence of this prisoner was known and excited curiosity. On October 15, 1711, the Princess Palatine wrote about the case to the Electress Sophia of Hanover, "A man lived for long years in the Bastille, masked, and masked he died there. Two musketeers were by his side to shoot him if ever he unmasked. He ate and slept in his mask. There must, doubtless, have been some good reason for this, as otherwise he was very well treated, well lodged, and had everything given to him that he wanted. He took the Communion masked; was very devout, and read perpetually."

On October 22, 1711, the Princess writes that the Mask was an English nobleman, mixed up in the plot of the Duke of Berwick against William III.—Fenwick's affair is meant. He was imprisoned and masked that the Dutch usurper might never know what had become of him.[1]

[1] Op. cit. 98, note I.

The legend was now afloat in society. The sub-commandant of the Bastille from 1749 to 1787, Chevalier, declared, obviously on the evidence of tradition, that all the Mask's furniture and clothes were destroyed at his death, lest they might yield a clew to his identity. Louis XV. is said to have told Madame de Pompadour that the Mask was "the minister of an Italian prince." Louis XVI. told Marie Antoinette (according to Madame de Campan) that the Mask was a Mantuan intriguer, the same person as Louis XV. indicated. Perhaps he was, it is one of two possible alternatives. Voltaire, in the first edition of his "Siecle de Louis XIV.," merely spoke of a young, handsome, masked prisoner, treated with the highest respect by Louvois, the Minister of Louis XIV. At last, in "Questions sur l'Encyclopedie" (second edition), Voltaire averred that the Mask was the son of Anne of Austria and Mazarin, an elder brother of Louis XIV. Changes were rung on this note: the Mask was the actual King, Louis XIV. was a bastard. Others held that he was James, Duke of Monmouth—or Moliere! In 1770 Heiss identified him with Mattioli, the Mantuan intriguer, and especially after the appearance of the book by Roux Fazaillac, in 1801, that was the generally accepted opinion.

It MAY be true, in part. Mattioli MAY have been the prisoner who died in the Bastille in November 1703, but the legend of the Mask's prison life undeniably arose out of the adventure of our valet, Martin or Eustache Dauger.

II

THE VALET'S HISTORY

After reading the arguments of the advocates of Mattioli, I could not but perceive that, whatever captive died, masked, at the Bastille in 1703, the valet Dauger was the real source of most of the legends about the Man in the Iron Mask. A study of M. Lair's book "Nicholas Fouquet" (1890) confirmed this opinion. I therefore pushed the inquiry into a source neglected by the French historians, namely, the correspondence of the English ambassadors, agents, and statesmen for the years 1668, 1669.[1] One result is to confirm a wild theory of my own to the effect that the Man in the Iron Mask (if Dauger were he) may have been as great a mystery to himself as to historical inquirers. He may not have known WHAT he was imprisoned for doing! More important is the probable conclusion that the long and mysterious captivity of Eustache Dauger, and of another perfectly harmless valet and victim, was the mere automatic result of "red tape" of the old French absolute monarchy. These wretches were caught in the toils of the system, and suffered to no purpose, for no crime. The two men, at least Dauger, were apparently mere supernumeraries in the obscure intrigue of a conspirator known as Roux de Marsilly.

[1] The papers are in the Record Office; for the contents see the following essay, The Valet's Master.

This truly abominable tragedy of Roux de Marsilly is "another story," narrated in the following essay. It must suffice here to say that, in 1669, while Charles II. was negotiating the famous, or infamous, secret treaty with Louis XIV.—the treaty of alliance against Holland, and in favor of the restoration of Roman Catholicism in England—Roux de Marsilly, a French Huguenot, was dealing with Arlington and others, in favor of a Protestant league against France.

When he started from England for Switzerland in February, 1669, Marsilly left in London a valet called by him "Martin," who had quitted his service and was living with his own family. This man is the "Eustache Dauger" of our mystery. The name is his prison pseudonym, as "Lestang" was that of Mattioli. The French Government was anxious to lay hands on him, for he had certainly, as the letters of Marsilly prove, come and gone freely between that conspirator and his English employers. How much Dauger knew, what amount of mischief he could effect, was uncertain. Much or little, it was a matter which, strange to say, caused the greatest anxiety to Louis XIV. and to his Ministers for very many years. Probably long before Dauger died (the date is unknown, but it was more than twenty-five years after Marsilly's execution), his secret, if secret he possessed, had ceased to be of importance. But he was now in the toils of the French red tape, the system of secrecy which rarely released its victim. He was guarded, we shall see with such unheard-of rigor that popular fancy at once took him for some great, perhaps royal, personage.

Marsilly was publicly tortured to death in Paris on June 22, 1669. By July 19 his ex-valet, Dauger, had entered on his mysterious term of captivity. How the French got possession of him, whether he yielded to cajolery, or was betrayed by Charles II., is uncertain. The French ambassador at St. James's, Colbert (brother of the celebrated Minister), writes thus to M. de Lyonne, in Paris, on July I, 1669:[1] "Monsieur Joly has spoken to the man Martin" (Dauger), "and has really persuaded him that, by going to France and telling all that he knows against Roux, he will play the part of a lad of honor and a good subject."

[1] Transcripts from Paris MSS., Vol. xxxiii., Record Office.

But Martin, after all, was NOT persuaded!

Martin replied to Joly that he knew nothing at all, and that, once in France, people would think he was well acquainted with the traffickings of Roux, "and so he would be kept in prison to make him divulge what he did not know." The possible Man in the Iron Mask did not know his own secret! But, later in the conversation, Martin foolishly admitted that he knew a great deal; perhaps he did this out of mere fatal vanity. Cross to France, however, he would not, even when offered a safe-conduct and promise of reward. Colbert therefore proposes to ask Charles to surrender the valet, and probably Charles descended to the meanness. By July 19, at all events, Louvois, the War Minister of Louis XIV., was bidding Saint- Mars, at Pignerol in Piedmont, expect from Dunkirk a prisoner of the very highest importance—a valet! This valet, now called "Eustache Dauger," can only have been Marsilly's valet, Martin, who, by one means or another, had been brought from England to Dunkirk. It is hardly conceivable, at least, that when a valet, in England, is "wanted" by the French police on July 1, for political reasons, and when by July 19 they have caught a valet of extreme political importance, the two valets should be two different men. Martin must be Dauger.

Here, then, by July 19, 1669, we find our unhappy serving man in the toils. Why was he to be handled with such mysterious rigor? It is true that State prisoners of very little account were kept with great secrecy. But it cannot well be argued that they were all treated with the extraordinary precautions which, in the case of Dauger, were not relaxed for twenty-five or thirty years. The King says, according to Louvois, that the safe keeping of Dauger is "of the last importance to his service." He must have intercourse with nobody. His windows must be where nobody can pass; several bolted doors must cut him off from the sound of human voices. Saint-Mars himself, the commandant, must feed the valet daily. "You must never, under any pretenses listen to what he may wish to tell you. You must threaten him with death if he speaks one word except about his actual needs. He is only a valet, and does not need much furniture."[1]

[1] The letters are printed by Roux Fazaillac, Jung, Lair, and others.

Saint-Mars replied that, in presence of M. de Vauroy, the chief officer of Dunkirk (who carried Dauger thence to Pignerol), he had threatened to run Dauger through the body if he ever dared to speak, even to him, Saint-Mars. He has mentioned this prisoner, he says, to no mortal. People believe that Dauger is a Marshal of France, so strange and unusual are the precautions taken for his security.

A Marshal of France! The legend has begun. At this time (1669) Saint-Mars had in charge Fouquet, the great fallen Minister, the richest and most dangerous subject of Louis XIV. By-and-by he also held Lauzun, the adventurous wooer of la Grande Mademoiselle. But it was not they, it was the valet, Dauger, who caused "sensation."

On February 20, 1672, Saint-Mars, for the sake of economy, wished to use Dauger as valet to Lauzun. This proves that Saint-Mars did not, after all, see the necessity of secluding Dauger or thought the King's fears groundless. In the opinion of Saint-Mars, Dauger did not want to be released, "would never ask to be set free." Then why was he so anxiously guarded? Louvois refused to let Dauger be put with Lauzun as valet. In 1675, however, he allowed Dauger to act as valet to Fouquet, but with Lauzun, said Louvois, Dauger must have no intercourse. Fouquet had then another prisoner valet, La Riviere. This man had apparently been accused of no crime. He was of a melancholy character, and a dropsical habit of body: Fouquet had amused himself by doctoring him and teaching him to read.

In the month of December, 1678, Saint-Mars, the commandant of the prison, brought to Fouquet a sealed letter from Louvois, the seal unbroken. His own reply was also to be sealed, and not to be seen by Saint-Mars. Louvois wrote that the King wished to know one thing, before giving Fouquet ampler liberty. Had his valet, Eustache Dauger, told his other valet, La Riviere, what he had done before coming to Pignerol? (de ce a quoi il a ete employe aupravant que d'etre a Pignerol). "His Majesty bids me ask you [Fouquet] this question, and expects that you will answer without considering anything but the truth, that he may know what measures to take," these depending on whether Dauger has, or has not, told La Riviere the story of his past life.[1] Moreover, Lauzun was never, said Louvois, to be allowed to enter Fouquet's room when Dauger was present. The humorous point is that, thanks to a hole dug in the wall between his room and Fouquet's, Lauzun saw Dauger whenever he pleased.

[1] Lair, Nicholas Foucquet, ii. pp. 463, 464.

From the letter of Louvois to Fouquet, about Dauger (December 23, 1678), it is plain that Louis XIV. had no more pressing anxiety, nine years after Dauger's arrest, than to conceal what it was that Dauger had done. It is apparent that Saint-Mars himself either was unacquainted with this secret, or was supposed by Louvois and the King to be unaware of it. He had been ordered never to allow Dauger to tell him; he was not allowed to see the letters on the subject between Lauzun and Fouquet. We still do not know, and never shall know, whether Dauger himself knew his own secret, or whether (as he had anticipated) he was locked up for not divulging what he did not know.

The answer of Fouquet to Louvois must have satisfied Louis that Dauger had not imparted his secret to the other valet, La Riviere, for Fouquet was now allowed a great deal of liberty. In 1679, he might see his family, the officers of the garrison, and Lauzun—it being provided that Lauzun and Dauger should never meet. In March, 1680, Fouquet died, and henceforth the two valets were most rigorously guarded; Dauger, because he was supposed to know something; La Riviere, because Dauger might have imparted the real or fancied secret to him. We shall return to these poor serving men, but here it is necessary to state that, ten months before the death of their master, Fouquet, an important new captive had been brought to the prison of Pignerol.

This captive was the other candidate for the honors of the Mask, Count Mattioli, the secretary of the Duke of Mantua. He was kidnaped on Italian soil on May 2, 1679, and hurried to the mountain fortress of Pignerol, then on French ground. His offense was the betraying of the secret negotiations for the cession of the town and fortress of Casal, by the Duke of Mantua, to Louis XIV. The disappearance of Mattioli was, of course, known to the world. The cause of his enlevement, and the place of his captivity, Pignerol, were matters of newspaper comment at least as early as 1687. Still earlier, in 1682, the story of Mattioli's arrest and seclusion in Pignerol had been published in a work named "La Prudenza Trionfante di Casale."[1] There was thus no mystery, at the time, about Mattioli; his crime and punishment were perfectly well known to students of politics. He has been regarded as the mysterious Man in the Iron Mask, but, for years after his arrest, he was the least mysterious of State prisoners.

[1] Brentano, op. cit., p. 117.

Here, then, is Mattioli in Pignerol in May, 1679. While Fouquet then enjoyed relative freedom, while Lauzun schemed escapes or made insulting love to Mademoiselle Fouquet, Mattioli lived on the bread and water of affliction. He was threatened with torture to make him deliver up some papers compromising Louis XIV. It was expressly commanded that he should have nothing beyond the barest necessaries of life. He was to be kept dans la dure prison. In brief, he was used no better than the meanest of prisoners. The awful life of isolation, without employment, without books, without writing materials, without sight or sound of man save when Saint- Mars or his lieutenant brought food for the day, drove captives mad.

In January, 1680, two prisoners, a monk[1] and one Dubreuil, had become insane. By February 14, 1680, Mattioli was daily conversing with God and his angels. "I believe his brain is turned," says Saint-Mars. In March, 1680, as we saw, Fouquet died. The prisoners, not counting Lauzun (released soon after), were now five: (1) Mattioli (mad); (2) Dubreuil (mad); (3) The monk (mad); (4) Dauger, and (5) La Riviere. These two, being employed as valets, kept their wits. On the death of Fouquet, Louvois wrote to Saint-Mars about the two valets. Lauzun must be made to believe that they had been set at liberty, but, in fact, they must be most carefully guarded IN A SINGLE CHAMBER. They were shut up in one of the dungeons of the "Tour d'en bas." Dauger had recently done something as to which Louvois writes: "Let me know how Dauger can possibly have done what you tell me, and how he got the necessary drugs, as I cannot suppose that you supplied him with them" (July 10, 1680).[2]

[1] A monk, who MAY have been this monk, appears in the following essay, p. 34, infra.

[2] Lair, Nicholas Foucquet, ii., pp. 476, 477.

Here, then, by July, 1680, are the two valets locked in one dungeon of the "Tour d'en bas." By September Saint-Mars had placed Mattioli, with the mad monk, in another chamber of the same tower. He writes: "Mattioli is almost as mad as the monk," who arose from bed and preached naked. Mattioli behaved so rudely and violently that the lieutenant of Saint-Mars had to show him a whip, and threaten him with a flogging. This had its effect. Mattioli, to make his peace, offered a valuable ring to Blainvilliers. The ring was kept to be restored to him, if ever Louis let him go free—a contingency mentioned more than once in the correspondence.

Apparently Mattioli now sobered down, and probably was given a separate chamber and a valet; he certainly had a valet at Pignerol later. By May 1681, Dauger and La Riviere still occupied their common chamber in the "Tour d'en bas." They were regarded by Louvois as the most important of the five prisoners then at Pignerol. They, not Mattioli, were the captives about whose safe and secret keeping Louis and Louvois were most anxious. This appears from a letter of Louvois to Saint-Mars, of May 12, 1681. The jailer, Saint-Mars, is to be promoted from Pignerol to Exiles. "Thither," says Louvois, "the king desires to transport such of your prisoners as he thinks too important to have in other hands than yours." These prisoners are "the two in the low chamber of the tower," the two valets, Dauger and La Riviere.

From a letter of Saint-Mars (June, 1681) we know that Mattioli was not one of these. He says: "I shall keep at Exiles two birds (merles) whom I have here: they are only known as the gentry of the low room in the tower; Mattioli may stay on here at Pignerol with the other prisoners" (Dubreuil and the mad monk). It is at this point that Le Citoyen Roux (Fazaillac), writing in the Year IX. of the Republic (1801), loses touch with the secret.[1] Roux finds, in the State Papers, the arrival of Eustache Dauger at Pignerol in 1669, but does not know who he is, or what is his quality. He sees that the Mask must be either Mattioli, Dauger, the monk, one Dubreuil, or one Calazio. But, overlooking or not having access to the letter of Saint-Mars of June, 1681, Roux holds that the prisoners taken to Les Exiles were the monk and Mattioli. One of these must be the Mask, and Roux votes for Mattioli. He is wrong. Mattioli beyond all doubt remained at Pignerol.

[1] Recherches Historiques sur l'Homme au Masque de Fer, Paris. An. IX.

Mountains of argument have been built on these words, deux merles, "two jail-birds." One of the two, we shall see, became the source of the legend of the Man in the Iron Mask. "How can a wretched jail-bird (merle) have been the Mask?" asks M. Topin. "The rogue's whole furniture and table-linen were sold for 1l. 19s. He only got a new suit of clothes every three years." All very true; but this jail-bird and his mate, by the direct statement of Louvois, are "the prisoners too important to be intrusted to other hands than yours"—the hands of Saint-Mars—while Mattioli is so unimportant that he may be left at Pignerol under Villebois.

The truth is, that the offense and the punishment of Mattioli were well known to European diplomatists and readers of books. Casal, moreover, at this time was openly ceded to Louis XIV., and Mattioli could not have told the world more than it already knew. But, for some inscrutable reason, the secret which Dauger knew, or was suspected of knowing, became more and more a source of anxiety to Louvois and Louis. What can he have known? The charges against his master, Roux de Marsilly, had been publicly proclaimed. Twelve years had passed since the dealings of Arlington with Marsilly. Yet, Louvois became more and more nervous.

In accordance with commands of his, on March 2, 1682, the two valets, who had hitherto occupied one chamber at Exiles as at Pignerol, were cut off from all communication with each other. Says Saint-Mars, "Since receiving your letter I have warded the pair as strictly and exactly as I did M. Fouquet and M. Lauzun, who cannot brag that he sent or received any intelligence. Night and day two sentinels watch their tower; and my own windows command a view of the sentinels. Nobody speaks to my captives but myself, my lieutenant, their confessor, and the doctor, who lives eighteen miles away, and only sees them when I am present." Years went by; in January, 1687, one of the two captives died; we really do not know which with absolute certainty. However, the intensified secrecy with which the survivor was now guarded seems more appropriate to Dauger and M. Funck-Brentano and M. Lair have no doubt that it was La Riviere who expired. He was dropsical, that appears in the official correspondence, and the dead prisoner died of dropsy.

As for the strange secrecy about Dauger, here is an example. Saint-Mars, in January, 1687, was appointed to the fortress of the Isles Sainte-Marguerite, that sun themselves in the bay of Cannes. On January 20 he asks leave to go to see his little kingdom. He must leave Dauger, but has forbidden even his lieutenant to speak to that prisoner. This was an increase of precaution since 1682. He wishes to take the captive to the Isles, but how? A sedan chair covered over with oilcloth seems best. A litter might break down, litters often did, and some one might then see the passenger.

Now M. Funck-Brentano says, to minimize the importance of Dauger, "he was shut up like so much luggage in a chair hermetically closed with oilcloth, carried by eight Piedmontese relays of four."

Luggage is not usually carried in hermetically sealed sedan chairs, but Saint-Mars has explained why, by surplus of precaution, he did not use a litter. The litter might break down and Dauger might be seen. A new prison was built specially, at the cost of 5,000 lires, for Dauger at Sainte-Marguerite, with large sunny rooms. On May 3, 1687, Saint-Mars had entered on his island realm, Dauger being nearly killed by twelve days' journey in a closed chair. He again excited the utmost curiosity. On January 8, 1688, Saint-Mars writes that his prisoner is believed by the world to be either a son of Oliver Cromwell, or the Duc de Beaufort,[1] who was never seen again, dead or alive, after a night battle in Crete, on June 25, 1669, just before Dauger was arrested. Saint-Mars sent in a note of the TOTAL of Dauger's expenses for the year 1687. He actually did not dare to send the ITEMS, he says, lest they, if the bill fell into the wrong hands, might reveal too much.

[1] Duc de Beaufort whom Athos releases from prison in Dumas's Vingt Ans Apres.

Meanwhile, an Italian news-letter, copied into a Leyden paper, of August 1687, declared that Mattioli had just been brought from Pignerol to Sainte-Marguerite. There was no mystery about Mattioli, the story of his capture was published in 1682, but the press, on one point, was in error; Mattioli was still at Pignerol. The known advent of the late Commandant of Pignerol, Saint-Mars, with a single concealed prisoner, at the island, naturally suggested the erroneous idea that the prisoner was Mattioli. The prisoner was really Dauger, the survivor of the two valets.

From 1688 to 1691 no letter about Dauger has been published. Apparently he was then the only prisoner on the island, except one Chezut, who was there before Dauger arrived, and gave up his chamber to Dauger while the new cells were being built. Between 1689 and 1693 six Protestant preachers were brought to the island, while Louvois, the Minister, died in 1691, and was succeeded by Barbezieux. On August 13, 1691, Barbezieux wrote to ask Saint-Mars about "the prisoner whom he had guarded for twenty years." The only such prisoner was Dauger, who entered Pignerol in August, 1669. Mattioli had been a prisoner only for twelve years, and lay in Pignerol, not in Sainte-Marguerite, where Saint-Mars now was. Saint-Mars replied: "I can assure you that NOBODY HAS SEEN HIM BUT MYSELF."

By the beginning of March, 1694, Pignerol had been bombarded by the enemies of France; presently Louis XIV. had to cede it to Savoy. The prisoners there must be removed. Mattioli, in Pignerol, at the end of 1693, had been in trouble. He and his valet had tried to smuggle out letters written on the linings of their pockets. These were seized and burned. On March 20, 1694, Barbezieux wrote to Laprade, now commanding at Pignerol, that he must take his three prisoners, one by one, with all secrecy, to Sainte-Marguerite. Laprade alone must give them their food on the journey. The military officer of the escort was warned to ask no questions. Already (February 26, 1694) Barbezieux had informed Saint-Mars that these prisoners were coming. They are of more consequence, one of them at least, than the prisoners on the island, and must be put in the safest places." The "one" is doubtless Mattioli. In 1681 Louvois had thought Dauger and La Riviere more important than Mattioli, who, in March, 1694, came from Pignerol to Sainte- Marguerite. Now in April, 1694, a prisoner died at the island, a prisoner who, like Mattioli, HAD A VALET. We hear of no other prisoner on the island, except Mattioli who had a valet. A letter of Saint-Mars (January 6, 1696) proves that no prisoner THEN had a valet, for each prisoner collected his own dirty plates and dishes, piled them up, and handed them to the lieutenant.

M. Funck-Brentano argues that in this very letter (January 6, 1696) Saint-Mars speaks of "les valets de messieurs les prisonniers." But in THAT part of the letter Saint-Mars is not speaking of the actual state of things at Sainte-Marguerite, but is giving reminiscences of Fouquet and Lauzun, who, of course, at Piguerol, had valets, and had money, as he shows. Dauger had no money. M. Funck-Brentano next argues that early in 1694 one of the preacher prisoners, Melzac, died, and cites M. Jung ("La Verite sur le Masque de Fer," p. 91). This is odd, as M. Jung says that Melzac, or Malzac, "died in the end of 1692, or early in 1693." Why, then, does M. Funck-Brentano cite M. Jung for the death of the preacher early in 1694, when M. Jung (conjecturally) dates his decease at least a year earlier?[1] It is not a mere conjecture as, on March 3, 1693, Barbezieux begs Saint-Mars to mention his Protestant prisoners under nicknames. There are THREE, and Malzac is no longer one of them. Malzac, in 1692, suffered from a horrible disease, discreditable to one of the godly, and in October, 1692, had been allowed medical expenses. Whether they included a valet or not, Malzac seems to have been non-existent by March, 1693. Had he possessed a valet, and had he died in 1694, why should HIS valet have been "shut up in the vaulted prison"? This was the fate of the valet of the prisoner who died in April, 1694, and was probably Mattioli.

[1] M. Funck-Brentano's statement is in Revue Historique, lvi. p. 298. "Malzac died at the beginning of 1694," citing Jung, p. 91. Now on p. 91 M. Jung writes, "At the beginning of 1694 Saint-Mars had six prisoners, of whom one Melzac, dies." But M. Jung (pp. 269, 270) later writes, "It is probable that Melzac died at the end of 1692, or early in 1693," and he gives his reasons, which are convincing. M. Funck-Brentano must have overlooked M. Jung's change of opinion between his p. 91 and his pp. 269, 270.

Mattioli, certainly, had a valet in December, 1693, at Pignerol. He went to Sainte-Marguerite in March, 1694. In April, 1694, a prisoner with a valet died at Sainte-Marguerite. In January, 1696, no prisoner at Sainte-Marguerite had a valet. Therefore, there is a strong presumption that the "prisonnier au valet" who died in April, was Mattioli.

After December, 1693, when he was still at Pignerol, the name of Mattioli, freely used before, never occurs in the correspondence. But we still often hear of "l'ancien prisonnier," "the old prisoner." He was, on the face of it, Dauger, by far the oldest prisoner. In 1688, Saint-Mars, having only one prisoner (Dauger), calls him merely "my prisoner. In 1691, when Saint-Mars had several prisoners, Barbezieux styles Dauger "your prisoner of twenty years' standing." When, in 1696-1698, Saint-Mars mentions "mon ancien prisonnier," "my prisoner of long standing," he obviously means Dauger, not Mattioli—above all, if Mattioli died in 1694. M. Funck-Brentano argues that "mon ancien prisonnier" can only mean "my erstwhile prisoner, he who was lost and is restored to me"—that is, Mattioli. This is not the view of M. Jung, or M. Lair, or M. Loiseleur.

Friends of Mattioli's claims rest much on this letter of Barbezieux to Saint-Mars (November

17, 1697): "You have only to watch over the security of all your prisoners, without ever explaining to anyone what it is that your prisoner of long standing did." That secret, it is argued, MUST apply to Mattioli. But all the world knew what Mattioli had done! Nobody knew, and nobody knows, what Eustache Dauger had done. It was one of the arcana imperii. It is the secret enforced ever since Dauger's arrest in 1669. Saint-Mars (1669) was not to ask. Louis XIV. could only lighten the captivity of Fouquet (1678) if his valet, La Riviere, did not know what Dauger had done. La Riviere (apparently a harmless man) lived and died in confinement, the sole reason being that he might perhaps know what Dauger had done. Consequently there is the strongest presumption that the "ancien prisonnier" of 1697 is Dauger, and that "what he had done" (which Saint-Mars must tell to no one) was what Dauger did, not what Mattioli did. All Europe knew what Mattioli had done; his whole story had been published to the world in 1682 and 1687.

On July 19, 1698, Barbezieux bade Saint-Mars come to assume the command of the Bastille. He is to bring his "old prisoner," whom not a soul is to see. Saint-Mars therefore brought his man MASKED, exactly as another prisoner was carried masked from Provence to the Bastille in 1695. M. Funck-Brentano argues that Saint-Mars was now quite fond of his old Mattioli, so noble, so learned.

At last, on September 18, 1698, Saint-Mars lodged his "old prisoner" in the Bastille, "an old prisoner whom he had at Pignerol," says the journal of du Junca, Lieutenant of the Bastille. His food, we saw, was brought him by Rosarges alone, the "Major," a gentleman who had always been with Saint-Mars. Argues M. Funck-Brentano, all this proves that the captive was a gentleman, not a valet. Why? First, because the Bastille, under Louis XIV., was "une prison de distinction." Yet M. Funck-Brentano tells us that in Mazarin's time "valets mixed up with royal plots" were kept in the Bastille. Again, in 1701, in this "noble prison," the Mask was turned out of his room to make place for a female fortune-teller, and was obliged to chum with a profligate valet of nineteen, and a "beggarly" bad patriot, who "blamed the conduct of France, and approved that of other nations, especially the Dutch." M. Funck-Brentano himself publishes these facts (1898), in part published earlier (1890) by M. Lair.[1] Not much noblesse here! Next, if Rosarges, a gentleman, served the Mask, Saint-Mars alone (1669) carried his food to the valet, Dauger. So the service of Rosarges does not ennoble the Mask and differentiate him from Dauger, who was even more nobly served, by Saint-Mars.

[1] Legendes de la Bastille, pp. 86-89. Citing du Junca's Journal, April 30, 1701.

On November 19, 1703, the Mask died suddenly (still in his velvet mask), and was buried on the 20th. The parish register of the church names him "Marchialy" or "Marchioly," one may read it either way; du Junca, Lieutenant of the Bastille, in his contemporary journal, calls him "M. de Marchiel." Now, Saint-Mars often spells Mattioli, "Marthioly."

This is the one strength of the argument for Mattioli's claims to the Mask. M. Lair replies, "Saint-Mars had a mania for burying prisoners under fancy names," and gives examples. One is only a gardener, Francois Eliard (1701), concerning whom it is expressly said that, as he is a prisoner, his real name is not to be given, so he is registered as Pierre Maret (others read Navet, "Peter Turnip"). If Saint-Mars, looking about for a false name for Dauger's burial register, hit on Marsilly (the name of Dauger's old master), that MIGHT be miswritten Marchialy. However it be, the age of the Mask is certainly falsified; the register gives "about forty-five years old." Mattioli would have been sixty-three; Dauger cannot have been under fifty-three.

There the case stands. If Mattioli died in April, 1694, he cannot be the Man in the Iron Mask.

Of Dauger's death we find no record, unless he was the Man in the Iron Mask, and died, in 1703, in the Bastille. He was certainly, in 1669 and 1688, at Pignerol and at Sainte-Marguerite, the center of the mystery about some great prisoner, a Marshal of France, the Duc de Beaufort, or a son of Oliver Cromwell. Mattioli was not mystery, no secret. Dauger is so mysterious that probably the secret of his mystery was unknown to himself. By 1701, when obscure wretches were shut up with the Mask, the secret, whatever its nature, had ceased to be of moment. The captive was now the mere victim of cruel routine. But twenty years earlier, Saint-Mars had said that Dauger "takes things easily, resigned to the will of God and the King."

To sum up, on July 1, 1669, the valet of the Huguenot intriguer, Roux de Marsilly, the valet resident in England, known to his master as "Martin," was "wanted" by the French secret police. By July 19, a valet, of the highest political importance, had been brought to Dunkirk, from England, no doubt. My hypothesis assumes that this valet, though now styled "Eustache Dauger," was the "Martin of Roux de Marsilly. He was kept with so much mystery at Pigernol that already the legend began its course; the captive valet was said to be a Marshal of France! We then follow Dauger from Pignerol to Les Exiles, till January, 1687, when one valet out of a pair, Dauger being one of them, dies. We presume that Dauger is the survivor, because the great mystery still is "what he HAS DONE," whereas the other valet had done nothing, but may have known Dauger's secret. Again the other valet had long been dropsical, and the valet who died in 1687 died of dropsy.

In 1688, Dauger, at Sainte-Marguerite, is again the source and center of myths; he is taken for a son of Oliver Cromwell, or for the Duc de Beufort. In June 1692, one of the Huguenot preachers at Saint-Marguerite writes on his shirt and pewter plate and throws them out of the window.[1] Legend attributes these acts to the Man in the Iron Mask, and transmutes a pewter into a silver plate. Now, in 1689-1693, Mattioli was at Pignerol, but Dauger was at Sainte-Marguerite, and the Huguenot's act is attributed to him. Thus Dauger, not Mattioli, is the center round which the myths crystallize: the legends concern him, not Mattioli, whose case is well known, and gives rise to no legend. Finally, we have shown that Mattioli probably died at Sainte-Marguerite in April, 1694. If so, then nobody but Dauger can be the "old prisoner" whom Saint-Mars brought, masked, to the Bastille, in September, 1698, and who died there in November, 1703. However suppose that Mattioli did not die in 1694, but was the masked man who died in the Bastille in 1703, then the legend of Dauger came to be attributed to Mattioli: these two men's fortunes are combined in the one myth.

[1] Saint-Mars au Ministre, June 4, 1692.

The central problem remains unsolved.

What had the valet, Eustache Dauger, done?[1]

[1] One marvels that nobody has recognized, in the mask, James Stuart (James de la Cloche), eldest of the children of Charles II. He came to England in 1668, was sent to Rome, and "disappears from history." See infra, "The Mystery of James de la Cloche."

III

THE VALET'S MASTER

The secret of the Man in the Iron Mask, or at least of one of the two persons who have claims to be the Mask, was "What had Eustache Dauger done?" To guard this secret the most extraordinary precautions were taken, as we have shown in the foregoing essay. And yet, if secret there was, it might have got wind in the simplest fashion. In the "Vicomte de Bragelonne," Dumas describes the tryst of the Secret-hunters with the dying Chief of the Jesuits at the inn in Fontainebleau. They come from many quarters, there is a Baron of Germany and a laird from Scotland, but Aramis takes the prize. He knows the secret of the Mask, the most valuable of all to the intriguers of the Company of Jesus.

Now, despite all the precautions of Louvois and Saint-Mars, despite sentinels for ever posted under Dauger's windows, despite arrangements which made it impossible for him to signal to people on the hillside at Les Exiles, despite the suppression even of the items in the accounts of his expenses, his secret, if he knew it, could have been discovered, as we have remarked, by the very man most apt to make mischievous use of it—by Lauzun. That brilliant and reckless adventurer could see Dauger, in prison at Pignerol, when he pleased, for he had secretly excavated a way into the rooms of his fellow prisoner, Fouquet, on whom Dauger attended as valet. Lauzun was released soon after Fouquet's death. It is unlikely that he bought his liberty by the knowledge of the secret and there is nothing to suggest that he used it (if he possessed it) in any other way.

The natural clew to the supposed secret of Dauger is a study of the career of his master, Roux de Marsilly. As official histories say next to nothing about him, we may set forth what can be gleaned from the State Papers in our Record Office. The earliest is a letter of Roux de Marsilly to Mr. Joseph Williamson, secretary of Lord Arlington (December, 1668). Marsilly sends Martin (on our theory Eustache Dauger) to bring back from Williamson two letters from his own correspondent in Paris. He also requests Williamson to procure for him from Arlington a letter of protection, as he is threatened with arrest for some debt in which he is not really concerned. Martin will explain. The next paper is indorsed "Received December 28, 1668, Mons. de Marsilly." As it is dated December 27, Marsilly must have been in England. The contents of this piece deserve attention, because they show the terms on which Marsilly and Arlington were, or, at least, how Marsilly conceived them.

(1) Marsilly reports, on the authority of his friends at Stockholm, that the King of Sweden intends, first to intercede with Louis XIV. in favor of the French Huguenots, and next, if diplomacy fails, to join in arms with the other Protestant Powers of Europe.

(2) His correspondent in Holland learns that if the King of England invites the States to any "holy resolution," they will heartily lend forces. No leader so good as the English King—Charles II.! Marsilly had shown ARLINGTON'S LETTER to a Dutch friend, who bade him approach the Dutch ambassador in England. He has dined with that diplomatist. Arlington had, then, gone so far as to write an encouraging letter. The Dutch ambassador had just told Marsilly that he had received the same news, namely, that, Holland would aid the Huguenots, persecuted by Louis XIV.

(3) Letters from Provence, Languedoc, and Dauphine say that the situation there is unaltered.

(4) The Canton of Zurich write that they will keep their promises and that Berne is anxious to please the King of Great Britain, and that it is ready to raise, with Zurich, 15,000 men. They are not afraid of France.

(5) Zurich fears that, if Charles is not represented at the next Diet, Bale and Saint Gall will be intimidated, and not dare to join the Triple Alliance of Spain, Holland, and England. The best plan will be for Marsilly to represent England at the Diet of January 25, 1669, accompanied by the Swiss General Balthazar. This will encourage friends "to give His Britannic Majesty the satisfaction which he desires, and will produce a close union between Holland, Sweden, the Cantons, and other Protestant States."

This reads as if Charles had already expressed some "desire."

(6) Geneva grumbles at a reply of Charles "through a bishop who is their enemy," the Bishop of London, "a persecutor of our religion," that is, of Presbyterianism. However, nothing will dismay the Genevans, "si S. M. B. ne change."

Then comes a blank in the paper. There follows a copy of a letter as if from Charles II. himself, to "the Right High and Noble Seigneurs of Zurich." He has heard of their wishes from Roux de Marsilly, whom he commissions to wait upon them. "I would not have written by my Bishop of London had I been better informed, but would myself have replied to your obliging letter, and would have assured you, as I do now, that I desire. . . ."

It appears as if this were a draft of a kind of letter which Marsilly wanted Charles to write to Zurich, and there is a similar draft of a letter for Arlington to follow, if he and Charles wish to send Marsilly to the Swiss Diet. The Dutch ambassador, with whom Marsilly dined on December 26, the Constable of Castille, and other grandees, are all of opinion that he should visit the Protestant Swiss, as from the King of England. The scheme is for an alliance of England, Holland, Spain, and the Protestant Cantons, against France and Savoy.

Another letter of Marsilly to Arlington, only dated Jeudi, avers that he can never repay Arlington for his extreme kindness and liberality. "No man in England is more devoted to you than I am, and shall be all my life."[1]

[1] State Papers, France, vol. 125, 106.

On the very day when Marsilly drafted for Charles his own commission to treat with Zurich for a Protestant alliance against France, Charles himself wrote to his sister, Madame (Henriette d'Orleans). He spoke of his secret treaty with France. "You know how much secrecy is necessary for the carrying on of the business, and I assure you that nobody does, nor shall, know anything of it here, but myself and that one person more, till it be fit to be public."[1] (Is "that one person" de la Cloche?)

[1] Madame, by Julia Cartwright, p. 275.

Thus Marsilly thought Charles almost engaged for the Protestant
League, while Charles was secretly allying himself with France
against Holland. Arlington was probably no less deceived by
Charles than Marsilly was.

The Bishop of London's share in the dealing with Zurich is obscure.

It appears certain that Arlington was not consciously deceiving Marsilly. Madame wrote, on February 12, as to Arlington, "The man's attachment to the Dutch and his inclination towards Spain are too well known."[1] Not till April 25, 1669, does Charles tell his sister that Arlington has an inkling of his secret dealings with France; how he knows, Charles cannot tell.[2] It is impossible for us to ascertain how far Charles himself deluded Marsilly, who went to the Continent early in spring, 1669. Before May 15-25, 1669, in fact on April 14, Marsilly had been kidnaped by agents of Louis XIV., and his doom was dight. Here is the account of the matter, written to —— by Perwich in Paris:

[1] Ibid., p. 281.
[2] Ibid., p. 285.

"W. Perwich to ——

"Paris, May 25, '69.

"Honored Sir,

"The Cantons of Switzerland are much troubled at the French King's having sent fifteen horsemen into Switzerland from whence the Sr de Manille, the King's resident there, had given information of the Sr Roux de Marsilly's being there negotiating the bringing the Cantons into the Triple League by discourses much to the disadvantage of France, giving them very ill impressions of the French King's Government, who was betrayed by a monk that kept him company and intercepted by the said horsemen brought into France and is expected at the Bastille. I believe you know the man. . . . I remember him in England."

Can this monk be the monk who went mad in prison at Pignerol, sharing the cell of Mattioli? Did he, too, suffer for his connection with the secret? We do not know, but the position of Charles was awkward. Marsilly, dealing with the Swiss, had come straight from England, where he was lie with Charles's minister, Arlington, and with the Dutch and Spanish ambassadors. The King refers to the matter in a letter to his sister of May 24, 1669 (misdated by Miss Cartwright, May 24, 1668.)[1]

[1] Madame, by Julia Cartwright, p. 264.

"You have, I hope, received full satisfaction by the last post in the matter of Marsillac [Marsilly], for my Ld. Arlington has sent to Mr. Montague [English ambassador at Paris] his history all the time he was here, by which you will see how little credit he had here, and that particularly my Lord Arlington was not in his good graces, because he did not receive that satisfaction, in his negotiation, he expected, and that was only in relation to the Swissers, and so I think I have said enough of this matter."

Charles took it easily!

On May 15/25 Montague acknowledged Arlington's letter to which Charles refers; he has been approached, as to Marsilly, by the Spanish resident, "but I could not tell how to do anything in the business, never having heard of the man, or that he was employed by my Master [Charles] in any business. I have sent you also a copy of a letter which an Englishman writ to me that I do not know, in behalf of Roux de Marsilly, but that does not come by the post," being too secret.[1]

[1] State Papers, France, vol. 126.

France had been well-informed about Marsilly while he was in England. He then had a secretary, two lackeys, and a valet de chambre, and was frequently in conference with Arlington and the Spanish ambassador to the English Court. Colbert, the French ambassador in London, had written all this to the French Government, on April 25, before he heard of Marsilly's arrest.[1]

[1] Bibl. Nat., Fonds. Francais, No. 10665.

The belief that Marsilly was an agent of Charles appears to have been general, and, if accepted by Louis XIV., would interfere with Charles's private negotiations for the Secret Treaty with France. On May 18 Prince d'Aremberg had written on the subject to the Spanish ambassador in Paris. Marsilly, he says, was arrested in Switzerland, on his way to Berne, with a monk who was also seized, and, a curious fact, Marsilly's valet was killed in the struggle. This valet, of course, was not Dauger, whom Marsilly had left in England. Marsilly "doit avoir demande la protection du Roy de la Grande Bretagne en faveur des Religionaires (Huguenots) de France, et passer en Suisse avec quelque commission de sa part." D'Aremberg begs the Spanish ambassador to communicate all this to Montague, the English ambassador at Paris, but Montague probably, like Perwich, knew nothing of the business any more than he knew of Charles's secret dealings with Louis through Madame.[1]

[1] State Papers, France. vol. 126.

To d'Aremberg's letter is pinned an unsigned English note, obviously intended for Arlington's reading.

"Roux de Marsilly is still in the Bastille though they have a mind to hang him, yet they are much puzzled what to do with him. De Lionne has beene to examine him twice or thrice, but there is noe witnes to prove anything against him. I was told by one that the French king told it to, that in his papers they find great mention of the Duke of Bucks: and your name, and speak as if he were much trusted by you. I have enquired what this Marsilly is, and I find by one Mr. Marsilly that I am acquainted withall, and a man of quality, that this man's name is onely Roux, and borne at Nismes and having been formerly a soldier in his troope, ever since has taken his name to gain more credit in Switserland where hee, Marsilly, formerly used to bee employed by his Coll: the Mareschall de Schomberg who invaded Switserland."

We next find a very curious letter, from which it appears that the French Government inclined to regard Marsilly as, in fact, an agent of Charles, but thought it wiser to trump up against him a charge of conspiring against the life of Louis XIV. On this charge, or another, he was executed, while the suspicion that he was an agent of English treachery may have been the real cause of the determination to destroy him. The Balthazar with whom Marsilly left his papers is mentioned with praise by him in his paper for Arlington, of December 27, 1668. He is the General who should have accompanied Marsilly to the Diet.

The substance of the letter (given in full in Note I.) is to the following effect. P. du Moulin (Paris, May 19/29 1669) writes to Arlington. Ever since, Ruvigny, the late French ambassador, a Protestant, was in England, the French Government had been anxious to kidnap Roux de Marsilly. They hunted him in England, Holland, Flanders, and Franche-Comte. As we know from the case of Mattioli, the Government of Louis XIV. was unscrupulously daring in breaking the laws of nations, and seizing hostile personages in foreign territory, as Napoleon did in the affair of the Duc d'Enghien. When all failed Louis bade Turenne capture Roux de Marsilly wherever he could find him. Turenne sent officers and gentlemen abroad, and, after four months' search they found Marsilly in Switzerland. They took him as he came out of the house of his friend, General Balthazar, and carried him to Gex. No papers were found on him, but he asked his captors to send to Balthazar and get "the commission he had from England," which he probably thought would give him the security of an official diplomatic position. Having got this document, Marsilly's captors took it to the French Ministers. Nothing could be more embarrassing, if this were true, to Charles's representative in France, Montague, and to Charles's secret negotiations, also to Arlington, who had dealt with Marsilly. On his part, the captive Marsilly constantly affirmed that he was the envoy of the King of England. The common talk of Paris was that an agent of Charles was in the Bastille, "though at Court they pretended to know nothing of it." Louis was overjoyed at Marsilly's capture, giving out that he was conspiring against his life. Monsieur told Montague that he need not beg for the life of a would-be murderer like Marsilly. But as to this idea, "they begin now to mince it at Court," and Ruvigny assured du Moulin "that they had no such thoughts." De Lyonne had seen Marsilly and observed that it was a blunder to seize him. The French Government was nervous, and Turenne's secretary had been "pumping" several ambassadors as to what they thought of Marsilly's capture on foreign territory. One ambassador replied with spirit that a crusade of all Europe against France, as of old against the Moslems, would be necessary. Would Charles, du Moulin asked, own or disown Marsilly?

Montague's position was now awkward. On May 23, his account of the case was read, at

Whitehall, to the Foreign Committee in London. (See Note II. for the document.) He did not dare to interfere in Marsilly's behalf, because he did not know whether the man was an agent of Charles or not. Such are the inconveniences of a secret royal diplomacy carried on behind the backs of Ministers. Louis XV. later pursued this method with awkward consequences.[1] The French Court, Montague said, was overjoyed at the capture of Marsilly, and a reward of 100,000 crowns, "I am told very privately, is set upon his head." The French ambassador in England, Colbert, had reported that Charles had sent Marsilly "to draw the Swisses into the Triple League" against France. Montague had tried to reassure Monsieur (Charles's brother-in-law), but was himself entirely perplexed. As Monsieur's wife, Charles's sister, was working with Charles for the secret treaty with Louis, the State and family politics were clearly in a knot. Meanwhile, the Spanish ambassador kept pressing Montague to interfere in favor of Marsilly. After Montague's puzzled note had been read to the English Foreign Committee on May 23, Arlington offered explanations. Marsilly came to England, he said, when Charles was entering into negotiations for peace with Holland, and when France seemed likely to oppose the peace. No proposition was made to him or by him. Peace being made, Marsilly was given money to take him out of the country. He wanted the King to renew his alliance with the Swiss cantons, but was told that the cantons must first expel the regicides of Charles I. He undertook to arrange this, and some eight months later came back to England. "He was coldly used, and I was complained of for not using so important a man well enough."

[1] Cf. Le Secret du Roi, by the Duc de Broglie.

As we saw, Marsilly expressed the most effusive gratitude to Arlington, which does not suggest cold usage. Arlington told the complainers that Marsilly was "another man's spy," what man's, Dutch, Spanish, or even French, he does not explain. So Charles gave Marsilly money to go away. He was never trusted with anything but the expulsion of the regicides from Switzerland. Arlington was ordered by Charles to write a letter thanking Balthazar for his good offices.

These explanations by Arlington do not tally with Marsilly's communications to him, as cited at the beginning of this inquiry. Nothing is said in these about getting the regicides of Charles I. out of Switzerland: the paper is entirely concerned with bringing the Protestant Cantons into anti-French League with England, Holland, Spain, and even Sweden. On the other hand, Arlington's acknowledged letter to Balthazar, carried by Marsilly, may be the "commission" of which Marsilly boasted. In any case, on June 2, Charles gave Colbert, the French ambassador, an audience, turning even the Duke of York out of the room. He then repeated to Colbert the explanations of Arlington, already cited, and Arlington, in a separate interview, corroborated Charles. So Colbert wrote to Louis (June 3, 1669); but to de Lyonne, on the same day, "I trust that you will extract from Marsilly much matter for the King's service. It seemed to me that milord d'Arlington was uneasy about it [en avait de l'inquietude]. . . . There is here in England one Martin" (Eustace Dauger), "who has been that wretch's valet, and who left him discontent." Colbert then proposes to examine Martin, who may know a good deal, and to send him into France. On June 10, Colbert writes to Louis that he expects to see Martin.[1]

[1] Bibl. Nat., Fonds. Francais, No. 10665.

On June 24, Colbert wrote to Louis about a conversation with Charles. It is plain that proofs of a murder-plot by Marsilly were scanty or non-existent, though Colbert averred that Marsilly had discussed the matter with the Spanish Ministers. "Charles knew that he had had much conference with Isola, the Spanish ambassador." Meanwhile, up to July 1, Colbert was trying to persuade

Marsilly's valet to go to France, which he declined to do, as we have seen. However, the luckless lad, by nods and by veiled words, indicated that he knew a great deal. But not by promise of security and reward could the valet be induced to return to France. "I might ask the King to give up Martin, the valet of Marsilly, to me," Colbert concludes, and, by hook or by crook, he secured the person of the wretched man, as we have seen. In a postcript, Colbert says that he has heard of the execution of Marsilly.

By July 19, as we saw in the previous essay, Louvois was bidding Saint-Mars expect, at Pignerol from Dunkirk, a prisoner of the highest political importance, to be guarded with the utmost secrecy, yet a valet. That valet must be Martin, now called Eustache Dauger, and his secret can only be connected with Marsilly. It may have been something about Arlington's negotiations through Marsilly, as compromising Charles II. Arlington's explanations to the Foreign Committee were certainly incomplete and disingenuous. He, if not Charles, was more deeply engaged with Marsilly than he ventured to report. But Marsilly himself avowed that he did not know why he was to be executed.

Executed he was, in circumstances truly hideous. Perwich, June 5, wrote to an unnamed correspondent in England: "They have all his papers, which speak much of the Triple Alliance, but I know not whether they can lawfully hang him for this, having been naturalized in Holland, and taken in a privileged country" (Switzerland). Montague (Paris, June 22, 1669) writes to Arlington that Marsilly is to die, so it has been decided, for "a rape which he formerly committed at Nismes," and after the execution, on June 26, declares that, when broken on the wheel, Marsilly "still persisted that he was guilty of nothing, nor did know why he was put to death."

Like Eustache Dauger, Marsilly professed that he did not know his own secret. The charge of a rape, long ago, at Nismes, was obviously trumped up to cover the real reason for the extraordinary vindictiveness with which he was pursued, illegally taken, and barbarously slain. Mere Protestant restlessness on his part is hardly an explanation. There was clearly no evidence for the charge of a plot to murder Louis XIV., in which Colbert, in England, seems to have believed. Even if the French Government believed that he was at once an agent of Charles II., and at the same time a would-be assassin of Louis XIV., that hardly accounts for the intense secrecy with which his valet, Eustache Dauger, was always surrounded. Did Marsilly know of the Secret Treaty, and was it from him that Arlington got his first inkling of the royal plot? If so, Marsilly would probably have exposed the mystery in Protestant interests. We are entirely baffled.

In any case, Francis Vernon, writing from Paris to Williamson (?) (June 19/25, 1669), gave a terrible account of Marsilly's death. (For the letter, see Note V.) With a broken piece of glass (as we learn from another source), Marsilly, in prison, wounded himself in a ghastly manner, probably hoping to die by loss of blood. They seared him with a red-hot iron, and hurried on his execution. He was broken on the wheel, and was two hours in dying (June 22). Contrary to usage, a Protestant preacher was brought to attend him on the scaffold. He came most reluctantly, expecting insult, but not a taunt was uttered by the fanatic populace. "He came up the scaffold, great silence all about," Marsilly lay naked, stretched on a St. Andrew's cross. He had seemed half dead, his head hanging limp, "like a drooping calf." To greet the minister of his own faith, he raised himself, to the surprise of all, and spoke out loud and clear. He utterly denied all share in a scheme to murder Louis. The rest may be read in the original letter (p. 51).

So perished Roux de Marsilly; the history of the master throws no light on the secret of the servant. That secret, for many years, caused the keenest anxiety to Louis XIV. and Louvois. Saint-

Mars himself must not pry into it. Yet what could Dauger know? That there had been a conspiracy against the King's life? But that was the public talk of Paris. If Dauger had guilty knowledge, his life might have paid for it; why keep him a secret prisoner? Did he know that Charles II. had been guilty of double dealing in 1668- 1669? Probably Charles had made some overtures to the Swiss, as a blind to his private dealings with Louis XIV., but, even so, how could the fact haunt Louis XIV. like a ghost? We leave the mystery much darker than we found it, but we see good reason why diplomatists should have murmured of a crusade against the cruel and brigand Government which sent soldiers to kidnap, in neighboring states, men who did not know their own crime.

To myself it seems not improbable that the King and Louvois were but stupidly and cruelly nervous about what Dauger MIGHT know. Saint-Mars, when he proposed to utilize Dauger as a prison valet, manifestly did not share the trembling anxieties of Louis XIV. and his Minister; anxieties which grew more keen as time went on. However, "a soldier only has his orders," and Saint-Mars executed his orders with minute precision, taking such unheard-of precautions that, in legend, the valet blossomed into the rightful kind of France.

ORIGINAL PAPERS IN THE CASE OF ROUX DE MARSILLY.[1]

[1] State Papers, France, vol. 126.

I. Letter of Mons. P. du Moulin to Arlington.

Paris, May ye , 1669.

My Lord,

Ever since that Monsieur de Ruvigny was in England last, and upon the information he gave, this King had a very great desire to seize if it were possible this Roux de Marsilly, and several persons were sent to effect it, into England, Holland, Flanders, and Franche Compte: amongst the rest one La Grange, exempt des Gardes, was a good while in Holland with fifty of the guards dispersed in severall places and quarters; But all having miscarried the King recommended the thing to Monsieur de Turenne who sent some of his gentlemen and officers under him to find this man out and to endeavor to bring him alive. These men after foure months search found him att last in Switzerland, and having laid waite for him as he came out from Monsr Baithazar's house (a commander well knowne) they took him and carryed him to Gex before they could be intercepted and he rescued. This was done only by a warrant from Monsieur de Turenne but as soone as they came into the french dominions they had full powers and directions from this court for the bringing of him hither. Those that tooke him say they found no papers about him, but that he desired them to write to Monsr Balthazar to desire him to take care of his papers and to send him the commission he had from England and a letter being written to that effect it was signed by the prisoner and instead of sending it as they had promised, they have brought it hither along with them. They do all unanimously report that he did constantly affirme that he was imployed by the King of Great Brittain and did act by his commission; so that the general discourse here in towne is that one of the King of England's agents is in the Bastille; though att Court they pretend to know nothing of it and would have the world think they are persuaded he had no relacion to his Majesty. Your Lordship hath heard by the publique newes how overjoyed this King was att the bringing of this prisoner, and how farr he expressed his thanks to the chiefe person employed in it, declaring openly that this man had long since conspired against his life, and agreeable to this, Monsieur, fearing that Mylord Ambr. was come to interpose on the prisoner's behalfe asked him on Friday last att St. Germains whether that was the cause of his coming, and told him that he did not think he would speake for a man that attempted to kill the King. The same report hath been hitherto in everybody's mouth but they begin now to mince it att court, and Monsieur de Ruvigny would have persuaded me yesterday, they had no such thoughts. The truth is I am apt to believe they begin now to be ashamed of it: and I am informed from a very good hand that Monsieur de Lionee who hath confessed since that he can find no ground for this pretended attempting to the King's life, and that upon the whole he was of opinion that this man had much better been left alone than taken, and did look upon what he had done as the intemperancy of an ill-settled braine. And to satisfy your Lordship that they are nettled here, and are concerned to know what may be the issue of all this, Monsieur de Turenne's secretary was on Munday last sent to several foreigne Ministers to pump them and to learne what their thoughts were concerning this violence committed in the Dominions of a sovereign and an allye whereupon he was told by one of them that such proceedings would bring Europe to the necessity of entering into a Croisade against them, as formerly against the infidels. If I durst I would acquaint your Lordship with the reflexions of all publique ministers here and of other unconcerned persons in relation to his Majesty's owning or disowning this man; but not knowing the particulars of his case, nor the grounds his Maty may go upon, I shall forbeare entering upon this discourse. . . .

Your Lordships' &c.

P. DU MOULIN.

II. Paper endorsed "Mr. Montague originally in Cypher. Received

May 19, '69. Read in foreigne Committee, 23 May. Roux de

Marsilli."[1]

[1] State Papers, France, vol. 126.

I durst not venture to sollicite in Monsr Roux Marsilly's behalfe because I doe not know whether the King my Master hath imployed him or noe; besides he is a man as I have been tolde by many people here of worth, that has given out that he is resolved to kill the French king at one time or other, and I think such men are as dangerous to one king as to another: hee is brought to the Bastille and I believe may be proceeded against and put to death, in very few daies. There is great joy in this Court for his being taken, and a hundred thousand crownes, I am told very privately, set upon his head; the French Ambassador in England wacht him, and hee has given the intelligence here of his being employed by the King, and sent into Switzerland by my Master to draw the Swisses into the Triple League. Hee aggravates the business as much as hee can to the prejudice of my Master to value his owne service the more, and they seeme here to wonder that the King my Master should have imployed or countenanced a man that had so base a design against the King's Person, I had a great deal of discourse with Monsieur about it, but I did positively say that he had noe relation to my knowledge to the King my Master, and if he should have I make a question or noe whither in this case the King will owne him. However, my Lord, I had nothing to doe to owne or meddle in a business that I was so much a stranger to. . . .

This Roux Marsilly is a great creature of the B. d'Isola's, wch makes them here hate him the more. The Spanish Resident was very earnest with mee to have done something in behalfe of Marsilly, but I positively refused.

III. [A paper endorsed "Roux de Marsilli. Read in for. Committee, 23d May."][1]

[1] State Papers, France, vol. 126.

Roux de Marsilli came hither when your Majesty had made a union with Holland for making the Peace betwix the two Crownes and when it was probable the opposition to the Peace would bee on the side of France.

Marsilly was heard telling of longe things but noe proposition made to him or by him.

Presently the Peace was made and Marsilly told more plainly wee had no use of him. A little summe of money was given him to returne as he said whither he was to goe in Switzerland. Upon which hee wishing his Maty would renew his alience wth the Cantons hee was answered his Maty would not enter into any comerce with them till they had sent the regicides out of their Country, hee undertooke it should bee done. Seven or eight months after wth out any intimation given him from hence or any expectation of him, he comes hither, but was so coldly used I was complained off for not using so important a man well enough. I answered I saw noe use the King could make of him, because he had no credit in Switzerlande and for any thing else I thought him worth nothing to us, but above all because I knew by many circumstances HEE WAS ANOTHER MAN'S SPY and soe ought not to be paid by his Majesty. Notwithstanding this his Maty being moved from compassion commanded hee should have some money given him to carry him away and that I should write to Monsieur Balthazar thanking him in the King's name for the good offices hee rendered in advancing a good understanding betwixt his Maty and the Cantons and desiring him to continue them in all occasions.

The man was always looked upon as a hot headed and indiscreete man, and soe accordingly handled, hearing him, but never trusting him with anything but his own offered and undesired endeavours to gett the Regicides sent out of Switzerland.

IV. Letter of W. Perwich to ———.[1]

[1] State Papers, France, vol. 126.

Paris: June 5, 1669.

Honored Sir,

Roux Marsilly has prudently declared hee had some what of importance to say but it should bee to the King himselfe wch may be means of respiting his processe and as he hopes intercession may bee made for him; but people talk so variously of him that I cannot tell whether hee ought to bee owned by any Prince; the Suisses have indeed the greatest ground to reclayme him as being taken in theirs. They have all his papers which speake much of the Triple Alliance; if they have no other pretext of hanging him I know not whether they can lawfully for this, hee having been naturallised in Holland and taken in a priviledged Country. . . .

V. Francis Vernon to [Mr. Williamson?].[1]

[1] State Papers, France, vol. 126.

Paris: June 19/25, 1669.

Honored Sir,

My last of the 26th Currt was soe short and soe abrupt that I fear you can peck butt little satisfaction out of it.

I did intend to have written something about Marsilly but that I had noe time then. In my letter to my Lord Arlington I writt that Friday 21 Currt hee wounded himself wch he did not because hee was confronted with Ruvigny as the Gazettes speake. For he knew before hee should dye, butt he thought by dismembering himself that the losse of blood would carry him out of the world before it should come to bee knowne that he had wounded himselfe. And when the Governor of the Bastille spied the blood hee said It was a stone was come from him which caused that effusion. However the governor mistrusted the worst and searcht him to see what wound he had made. So they seared him and sent word to St. Germaines which made his execution be hastened. Saturday about 1 of the clock he was brought on the skaffold before the Chastelet and tied to St. Andrew's Crosse all wch while he acted the Dying man and scarce stirred, and seemed almost breathless and fainting. The Lieutenant General prest him to confesse and there was a doctor of the Sorbon who was a counsellr of the Castelet there likewise to exhort him to disburthen his mind of any thing which might be upon it. Butt he seemed to take no notice and lay panting.

Then the Lieutenant Criminel bethought himself that the only way to make him speake would bee to sende for a ministre soe hee did to Monsr Daillie but hee because the Edicts don't permitt ministres to come to condemned persons in publique but only to comfort them in private before they goe out of prison refused to come till hee sent a huissier who if he had refused the second time would have brought him by force. At this second summons hee came butt not without great expectations to bee affronted in a most notorious manner beeing the first time a ministre came to appeare on a scaffold and that upon soe sinister an occasion. Yet when he came found a great presse of people. All made way, none lett fall soe much as a taunting word. Hee came up the Scaffold, great silence all about. Hee found him lying bound stretched on St. Andrew's Crosse naked ready for execution. Hee told him hee was sent for to exhort him to die patiently and like a Christian. Then immediately they were all surprized to see him hold up his head wch he lett hang on one side before like a drooping calfe and speake as loud and clear as the ministre, to whom he said with a cheerful air hee was glad to see him, that hee need not question butt that hee would dye like a Christian and patiently too. Then hee went and spoke some places of Scripture to encourage him which he heard with great attention. They afterward came to mention some things to move him to contrition, and there hee tooke an occasion to aggravate the horrour of a Crime of attempting against the King's person. Hee said hee did not know what hee meant. For his part hee never had any evill intention against the Person of the King.

The Lieutenant Criminel stood all the while behind Monsieur Daillie and hearkened to all and prompted Monsr Daillie to aske him if hee had said there were 10 Ravillacs besides wch would doe the King's businesse. Hee protested solemnly hee never said any such words or if hee did hee never remembered, butt if hee had it was with no intention of Malice. Then Monsieur Daillie turned to the people and made a discourse in vindication of those of the Religion that it was no Principle of theirs attempts on the persons of King[s] butt only loyalty and obedience. This ended hee went away; hee staid about an hour in all, and immediately as soon as he was gone, they went to their worke and gave him eleven blows with a barre and laid him on the wheele. He was two houres dying. All about Monsr Daillie I heard from his own mouth for I went to wait on him because it was reported hee had said something concerning the King of England butt hee could tell mee nothing of that. There was a flying report that he should say going from the Chastelet— The Duke of York hath done mee a great injury. The Swisses they say resented his [Marsilly's] taking and misst but 1/2 an hour to take them which betrayed him [the monk] after whom they sent. When he was on the wheele he was heard to say Le Roy est grand tyrant, Le Roy me traitte d'un facon fort barbare. All that you read concerning oaths and dying en enrage is false all the oaths hee used being only asseverations to Monsr Daillie that he was falsely accused as to the King's person

Sr I am &c

FRANS. VERNON.

VI. The Ambassador Montague to Arlington.[1]

[1] State Papers, France, vol. 126.

Paris: June 22, 1669.

My Lord,

The Lieutenant criminel hath proceeded pretty farre with Le Roux Marsilly. The crime they forme their processe on beeing a rape which he had formerly committed at Nismes soe that he perceiving but little hopes of his life, sent word to the King if hee would pardon him he could reveale things to him which would concerne him more and be of greater consequence to him, than his destruction.

VII. The same to the same.

Paris: June 26, '69.

My Lord,

I heard that Marsilly was to be broke on the wheel and I gave order then to one of my servants to write Mr. Williamson word of it, soe I suppose you have heard of it already: they hastened his execution for feare he should have dyed of the hurt he had done himself the day before; they sent for a minister to him when he was upon the scaffold to see if he would confesse anything, but he still persisted that he was guilty of nothing nor did not know why he was put to death. . . .

PART II—True Stories of Modern Magic

M. Robert-Houdin

A Conjurer's Confessions

I

SELF-TRAINING

[Sleight-of-hand theories alone cannot explain the mysteries of "magic" as practiced by that eminent Frenchman who revolutionized the entire art, and who was finally called upon to help his government out of a difficulty—Robert-Houdin. The success of his most famous performances hung not only on an incredible dexterity, but also on high ingenuity and moral courage, as the following pages from his "Memoirs" will prove to the reader. The story begins when the young man of twenty was laboring patiently as apprentice to a watchmaker.]

In order to aid my progress and afford me relaxation, my master recommended me to study some treatises on mechanics in general, and on clockmaking in particular. As this suited my taste exactly, I gladly assented, and I was devoting myself passionately to this attractive study, when a circumstance, apparently most simple, suddenly decided my future life by revealing to me a vocation whose mysterious resources must open a vast field for my inventive and fanciful ideas.

One evening I went into a bookseller's shop to buy Berthoud's "Treatise on Clockmaking," which I knew he had. The tradesman being engaged at the moment on matters more important, took down two volumes from the shelves and handed them to me without ceremony. On returning home I sat down to peruse my treatise conscientiously, but judge of my surprise when I read on the back of one of the volumes "SCIENTIFIC AMUSEMENTS." Astonished at finding such a title on a professional work, I opened it impatiently, and, on running through the table of contents, my surprise was doubled on reading these strange phrases:

The way of performing tricks with the cards—How to guess a person's thoughts—To cut off a pigeon's head, to restore it to life, etc., etc.

The bookseller had made a mistake. In his haste, he had given me two volumes of the

Encyclopaedia instead of Berthoud. Fascinated, however, by the announcement of such marvels, I devoured the mysterious pages, and the further my reading advanced, the more I saw laid bare before me the secrets of an art for which I was unconsciously predestined.

I fear I shall be accused of exaggeration, or at least not be understood by many of my readers, when I say that this discovery caused me the greatest joy I had ever experienced. At this moment a secret presentiment warned me that success, perhaps glory, would one day accrue to me in the apparent realization of the marvelous and impossible, and fortunately these presentiments did not err.

The resemblance between two books, and the hurry of a bookseller, were the commonplace causes of the most important event in my life.

It may be urged that different circumstances might have suggested this profession to me at a later date. It is probable; but then I should have had no time for it. Would any workman, artisan, or tradesman give up a certainty, however slight it may be, to yield to a passion which would be surely regarded as a mania? Hence my irresistible penchant for the mysterious could only be followed at this precise period of my life.

How often since have I blessed this providential error, without which I should have probably vegetated as a country watchmaker! My life would have been spent in gentle monotony; I should have been spared many sufferings, emotions, and shocks: but, on the other hand, what lively sensations, what profound delight would have been sacrificed!

I was eagerly devouring every line of the magic book which described the astounding tricks; my head was aglow, and I at times gave way to thoughts which plunged me in ecstasy.

The author gave a very plain explanation of his tricks; still, he committed the error of supposing his readers possessed of the necessary skill to perform them. Now, I was entirely deficient in this skill, and though most desirous of acquiring it, I found nothing in the book to indicate the means. I was in the position of a man who attempts to copy a picture without possessing the slightest notion of drawing and painting.

In the absence of a professor to instruct me, I was compelled to create the principles of the science I wished to study. In the first place, I recognized the fundamental principle of sleight-of-hand, that the organs performing the principal part are the sight and touch. I saw that, in order to attain any degree of perfection, the professor must develop these organs to their fullest extent—for, in his exhibitions, he must be able to see everything that takes place around him at half a glance, and execute his deceptions with unfailing dexterity.

I had been often struck by the ease with which pianists can read and perform at sight the most difficult pieces. I saw that, by practice, it would be possible to create a certainty of perception and facility of touch, rendering it easy for the artist to attend to several things simultaneously, while his hands were busy employed with some complicated task. This faculty I wished to acquire and apply to sleight-of-hand; still, as music could not afford me the necessary elements, I had recourse to the juggler's art, in which I hoped to meet with an analogous result.

It is well known that the trick with the balls wonderfully improves the touch, but does it not improve the vision at the same time? In fact, when a juggler throws into the air four balls crossing each other in various directions, he requires an extraordinary power of sight to follow the direction his hands have given to each of the balls. At this period a corn-cutter resided at Blois, who possessed the double talent of juggling and extracting corns with a skill worthy of the lightness of his hands. Still, with both these qualities, he was not rich, and being aware of that fact,

I hoped to obtain lessons from him at a price suited to my modest finances. In fact, for ten francs he agreed to initiate me in the juggling art.

I practiced with so much zeal, and progressed so rapidly, that in less than a month I had nothing more to learn; at least, I knew as much as my master, with the exception of corn-cutting, the monopoly in which I left him. I was able to juggle with four balls at once. But this did not satisfy my ambition; so I placed a book before me, and, while the balls were in the air, I accustomed myself to read without any hesitation.

This will probably seem to my readers very extraordinary; but I shall surprise them still more, when I say that I have just amused myself by repeating this curious experiment. Though thirty years have elapsed since the time of which I am writing, and though I scarcely once touched the balls during that period, I can still manage to read with ease while keeping three balls up.

The practice of this trick gave my fingers a remarkable degree of delicacy and certainty, while my eye was at the same time acquiring a promptitude of perception that was quite marvelous. Presently I shall have to speak of the service this rendered me in my experiment of second sight. After having thus made my hands supple and docile, I went on straight to sleight-of-hand, and I more especially devoted myself to the manipulation of cards and palmistry.

This operation requires a great deal of practice; for, while the hand is held apparently open, balls, corks, lumps of sugar, coins, etc., must be held unseen, the fingers remaining perfectly free and limber.

Owing to the little time at my disposal, the difficulties connected with these new experiments would have been insurmountable had I not found a mode of practicing without neglecting my business. It was the fashion in those days to wear coats with large pockets on the hips, called a la proprietaire, so whenever my hands were not otherwise engaged they slipped naturally into my pockets, and set to work with cards, coins, or one of the objects I have mentioned. It will be easily understood how much time I gained by this. Thus, for instance, when out on errands my hands could be at work on both sides; at dinner, I often ate my soup with one hand while I was learning to sauter la coupe with the other—in short, the slightest moment of relaxation was devoted to my favorite pursuit.

II

"SECOND SIGHT"

[A thousand more trials of patience and perseverance finally brought to the conjurer a Parisian theater and an appreciative clientele. But he never ceased to labor and improve the quality of his marvelous effects.]

The experiment, however, to which I owed my reputation was one inspired by that fantastic god to whom Pascal attributes all the discoveries of this sublunary world: it was chance that led me straight to the invention of SECOND SIGHT.

My two children were playing one day in the drawing-room at a game they had invented for their own amusement. The younger had bandaged his elder brother's eyes, and made him guess the objects he touched, and when the latter happened to guess right, they changed places. This simple game suggested to me the most complicated idea that ever crossed my mind.

Pursued by the notion, I ran and shut myself up in my workroom, and was fortunately in that happy state when the mind follows easily the combinations traced by fancy. I rested my hand in my hands, and, in my excitement, laid down the first principles of second sight.

My readers will remember the experiment suggested to me formerly by the pianist's dexterity, and the strange faculty I succeeded in attaining: I could read while juggling with four balls. Thinking seriously of this, I fancied that this "perception by appreciation" might be susceptible of equal development, if I applied its principles to the memory and the mind.

I resolved, therefore, on making some experiments with my son Emile, and, in order to make my young assistant understand the nature of the exercise we were going to learn, I took a domino, the cinq-quatre for instance, and laid it before him. Instead of letting him count the points of the two numbers, I requested the boy to tell me the total at once.

"Nine," he said.

Then I added another domino, the quarter-tray.

"That makes sixteen," he said, without any hesitation. I stopped the first lesson here; the next day we succeeded in counting at a single glance four dominoes, the day after six, and thus we at length were enabled to give instantaneously the product of a dozen dominoes.

This result obtained, we applied ourselves to a far more difficult task, over which we spent a month. My son and I passed rapidly before a toy-shop, or any other displaying a variety of wares, and cast an attentive glance upon it. A few steps farther on we drew paper and pencil from our pockets, and tried which could describe the greater number of objects seen in passing. I must own that my son reached a perfection far greater than mine, for he could often write down forty objects, while I could scarce reach thirty. Often feeling vexed at this defeat, I would return to the shop and verify his statement, but he rarely made a mistake.

My male readers will certainly understand the possibility of this, but they will recognize the difficulty. As for my lady readers, I am convinced beforehand they will not be of the same opinion, for they daily perform far more astounding feats. Thus, for instance, I can safely assert that a lady seeing another pass at full speed in a carriage, will have had time to analyze her toilet from her bonnet to her shoes, and be able to describe not only the fashion and quality of the stuffs, but also say if the lace be real or only machine-made. I have known ladies do this.

This natural, or acquired, faculty among ladies, but which my son and I had only gained by constant practice, was of great service in my performances, for while I was executing my tricks, I could see everything that passed around me, and thus prepare to foil any difficulties presented me. This exercise had given me, so to speak, the power of following two ideas simultaneously, and nothing is more favorable in conjuring than to be able to think at the same time both of what you are saying and of what you are doing. I eventually acquired such a knack in this that I frequently invented new tricks while going through my performances. One day, even, I made a bet I would solve a problem in mechanics while taking my part in conversation. We were talking of the pleasure of a country life, and I calculated during this time the quantity of wheels and pinions, as well as the necessary cogs, to produce certain revolutions required, without once failing in my reply.

This slight explanation will be sufficient to show what is the essential basis of second sight, and I will add that a secret and unnoticeable correspondence[1] existed between my son and myself, by which I could announce to him the name, nature, and bulk of objects handed me by spectators.

[1] "Telegraphy."

As none understood my mode of action, they were tempted to believe in something extraordinary, and, indeed, my son Emile, then aged twelve, possessed all the essential qualities to produce this opinion, for his pale, intellectual, and ever thoughtful face represented the type of a boy gifted with some supernatural power.

Two months were incessantly employed in erecting the scaffolding of our tricks, and when we were quite confident of being able to contend against the difficulties of such an undertaking, we announced the first representation of second sight. On the 12th of February, 1846, I printed in the center of my bill the following singular announcement:

"In this performance M. Robert-Houdin's son, who is gifted with a marvelous second sight, after his eyes have been covered with a thick bandage, will designate every object presented to him by the audience."

I cannot say whether this announcement attracted any spectators, for my room was constantly crowded, still I may affirm, what may seem very extraordinary, that the experiment of second sight, which afterwards became so fashionable, produced no effect on the first performance. I am inclined to believe that the spectators fancied themselves the dupes of accomplices, but I was much annoyed by the result, as I had built on the surprise I should produce; still, having no reason to doubt its ultimate success, I was tempted to make a second trial, which turned out well.

The next evening I noticed in my room several persons who had been present on the previous night, and I felt they had come a second time to assure themselves of the reality of the experiment. It seems they were convinced, for my success was complete, and amply compensated for my former disappointment.

I especially remember a mark of singular approval with which one of my pit audience favored me. My son had named to him several objects he offered in succession; but not feeling satisfied, my incredulous friend, rising, as if to give more importance to the difficulty he was about to present, handed me an instrument peculiar to cloth merchants, and employed to count the number of threads. Acquiescing in his wish, I said to my boy, "What do I hold in my hand?"

"It is an instrument to judge the fineness of cloth, and called a thread counter."

"By Jove!" my spectator said, energetically, "it is marvelous. If

I had paid ten francs to see it, I should not begrudge them."

From this moment my room was much too small, and was crowded every evening.

Still, success is not entirely rose-colored, and I could easily narrate many disagreeable scenes produced by the reputation I had of being a sorcerer; but I will only mention one, which forms a resume of all I pass over:

A young lady of elegant manners paid me a visit one day, and although her face was hidden by a thick veil, my practiced eyes perfectly distinguished her features. She was very pretty.

My incognita would not consent to sit down till she was assured we were alone, and that I was the real Robert-Houdin. I also seated myself, and assuming the attitude of a man prepared to listen, I bent slightly to my visitor, as if awaiting her pleasure to explain to me the object of her mysterious visit. To my great surprise, the young lady, whose manner betrayed extreme emotion, maintained the most profound silence, and I began to find the visit very strange, and was on the point of forcing an explanation, at any hazard, when the fair unknown timidly ventured these words:

"Good Heavens! sir, I know not how you will interpret my visit."

Here she stopped, and let her eyes sink with a very embarrassed air; then, making a violent effort, she continued:

"What I have to ask of you, sir, is very difficult to explain."

"Speak, madam, I beg," I said, politely, "and I will try to guess what you cannot explain to me."

And I began asking myself what this reserve meant.

"In the first place," the young lady said, in a low voice, and looking round her, "I must tell you confidentially that I loved, my love was returned, and I—I am betrayed."

At the last word the lady raised her head, overcame the timidity she felt, and said, in a firm and assured voice:

"Yes, sir—yes, I am betrayed, and for that reason I have come to you."

"Really, madam," I said, much surprised at this strange confession,

"I do not see how I can help you in such a matter."

"Oh, sir, I entreat you," said my fair visitor, clasping her hands—

"I implore you not to abandon me!"

I had great difficulty in keeping my countenance, and yet I felt an extreme curiosity to know the history concealed behind this mystery.

"Calm yourself, madam," I remarked, in a tone of tender sympathy; "tell me what you would of me, and if it be in my power—"

"If it be in your power!" the young lady said, quickly; "why, nothing is more easy, sir."

"Explain yourself, madam."

"Well, sir, I wish to be avenged."

"In what way?"

"How, you know better than I, sir; must I teach you? You have in your power means to—"

"I, madam?"

"Yes, sir, you! for you are a sorcerer, and cannot deny it."

At this word sorcerer, I was much inclined to laugh; but I was restrained by the incognita's evident emotion. Still, wishing to put an end to a scene which was growing ridiculous, I said, in a politely ironical tone:

"Unfortunately, madam, you give me a title I never possessed."

"How, sir!" the young woman exclaimed, in a quick tone, "you will not allow you are—"

"A sorcerer, madam? Oh, no, I will not."

"You will not?"

"No, a thousand times no, madam."

At these words my visitor rose hastily, muttered a few incoherent words, appeared suffering from terrible emotion, and then drawing near me with flaming eyes and passionate gestures, repeated:

"Ah, you will not! Very good; I now know what I have to do."

Stupefied by such an outbreak, I looked at her fixedly, and began to suspect the cause of her extraordinary conduct.

"There are two modes of acting," she said, with terrible volubility, "toward people who devote themselves to magic arts— entreaty and menaces. You would not yield to the first of these means, hence, I must employ the second. Stay," she added, "perhaps this will induce you to speak."

And, lifting up her cloak, she laid her hand on the hilt of a dagger passed through her girdle. At the same time she suddenly threw back her veil, and displayed features in which all the signs of rage and madness could be traced. No longer having a doubt as to the person I had to deal with, my first movement was to rise and stand on my guard; but this first feeling overcome, I repented the thought of a struggle with the unhappy woman, and determined on employing a method almost always successful with those deprived of reason. I pretended to accede to her wishes.

"If it be so, madam, I yield to your request. Tell me what you require."

"I have told you, sir; I wish for vengeance, and there is only one method to—"

Here there was a fresh interruption, and the young lady, calmed by my apparent submission, as well as embarrassed by the request she had to make of me, became again timid and confused.

"Well, madam?"

"Well, sir, I know not how to tell you—how to explain to you—but I fancy there are certain means—certain spells—which render it impossible—impossible for a man to be—unfaithful."

"I now understand what you wish, madam. It is a certain magic practice employed in the middle ages. Nothing is easier, and I will satisfy you."

Decided on playing the farce to the end, I took down the largest book I could find in my library, turned over the leaves, stopped at a page which I pretended to scan with profound attention, and then addressing the lady, who followed all my movements anxiously,

"Madam," I said confidentially, "the spell I am going to perform renders it necessary for me to know the name of the person; have the kindness, then, to tell it me."

"Julian!" she said, in a faint voice.

With all the gravity of a real sorcerer, I solemnly thrust a pin through a lighted candle, and pronounced some cabalistic words. After which, blowing out the candle, and turning to the poor creature, I said:

"Madam, it is done; your wish is accomplished."

"Oh, thank you, sir," she replied, with the expression of the profoundest gratitude; and at the same moment she laid a purse on the table and rushed away. I ordered my servant to follow her to her house, and obtain all the information he could about her, and I learned she had been a widow for a short time, and that the loss of an adored husband had disturbed her reason. The next day I visited her relatives, and, returning them the purse, I told them the scene the details of which the reader has just perused.

This scene, with some others that preceded and followed it, compelled me to take measures to guard myself against bores of every description. I could not dream, as formerly, of exiling myself in the country, but I employed a similar resource: this was to shut myself up in my workroom, and organize around me a system of defense against those whom I called, in my ill-temper, thieves of time.

I daily received visits from persons who were utter strangers to me; some were worth knowing, but the majority, gaining an introduction under the most futile pretexts, only came to kill a portion of their leisure time with me. It was necessary to distinguish the tares from the wheat, and this is the arrangement I made:

When one of these gentlemen rang at my door, an electric communication struck a bell in my workroom; I was thus warned and put on my guard. My servant opened the door, and, as is customary, inquired the visitor's name, while I, for my part, laid my ear to a tube, arranged for the purpose, which conveyed to me every word. If, according to his reply, I thought it as well not to receive him, I pressed a button, and a white mark that appeared in a certain part of the hall announced I was not at home to him. My servant then stated I was out, and begged the visitor to apply to the manager.

Sometimes it happened that I erred in my judgment, and regretted having granted an audience; but I had another mode of shortening a bore's visit. I had placed behind the sofa on which I sat an electric spring, communicating with a bell my servant could hear. In case of need, and while talking, I threw my arm carelessly over the back of the sofa, touching the spring, and the bell rang. Then my servant, playing a little farce, opened the front door, rang the bell, which could be heard from the room where I sat, and came to tell me that M. X—— (a name invented for the occasion) wished to speak to me. I ordered M. X—— to be shown into an adjoining room, and it was very rare that my bore did not raise the siege. No one can form an idea how much time I gained by this happy arrangement, or how many times I blessed my imagination and the celebrated savant to whom the discovery of galvanism is due!

This feeling can be easily explained, for my time was of inestimable value. I husbanded it like a treasure, and never sacrificed it, unless the sacrifice might help me to discover new experiments destined to stimulate public curiosity.

To support my determination in making my researches, I had ever before me this maxim:

IT IS MORE DIFFICULT TO SUPPORT ADMIRATION THAN TO EXCITE IT.

And this other, an apparent corollary of the preceding:

THE FASHION AN ARTIST ENJOYS CAN ONLY LAST AS HIS TALENT DAILY INCREASES.

Nothing increases a professional man's merit so much as the possession of an independent fortune; this truth may be coarse, but it is indubitable. Not only was I convinced of these principles of high economy, but I also knew that a man must strive to profit by the fickle favor of the public, which equally descends if it does not rise. Hence I worked my reputation as much as I could. In spite of my numerous engagements, I found means to give performances in all the principal theaters, though great difficulties frequently arose, as my performance did not end till half-past ten, and I could only fulfill my other engagements after that hour.

Eleven o'clock was generally the hour fixed for my appearance on a strange stage, and my readers may judge of the speed required to proceed to the theater in so short a time and make my preparations. It is true that the moments were as well counted as employed, and my curtain had hardly fallen than, rushing toward the stairs, I got before my audience, and jumped into a vehicle that bore me off at full speed.

But this fatigue was as nothing compared to the emotion occasionally produced by an error in the time that was to elapse between my two performances. I remember that, one night, having to wind up the performances at the Vaudeville, the stage manager miscalculated the time the pieces would take in performing, and found himself much in advance. He sent off an express to warn me that the curtain had fallen, and I was anxiously expected. Can my readers comprehend my wretchedness? My experiments, of which I could omit none, would occupy another quarter of an hour; but instead of indulging in useless recriminations, I resigned myself and continued my performance, though I was a prey to frightful anxiety. While speaking, I fancied I could hear that cadenced yell of the public to which the famous song, "Des lampions, des lampions," was set. Thus, either through preoccupation or a desire to end sooner, I found when my performance was over I had gained five minutes out of the quarter of an hour. Assuredly, it might he called the quarter of an hour's grace.

To jump into a carriage and drive to the Place de la Bourse was the affair of an instant; still, twenty minutes had elapsed since the curtain fell, and that was an enormous time. My son Emile and I proceeded up the actors' stairs at full speed, but on the first step we had heard the cries, whistling, and stamping of the impatient audience. What a prospect! I knew that frequently, either right or wrong, the public treated an artiste, no matter whom, very harshly, to remind him of punctuality. That sovereign always appears to have on its lips the words of another monarch: "I was obliged to wait." However, we hurried up the steps leading to the stage.

The stage manager, who had been watching, on hearing our hurried steps, cried from the landing:

"Is that you, M. Houdin?"

"Yes, sir—yes."

"Raise the curtain!" the same voice shouted.

"Wait, wait, it is imp—"

My breath would not allow me to finish my objection; I fell on a chair, unable to move.

"Come, M. Houdin," the manager said, "DO go on the stage, the curtain is up, and the public are so impatient."

The door at the back of the stage was open, but I could not pass through it; fatigue and emotion nailed me to the spot. Still, an idea occurred to me, which saved me from the popular wrath.

"Go on to the stage, my boy," I said to my son, "and prepare all that is wanting for the second-sight trick."

The public allowed themselves to be disarmed by this youth, whose face inspired a sympathizing interest; and my son, after gravely bowing to the audience, quietly made his slight preparations, that is to say, he carried an ottoman to the front of the stage, and placed on a neighboring table a slate, some chalk, a pack of cards, and a bandage.

This slight delay enabled me to recover my breath and calm my nerves, and I advanced in my turn with an attempt to assume the stereotyped smile, in which I signally failed, as I was so agitated. The audience at first remained silent, then their faces gradually unwrinkled, and soon, one or two claps having been ventured, they were carried away and peace was made. I was well rewarded, however, for this terrible ordeal, as my "second-sight" never gained a more brilliant triumph.

An incident greatly enlivened the termination of my performance.

A spectator, who had evidently come on purpose to embarrass us, had tried in vain for some minutes to baffle my son's clairvoyance, when, turning to me, he said, laying marked stress on his words:

"As your son is a soothsayer, of course he can guess the number of my stall?"

The importunate spectator doubtless hoped to force us into a confession of our impotence, for he covered his number, and the adjacent seats being occupied, it was apparently impossible to read the numbers. But I was on my guard against all surprises, and my reply was ready. Still, in order to profit as much as possible by the situation, I feigned to draw back.

"You know, sir," I said, feigning an embarrassed air, "that my son is neither sorcerer nor diviner; he reads through my eyes, and hence I have given this experiment the name of second sight. As I cannot see the number of your stall, and the seats close to you are occupied, my son cannot tell it you."

"Ah! I was certain of it," my persecutor said, in triumph, and turning to his neighbors: "I told you I would pin him."

"Oh, sir! you are not generous in your victory," I said, in my turn, in a tone of mockery. "Take care; if you pique my son's vanity too sharply, he may solve your problem, though it is so difficult."

"I defy him," said the spectator, leaning firmly against the back of his seat, to hide the number better—"yes, yes—I defy him!"

"You believe it to be difficult, then?"

"I will grant more: it is impossible."

"Well, then, sir, that is a stronger reason for us to try it. You will not be angry if we triumph in our turn?" I added, with a petulant smile.

"Come, sir; we understand evasions of that sort. I repeat it—I challenge you both."

The public found great amusement in this debate, and patiently awaited its issue.

"Emile," I said to my son, "prove to this gentleman that nothing can escape your second sight."

"It is number sixty-nine," the boy answered, immediately.

Noisy and hearty applause rose from every part of the theater, in which our opponent joined, for, confessing his defeat, he exclaimed, as he clapped his hands, "It is astounding— magnificent!"

The way I succeeded in finding out the number of the stall was this: I knew beforehand that in all theaters where the stalls are divided down the center by a passage, the uneven numbers are on the right, and the even on the left. As at the Vaudeville each row was composed of ten stalls, it followed that on the right hand the several rows must begin with one, twenty-one, forty-one, and so on, increasing by twenty each. Guided by this, I had no difficulty in discovering that my opponent was seated in number sixty-nine, representing the fifth stall in the fourth row. I had prolonged the conversation for the double purpose of giving more brilliancy to my experiment, and gaining time to make my researches. Thus I applied my process of two simultaneous thoughts, to which I have already alluded.

As I am now explaining matters, I may as well tell my readers some of the artifices that added material brilliancy to the second sight. I have already said this experiment was the result of a material communication between myself and my son which no one could detect. Its combinations enabled us to describe any conceivable object; but, though this was a splendid result, I saw that I should soon encounter unheard-of difficulties in executing it.

The experiment of second sight always formed the termination of my performance. Each evening I saw unbelievers arrive with all sorts of articles to triumph over a secret which they could not unravel. Before going to see Robert-Houdin's son a council was held, in which an object that must embarrass the father was chosen. Among these were half-effaced antique medals, minerals, books printed in characters of every description (living and dead languages), coats- of-arms, microscopic objects, etc.

But what caused me the greatest difficulty was in finding out the contents of parcels, often tied with a string, or even sealed up. But I had managed to contend successfully against all these attempts to embarrass me. I opened boxes, purses, pocketbooks, etc., with great ease, and unnoticed, while appearing to be engaged on something quite different. Were a sealed parcel offered me, I cut a small slit in the paper with the nail of my left thumb, which I always purposely kept very long and sharp, and thus discovered what it contained. One essential condition was excellent sight, and that I possessed to perfection. I owed it originally to my old trade, and practice daily improved it. An equally indispensable necessity was to know the name of every object offered me. It was not enough to say, for instance, "It is a coin"; but my son must give its technical name, its value, the country in which it was current, and the year in which it was struck. Thus, for instance, if an English crown were handed me, my son was expected to state that it was struck in the reign of George IV, and had an intrinsic value of six francs eighteen centimes.

Aided by an excellent memory, we had managed to classify in our heads the name and value of all foreign money. We could also describe a coat-of-arms in heraldic terms. Thus, on the arms of the house of X—— being handed me, my son would reply: "Field gules, with two croziers argent in pale." This knowledge was very useful to us in the salons of the Faubourg Saint Germain, where we were frequently summoned.

I had also learned the characters—though unable to translate a word—of an infinity of languages, such as Chinese, Russian, Turkish Greek, Hebrew, etc. We knew, too, the names of all surgical instruments, so that a surgical pocketbook, however complicated it might be, could not embarrass us. Lastly, I had a very sufficient knowledge of mineralogy, precious stones, antiquities, and curiosities; but I had at my command every possible resource for acquiring these studies, as one of my dearest and best friends, Aristide le Carpentier, a learned antiquary, and uncle of the talented composer of the same name, had, and still has, a cabinet of antique curiosities, which makes the keepers of the imperial museums fierce with envy. My son and I spent many long days in learning here names and dates of which we afterwards made a learned display. Le Carpentier taught me many things, and, among others, he described various signs by which to recognize old coins when the die is worn off. Thus, a Trajan, a Tiberius, or a Marcus Aurelius became as familiar to me as a five-franc piece.

Owing to my old trade, I could open a watch with ease, and do it with one hand, so as to be able to read the maker's name without the public suspecting it: then I shut up the watch again and the trick was ready; my son managed the rest of the business.

But that power of memory which my son possessed in an eminent degree certainly did us the greatest service. When we went to private houses, he needed only a very rapid inspection in order to know all the objects in a room, as well as the various ornaments worn by the spectators, such as chatelaines, pins, eyeglasses, fans, brooches, rings, bouquets, etc. He thus could describe these objects with the greatest ease, when I pointed them out to him by our secret communication. Here is an instance:

One evening, at a house in the Chaussee d'Antin, and at the end of a performance which had been as successful as it was loudly applauded, I remembered that, while passing through the next room to the one we were now in, I had begged my son to cast a glance at a library and remember the titles of some of the books, as well as the order they were arranged in. No one had noticed this rapid examination.

"To end the second-sight experiment, sir," I said to the master of the house, "I will prove to you that my son can read through a wall. Will you lend me a book?"

I was naturally conducted to the library in question, which I pretended now to see for the first time, and I laid my finger on a book.

"Emile," I said to my son, "what is the name of this work?"

"It is Buffon," he replied quickly.

"And the one by its side?" an incredulous spectator hastened to ask.

"On the right or left?" my son asked.

"On the right," the speaker said, having a good reason for choosing this book, for the lettering was very small.

"The Travels of Anacharsis the Younger," the boy replied. "But," he added, "had you asked the name of the book on the left, sir, I should have said Lamartine's Poetry. A little to the right of this row, I see Crebillon's works; below, two volumes of Fleury's Memoirs"; and my son thus named a dozen books before he stopped.

The spectators had not said a word during this description, as they felt so amazed; but when the experiment had ended, all complimented us by clapping their hands.

III

THE MAGICIAN WHO BECAME AN AMBASSADOR

[It is not generally known that Robert-Houdin once rendered his country an important service as special envoy to Algeria. Half a century ago this colony was an endless source of trouble to France. Although the rebel Arab chieftain Abd-del-Kader had surrendered in 1847, an irregular warfare was kept up against the French authority by the native Kabyles, stimulated by their Mohammedan priests, and particularly through so-called "miracles," such as recovery from wounds and burns self-inflicted by the Marabouts and other fanatic devotees of the Prophet.

Thus in 1856 the hopes of the French Foreign Office rested on Robert-Houdin. He was requested to exhibit his tricks in the most impressive form possible, with the idea of proving to the deluded Arabs that they had been in error in ascribing supernatural powers to their holy men.]

It was settled that I should reach Algiers by the next 27th of September, the day on which the great fetes annually offered by the capital of Algeria to the Arabs would commence.

I must say that I was much influenced in my determination by the knowledge that my mission to Algeria had a quasi-political character. I, a simple conjurer, was proud of being able to render my country a service.

It is known that the majority of revolts which have to be suppressed in Algeria are excited by intriguers, who say they are inspired by the Prophet, and are regarded by the Arabs as envoys of God on earth to deliver them from the oppression of the Roumi (Christians).

These false prophets and holy Marabouts, who are no more sorcerers than I am, and indeed even less so, still contrive to influence the fanaticism of their coreligionists by tricks as primitive as are the spectators before whom they are performed.

The government was, therefore, anxious to destroy their pernicious influence, and reckoned on me to do so. They hoped, with reason, by the aid of my experiments, to prove to the Arabs that the tricks of their Marabouts were mere child's play, and owing to their simplicity could not be done by an envoy from Heaven, which also led us very naturally to show them that we are their superiors in everything, and, as for sorcerers, there are none like the French.

Presently I will show the success obtained by these skillful tactics.

Three months were to elapse between the day of my acceptance and that of my departure which I employed in arranging a complete arsenal of my best tricks, and left St. Gervais on the 10th of September.

I will give no account of my passage, further than to say no sooner was I at sea than I wished I had arrived, and, after thirty-six hours' navigation, I greeted the capital of our colony with indescribable delight.

On the 28th of October, the day appointed for my first performance before the Arabs, I reached my post at an early hour, and could enjoy the sight of their entrance into the theater.

Each goum,[1] drawn up in companies, was introduced separately, and led in perfect order to the places chosen for it in advance. Then came the turn of the chiefs, who seated themselves with all the gravity becoming their character.

[1] Brigade of native soldiers under French command. It was this influential native faction that the Foreign Office wished particularly to impress, through Robert-Houdin's skill.—EDITOR.

Their introduction lasted some time, for these sons of nature could not understand that they were boxed up thus, side by side, to enjoy a spectacle, and our comfortable seats, far from seeming so to them, bothered them strangely. I saw them fidgeting about for some time, and trying to tuck their legs under them, after the fashion of European tailors.

The caids, agas, bash-agas, and other titled Arabs, held the places of honor, for they occupied the orchestra stalls and the dress circle.

In the midst of them were several privileged officers, and, lastly, the interpreters were mingled among the spectators, to translate my remarks to them.

I was also told that several curious people, having been unable to procure tickets, had assumed the Arab burnous, and, binding the camel's-hair cord round their foreheads, had slipped in among their new coreligionists.

This strange medley of spectators was indeed a most curious sight. The dress circle, more especially, presented an appearance as grand as it was imposing. Some sixty Arab chiefs, clothed in their red mantles (the symbol of their submission to France), on which one or more decorations glistened, gravely awaited my performance with majestic dignity.

I have performed before many brilliant assemblies, but never before one which struck me so much as this. However, the impression I felt on the rise of the curtain, far from paralyzing me, on the contrary inspired me with a lively sympathy for the spectators, whose faces seemed so well prepared to accept the marvels promised them. As soon as I walked on the stage, I felt quite at my ease, and enjoyed, in anticipation, the sight I was going to amuse myself with.

I felt, I confess, rather inclined to laugh at myself and my audience, for I stepped forth, wand in hand, with all the gravity of a real Sorcerer. Still, I did not give way, for I was here not merely to amuse a curious and kind public, I must produce a startling effect upon coarse minds and prejudices, for I was enacting the part of a French Marabout.

Compared with the simple tricks of their pretended sorcerers, my experiments must appear perfect miracles to the Arabs.

I commenced my performance in the most profound, I might almost say religious, silence, and the attention of the spectators was so great that they seemed petrified. Their fingers alone moving nervously, played with the beads of their rosaries, while they were, doubtless, invoking the protection of the Most High.

This apathetic condition did not suit me, for I had not come to Algeria to visit a waxwork exhibition. I wanted movement, animation, life in fact, around me.

I changed my batteries, and, instead of generalizing my remarks, I addressed them more especially to some of the Arabs, whom I stimulated by my words, and still more by my actions. The astonishment then gave way to a more expressive feeling, which was soon evinced by noisy outbursts.

This was especially the case when I produced cannon balls from a hat, for my spectators, laying aside their gravity, expressed their delighted admiration by the strangest and most energetic gestures.

Then came—greeted by the same success—the bouquet of flowers, produced instantaneously from a hat; the CORNUCOPIA, supplying a multitude of objects which I distributed, though unable to satisfy the repeated demands made on all sides, and still more by those who had their hands full already; the FIVE-FRANC PIECES, sent across the theater with a crystal box suspended above the spectators.

One trick I should much have liked to perform was the INEXHAUSTIBLE BOTTLE, so appreciated by the Parisians and the Manchester "hands"; but I could not employ it in this performance, for it is well known the followers of Mohammed drink no fermented liquor—at least not publicly. Hence, I substituted the following with considerable advantage:

I took a silver cup, like those called "punch bowls" in the Parisian cafes. I unscrewed the foot, and passing my wand through it showed that the vessel contained nothing; then, having refitted the two parts, I went to the center of the pit, when, at my command, the bowl was MAGICALLY filled with sweetmeats, which were found excellent.

The sweetmeats exhausted, I turned the bowl over, and proposed to fill it with excellent coffee; so, gravely passing my hand thrice over the bowl, a dense vapor immediately issued from it, and announced the presence of the precious liquid. The bowl was full of boiling coffee, which I poured into cups, and offered to my astounded spectators.

The first cups were only accepted, so to speak, under protest; for not an Arab would consent to moisten his lips with a beverage which he thought came straight from Shaitan's kitchen; but, insensibly seduced by the perfume of their favorite liquor, and urged by the interpreters, some of the boldest decided on tasting the magic liquor, and all soon followed their example.

The vessel, rapidly emptied, was repeatedly filled again with equal rapidity; and it satisfied all demands, like my inexhaustible bottle, and was borne back to the stage still full.

But it was not enough to amuse my spectators; I must also, in order to fulfill the object of my mission, startle and even terrify them by the display of a supernatural power.

My arrangements had all been made for this purpose, and I had reserved for the end of my performances three tricks, which must complete my reputation as a sorcerer.

Many of my readers will remember having seen at my performances a small but solidly built box, which, being handed to the spectators, becomes heavy or light at my order; a child might raise it with ease, and yet the most powerful man could not move it from its place.

I advanced, with my box in my hand, to the center of the "practicable," communicating from the stage to the pit; then, addressing the Arabs, I said to them:

"From what you have witnessed, you will attribute a supernatural power to me, and you are right. I will give you a new proof of my marvelous authority, by showing that I can deprive the most powerful man of his strength and restore it at my will. Anyone who thinks himself strong enough to try the experiment may draw near me." (I spoke slowly, in order to give the interpreter time to translate my words.)

An Arab of middle height, but well built and muscular, like many of the Arabs are, came to my side with sufficient assurance.

"Are you very strong?" I said to him, measuring him from head to foot.

"Oh, yes!" he replied carelessly.

"Are you sure you will always remain so?"

"Quite sure."

"You are mistaken, for in an instant I will rob you of your strength, and you shall become as a little child."

The Arab smiled disdainfully as a sign of his incredulity.

"Stay," I continued; "lift up this box."

The Arab stooped, lifted up the box, and said to me, coldly, "Is that all?"

"Wait—!" I replied.

Then, with all possible gravity, I made an imposing gesture, and solemnly pronounced the words:

"Behold! you are weaker than a woman; now, try to lift the box."

The Hercules, quite cool as to my conjuration, seized the box once again by the handle, and gave it a violent tug, but this time the box resisted, and, spite of his most vigorous attacks, would not budge an inch.

The Arab vainly expended on this unlucky box a strength which would have raised an enormous weight, until, at length, exhausted, panting, and red with anger, he stopped, became thoughtful, and began to comprehend the influences of magic.

He was on the point of withdrawing; but that would be allowing his weakness, and that he, hitherto respected for his vigor, had become as a little child. This thought rendered him almost mad.

Deriving fresh strength from the encouragements his friends offered him by word and deed, he turned a glance round them, which seemed to say: "You will see what a son of the desert can do."

He bent once again over the box: his nervous hands twined round the handle, and his legs, placed on either side like two bronze columns, served as a support for the final effort.

But, wonder of wonders! this Hercules, a moment since so strong and proud, now bows his head; his arms, riveted to the box, undergo a violent muscular contraction; his legs give way, and he falls on his knees with a yell of agony!

An electric shock, produced by an inductive apparatus, had been passed, on a signal from me, from the further end of the stage into the handle of the box. Hence the contortions of the poor Arab!

It would have been cruelty to prolong this scene.

I gave a second signal, and the electric current was immediately intercepted. My athlete, disengaged from his terrible bondage, raised his hands over his head.

"Allah! Allah!" he exclaimed, full of terror; then wrapping himself up quickly in the folds of his burnous, as if to hide his disgrace, he rushed through the ranks of the spectators and gained the front entrance.

With the exception of my stage boxes and the privileged spectators who appeared to take great pleasure in this experiment, my audience had become grave and silent, and I heard the words "Shaitan!" "Djenoum!" passing in murmur round the circle of credulous men, who, while gazing on me, seemed astonished that I possessed none of the physical qualities attributed to the angel of darkness.

I allowed my public a few moments to recover from the emotion produced by my experiment and the flight of the herculean Arab.

One of the means employed by the Marabouts to gain influence in the eyes of the Arabs is by causing a belief in their invulnerability.

One of them, for instance, ordered a gun to be loaded and fired at him from a short distance, but in vain did the flint produce a shower of sparks; the Marabout pronounced some cabalistic words, and the gun did not explode.

The mystery was simple enough; the gun did not go off because the Marabout had skillfully stopped up the vent.

Colonel de Neven explained to me the importance of discrediting such a miracle by opposing to it a sleight-of-hand trick far superior to it, and I had the very article.

I informed the Arabs that I possessed a talisman rendering me invulnerable, and I defied the best marksman in Algeria to hit me.

I had hardly uttered the words when an Arab, who had attracted my notice by the attention he had paid to my tricks, jumped over four rows of seats, and disdaining the use of the "practicable," crossed the orchestra, upsetting flutes, clarionets, and violins, escaladed the stage, while burning himself at the footlights, and then said, in excellent French:

"I will kill you!"

An immense burst of laughter greeted both the Arab's picturesque ascent and his murderous intentions, while an interpreter who stood near me told me I had to deal with a Marabout.

"You wish to kill me!" I replied, imitating his accent and the inflection of his voice. "Well, I reply, that though you are a sorcerer, I am still a greater one, and you will not kill me."

I held a cavalry pistol in my hand, which I presented to him.

"Here, take this weapon, and assure yourself it has undergone no preparation."

The Arab breathed several times down the barrel, then through the nipple, to assure himself there was a communication between them, and after carefully examining the pistol, said:

"The weapon is good, and I will kill you."

"As you are determined, and for more certainty, put in a double charge of powder, and a wad on the top."

"It is done."

"Now, here is a leaden ball; mark it with your knife, so as to be able to recognize it, and put it in the pistol, with a second wad."

"It is done."

"Now that you are quite sure your pistol is loaded, and that it will explode, tell me, do you feel no remorse, no scruple about killing me thus, although I authorize you to do so?"

"No, for I wish to kill you," the Arab repeated coldly.

Without replying, I put an apple on the point of a knife, and, standing a few yards from the Marabout, ordered him to fire.

"Aim straight at the heart," I said to him.

My opponent aimed immediately, without the slightest hesitation.

The pistol exploded, and the bullet lodged in the center of the apple.

I carried the talisman to the Marabout, who recognized the ball he had marked.

I could not say that this trick produced greater stupefaction than the ones preceding it: at any rate, my spectators, palsied by surprise and terror, looked round in silence, seeming to think, "Where the deuce have we got to here!"

A pleasant scene, however, soon unwrinkled many of their faces. The Marabout, though stupefied by his defeat, had not lost his wits; so, profiting by the moment when he returned me the pistol, he seized the apple, thrust it into his waist belt, and could not be induced to return it, persuaded as he was that he possessed in it an incomparable talisman.

For the last trick in my performance I required the assistance of an Arab.

At the request of several interpreters, a young Moor, about twenty years of age, tall, well built, and richly dressed, consented to come on the stage. Bolder and more civilized, doubtless, than his comrades of the plains, he walked firmly up to me.

I drew him toward the table that was in the center of the stage, and pointed out to him and to the other spectators that it was slightly built and perfectly isolated. After which, without further preface, I told him to mount upon it, and covered him with an enormous cloth cone, open at the top.

Then, drawing the cone and its contents on to a plank, the ends of which were held by my servant and myself, we walked to the footlights with our heavy burden, and upset it. The Moor had disappeared—the cone was perfectly empty!

Immediately there began a spectacle which I shall never forget.

The Arabs were so affected by this last trick, that, impelled by an irresistible feeling of terror, they rose in all parts of the house, and yielded to the influence of a general panic. To tell the truth, the crowd of fugitives was densest at the door of the dress circle, and it could be seen, from the agility and confusion of these high dignitaries, that they were the first to wish to leave the house.

Vainly did one of them, the Caid of the Beni-Salah, more courageous than his colleagues, try to restrain them by his words:

"Stay! stay! we cannot thus lose one of our coreligionists. Surely we must know what has become of him, or what has been done to him. Stay! stay!"

But the coreligionists only ran away the faster, and soon the courageous caid, led away by their example, followed them.

They little knew what awaited them at the door of the theater; but they had scarce gone down the steps when they found themselves face to face with the "resuscitated Moor."

The first movement of terror overcome, they surrounded the man, felt and cross-questioned him; but, annoyed by these repeated questions, he had no better recourse than to escape at full speed.

The next evening the second performance took place, and produced nearly the same effect as the previous one.

The blow was struck: henceforth the interpreters and all those who had dealings with the Arabs received orders to make them understand that my pretended miracles were only the result of skill, inspired and guided by an art called prestidigitation, in no way connected with sorcery.

The Arabs doubtless yielded to these arguments, for henceforth I was on the most friendly terms with them. Each time a chief saw me, he never failed to come up and press my hand. And, even more, these men whom I had so terrified, when they became my friends, gave me a precious testimony of their esteem—I may say, too, of their admiration, for that is their own expression.

IV

FACING THE ARAB'S PISTOL

[The severest trial of all was unexpectedly encountered during a visit paid by the conjurer and his wife to Bou-Allem-ben-Sherifa, Bash-Aga of the Djendel, a tribe of the desert interior.]

We entered a small room very elegantly decorated, in which were two divans.

"This," our host said, "is the room reserved for guests of distinction; you can go to bed when you like, but if you are not tired, I would ask your leave to present to you several chief men of my tribe, who, having heard of you, wish to see you."

"Let them come in," I said, after consulting Madame Houdin, "we will receive them with pleasure."

The interpreter went out, and soon brought in a dozen old men, among whom were a Marabout and several talebs, whom the bash-aga appeared to hold in great deference.

They sat down in a circle on carpets and kept up a very lively conversation about my performances at Algiers. This learned society discussed the probability of the marvels related by the chief of the tribe, who took great pleasure in depicting his impressions and those of his coreligionists at the sight of the MIRACLES I had performed.

Each lent an attentive ear to these stories, and regarded me with a species of veneration; the Marabout alone displayed a degree of skepticism, and asserted that the spectators had been duped by what he called a vision.

Jealous of my reputation as a French sorcerer, I thought I must perform before the unbeliever a few tricks as a specimen of my late performance. I had the pleasure of astounding my audience, but the Marabout continued to offer me a systematic opposition, by which his neighbors were visibly annoyed; the poor fellow did not suspect, though, what I had in store for him.

My antagonist wore in his sash a watch, the chain of which hung outside.

I believe I have already mentioned a certain talent I possess of filching a watch, a pin, a pocketbook, etc., with a skill by which several of my friends have been victimized.

I was fortunately born with an honest and upright heart, or this peculiar talent might have led me too far. When I felt inclined for a joke of this nature, I turned it to profit in a conjuring trick, or waited till my friend took leave of me, and then recalled him: "Stay," I would say, handing him the stolen article, "let this serve as a lesson to put you on your guard against persons less honest than myself."

But to return to our Marabout. I had stolen his watch as I passed near him and slipped into its place a five-franc piece.

To prevent his detecting it, and while waiting till I could profit by my larceny, I improvised a trick. After juggling away Bou- Allem's rosary, I made it pass into one of the numerous slippers left at the door by the guests; this shoe was next found to be full of coins, and to end this little scene comically, I made five-franc pieces come out of the noses of the spectators. They took such pleasure in this trick that I fancied I should never terminate it. "Douros! douros!"[1] they shouted, as they twitched their noses. I willingly acceded to their request, and the douros issued at command.

[1] Gold Arabic coin.

The delight was so great that several Arabs rolled on the ground; this coarsely expressed joy on the part of Mohammedans was worth frenzied applause to me.

I pretended to keep aloof from the Marabout, who, as I expected, remained serious and impassive.

When calm was restored, my rival began speaking hurriedly to his neighbors, as if striving to dispel their illusion, and, not succeeding, he addressed me through the interpreter:

"You will not deceive me in that way," he said, with a crafty look.

"Why so?"

"Because I don't believe in your power."

"Ah, indeed! Well, then, if you do not believe in my power, I will compel you to believe in my skill."

"Neither in one nor the other."

I was at this moment the whole length of the room from the Marabout.

"Stay," I said to him; "you see this five-franc piece."

"Yes."

"Close your hand firmly, for the piece will go into it in spite of yourself."

"I am ready," the Arab said, in an incredulous voice, as he held out his tightly closed fist.

I took the piece at the end of my fingers, so that the assembly might all see it, then, feigning to throw it at the Marabout, it disappeared at the word "Pass!"

My man opened his hand, and, finding nothing in it, shrugged his shoulders, as if to say, "You see, I told you so."

I was well aware the piece was not there, but it was important to draw the Marabout's attention momentarily from the sash, and for this purpose I employed the feint.

"That does not surprise me," I replied, "for I threw the piece with such strength that it went right through your hand, and has fallen into your sash. Being afraid I might break your watch by the blow, I called it to me: here it is!" And I showed him the watch in my hand.

The Marabout quickly put his hand in his waist belt, to assure himself of the truth, and was quite stupefied at finding the five-franc piece.

The spectators were astounded. Some among them began telling their beads with a vivacity evidencing a certain agitation of mind; but the Marabout frowned without saying a word, and I saw he was spelling over some evil design.

"I now believe in your supernatural power," he said; "you are a real sorcerer; hence, I hope you will not fear to repeat here a trick you performed in your theater"; and offering me two pistols he held concealed beneath his burnous, he added, "Come, choose one of these pistols; we will load it, and I will fire at you. You have nothing to fear, as you can ward off all blows."

I confess I was for a moment staggered; I sought a subterfuge and found none. All eyes were fixed upon me, and a reply was anxiously awaited.

The Marabout was triumphant.

Bou-Allem, being aware that my tricks were only the result of skill, was angry that his guest should be so pestered; hence he began reproaching the Marabout. I stopped him, however, for an idea had occurred to me which would save me from my dilemma, at least temporarily; then, addressing my adversary:

"You are aware," I said, with assurance, "that I require a talisman in order to be invulnerable, and, unfortunately, I have left mine at Algiers."

The Marabout began laughing with an incredulous air. "Still," I continued, "I can, by remaining six hours at prayers, do without the talisman, and defy your weapon. To-morrow morning, at eight o'clock, I will allow you to fire at me in the presence of these Arabs, who were witnesses of your challenge."

Bou-Allem, astonished at such a promise, asked me once again if this offer were serious, and if he should invite the company for the appointed hour. On my affirmative, they agreed to meet before the stone bench in the market place.

I did not spend my night at prayers, as may be supposed, but I employed about two hours in insuring my invulnerability; then, satisfied with the result, I slept soundly, for I was terribly tired.

By eight the next morning we had breakfasted, our horses were saddled, and our escort was awaiting the signal for our departure, which would take place after the famous experiment.

73

None of the guests were absent, and, indeed, a great number of Arabs came in to swell the crowd.

The pistols were handed me; I called attention to the fact that the vents were clear, and the Marabout put in a fair charge of powder and drove the wad home. Among the bullets produced, I chose one which I openly put in the pistol, and which was then also covered with paper.

The Arab watched all these movements, for his honor was at stake.

We went through the same process with the second pistol and the solemn moment arrived.

Solemn, indeed, it seemed to everybody—to the spectators who were uncertain of the issue, to Madame Houdin, who had in vain besought me to give up this trick, for she feared the result— and solemn also to me, for as my new trick did not depend on any of the arrangements made at Algiers, I feared an error, an act of treachery—I knew not what.

Still I posted myself at fifteen paces from the sheik, without evincing the slightest emotion.

The Marabout immediately seized one of the pistols, and, on my giving the signal, took a deliberate aim at me. The pistol went off, and the ball appeared between my teeth.

More angry than ever, my rival tried to seize the other pistol, but I succeeded in reaching it before him.

"You could not injure me," I said to him, "but you shall now see that my aim is more dangerous than yours. Look at that wall."

I pulled the trigger, and on the newly whitewashed wall appeared a large patch of blood, exactly at the spot where I had aimed.

The Marabout went up to it, dipped his finger in the blood, and, raising it to his mouth, convinced himself of the reality. When he acquired this certainty, his arms fell, and his head was bowed on his chest, as if he were annihilated.

It was evident that for the moment he doubted everything, even the Prophet.

The spectators raised their eyes to heaven, muttered prayers, and regarded me with a species of terror.

This scene was a triumphant termination to my performance. I therefore retired, leaving the audience under the impression I had produced. We took leave of Bou-Allem and his son, and set off at a gallop.

The trick I have just described, though so curious, is easily prepared. I will give a description of it, while explaining the trouble it took me.

As soon as I was alone in my room, I took out of my pistol case— without which I never travel—a bullet mold.

I took a card, bent up the four edges, and thus made a sort of trough, in which I placed a piece of wax taken from one of the candles. When it was melted, I mixed with it a little lampblack I had obtained by putting the blade of a knife over the candle, and then ran this composition in the bullet mold.

Had I allowed the liquid to get quite cold, the ball would have been full and solid; but in about ten seconds I turned the mold over, and the portions of the wax not yet set ran out, leaving a hollow ball in the mold. This operation is the same as that used in making tapers, the thickness of the outside depending on the time the liquid has been left in the mold.

I wanted a second ball, which I made rather more solid than the other; and this I filled with blood, and covered the orifice with a lump of wax. An Irishman had once taught me the way to draw blood from the thumb without feeling any pain, and I employed it on this occasion to fill my bullet.

Bullets thus prepared bear an extraordinary resemblance to lead, and are easily mistaken for that metal when seen at a short distance off.

With this explanation, the trick will be easily understood. After showing the leaden bullet to the spectators, I changed it for my hollow ball, and openly put the latter into the pistol. By pressing the wad tightly down, the wax broke into small pieces, and could not touch me at the distance I stood.

At the moment the pistol was fired, I opened my mouth to display the lead bullet I held between my teeth, while the other pistol contained the bullet filled with blood, which bursting against the wall, left its imprint, though the wax had flown to atoms.

It is no wonder that after such exhibitions Robert-Houdin's success was complete. The Arabs lost all confidence in Marabout "miracles," and thus a dangerous smoldering flame of disaffection to the French was entirely smothered.—EDITOR.

David P. Abbott

Fraudulent Spiritualism Unveiled[1]

[1] As to whether communication with the departed is possible, no discussion is here attempted. The episodes following, from experiences well authenticated, merely illustrate what sleight-of- hand experts have long known—that most "mediums," "astrologers," "mind readers," and the like, can be proven to be frauds. Their dupes are puzzled, and sometimes won over, in the name of Spiritualism, either by the tricks familiar to all "conjurers," or else by the psychology of deception (see page 280). Some of the cleverness displayed is marvelous, as the following pages show. The passages by Hereward Carrington are copyrighted by Herbert B. Turner & Co., 1907, and those by David P. Abbott are copyrighted by the Open Court Publishing Company, 1907—EDITOR.

THE METHODS OF A "DOCTOR OF THE OCCULT"

Not so very long ago I met a friend—a man of wealth, who was a firm believer in spiritualism, and who frequently conversed with his dead wife and daughter. I asked him if he could inform me whether or not there were any good mediums in the city, as I should like to consult one.

He replied that at present there were none in Omaha of any well- developed psychic powers; that he was entirely satisfied on the subject and did not require any demonstrations to convince himself of the truths of spiritual science. He informed me that the question was settled beyond all dispute; but that if I were skeptical, there was said to be a medium in Council Bluffs who possessed most wonderful powers.

I accordingly made other inquiries from those who were in a position to know; and I learned that this medium, a celebrated "Doctor of the Occult, Astrologer, Palmist and Spirit Medium," was at that time giving private sittings in Council Bluffs to earnest inquirers only, for the small sum of two dollars.

I was informed that his performances were of the most wonderful nature; that there was no possibility of trickery of any kind; that he told you whatever you desired to know, without your even asking him; that, in addition to this, he had powers over the elements of nature; and, in fact, I was led to believe that he was a true sorcerer of the olden days.

I determined at once to call on this renowned personage, and try to secure a little information from the unseen world. Accordingly, one Sunday afternoon I took the car that crossed the river, and in due time arrived at the apartments of this wonderful doctor.

I was met at the door by an attendant, who accepted the fee and directed me to enter the rooms of this mysterious person quietly; and if I found him employed, by no means to disturb him, but merely to await his pleasure; that he was frequently conversing with unseen beings, or deep in some astrological computation, and at such times it was not safe to disturb him.

With a beating heart I entered the room where he was to be found. This room was a large one. I did not see him at first. What attracted my attention was a large map or painting on a piece of canvas which hung on a wall space in the room. This painting had a representation of the sun in its center. This could be discovered by the rays which radiated from it in all directions. Around this sun were many stars, and an occasional planet, among which Saturn and its rings were very prominently depicted. There were numerous pictures of animals and men, and of queer monsters, scattered among the stars.

Beneath this picture stood a large golden oak table at which sat this delver into the occult, deeply engrossed in a study of this painting; while with a little brush he figured and calculated, in a queer sort of Chinese characters, which he drew on a sheet of paper. He also seemed to be making a strange drawing on the same paper. He was far too deeply engaged to notice my entrance, and continued at his labors for some time, while I stood quietly and watched him. Sitting on one end of this rather large table was a glass globe or vessel, supported by three nickeled rods, something like a tripod. Coming from the wall was a rather large nickeled tube or pipe which curved over above the glass vessel, and continually allowed drops of water to fall into the globe. From the side of this glass vessel there led a small nickeled pipe which evidently carried away the waste water.

Occasionally a little blue flame would appear on the surface of this water, play about, and disappear. When this happened the body of the medium was always convulsed slightly.

After a time he seemed to finish his calculation, and this seer condescended to leave the realms of the stars wherein dwelt the spirits that rule the universe and the destinies of men, and to descend to earth and for a time direct his gaze toward this humble mortal. He turned around and observed me for the first time. He was a large, portly, fine-looking gentleman of middle age, with very long black hair which gave him a strange appearance. He wore a pair of glasses low down on his nose; and from over these he condescended to direct his gaze at, and to study me for a moment as a naturalist might study some specimen that happened temporarily to attract his notice.

He soon informed me that the stars had told him something of my coming and of the question that was worrying me; and he asked me if I desired to consult the stars as to my destiny, to have him decipher it from the lines of my palm, or whether I should prefer to converse with the dead. The last was my choice.

Not far from a window at one side of the room there was a small table on which were a few articles. He directed me to be seated at this table, and handed me a slip of paper of a size of probably four by five inches. He directed me to write the question I desired answered on this paper, and when through to fold the paper in halves three times with the writing inside. I did so while he walked to his bowl of water apparently paying no attention to me, and then returned.

When he had returned to a position opposite me at the table, he reached to take my writing out of my hand; seeing which I quickly bent down one corner of the paper and gave it to him. He directed one sharp glance at me as I did this, at the same time picking up an envelope from the table with his other hand. He held this envelope open flap side toward me, and slowly inserted my paper into it. As he did this, looking sharply at me, he remarked, "I am no sleight-of-hand performer. You see your question is actually in the envelope." This was the case; for it was close to me and I could plainly see the top of it against the back of the envelope, the lower portions being inserted; and I could see the little corner folded down, as I had bent it, and I was certain he had not exchanged it. In fact he took occasion to use his hands in such manner that I could see there was nothing concealed about them, that he "palmed" nothing, and that he made no exchange. I was entirely satisfied that all was fair, and that no exchange had been made.

Next, he sealed the envelope, and holding it toward the window, called my attention to the fact that as the envelope was partly transparent I could see my paper within it and that it was actually there. This was really the case. He now took a match, and lighting it applied the flame to this identical envelope without its leaving my sight; and proceeded to burn the last vestige of it and the paper within it, allowing the ashes to drop into a small vessel on the table.

There was no doubt that he did not exchange envelopes and that he burned it before my very eyes. He now took the ashes and emptied them into the bowl of water on the side table. A little blue flame appeared on the surface of the water after that for a moment, and then disappeared.

He now brought from a drawer a number of slates—about eight or ten small slates with padded edges. They were the smallest size of slates, I should judge; and with them he brought another slate, a trifle larger, probably two inches both longer and wider. He requested me to examine thoroughly or to clean them all to my own satisfaction, and to stack the small ones on the table, one on top of the other; and when all were thus placed, to place the large slate on top of the stack.

While I was doing this he called to his attendant for a drink of water, and incidentally stepped into the hall to receive it, so that his menial would not profane this sanctuary with his presence.

Returning to the table he took a seat opposite me and placed one of my hands and one of his on top of the slates. In due time he took up the slates and we found nothing. He replaced them, and waited for a few moments; then seeming dissatisfied with conditions, he took up the top slate in his left hand and with his right hand began writing a message for me. He did this like mediums do automatic writing, with eyes half closed; and while writing his person was convulsed a few times. He then opened his eyes and read aloud what he had written, asking me if it answered my question. I replied that it did not, as it was entirely foreign to the subject. Then seeming dissatisfied, he moistened his fingers, erased the writing, and replaced the top slate on the stack of slates.

He now placed his hands on this slate again, and after a time examined it; but it was still free from writing. He lifted up some of the other slates; but as there was no writing, he scattered the slates around on the table and asked me to spread a large cloth over them which he handed to me. This I did, and under his direction placed my arms and hands over this. He walked to the bowl of water on the side table, and gazed into it. I watched him; and I saw a rather large flame appear on the surface of the water, dance about, and disappear.

He immediately informed me that he was certain that I now had a message. He remained at a distance while I examined the slates one by one. Finally, on one of them I found a message, neatly written and covering the entire slate. It read:

"Mrs. Piper is a genuine medium. She possesses powers of a very unusual nature. Her tests given Hyslop and others are genuine. Do not be a skeptic. You are making a mistake, dear friend. It is all plain to me now, and spirit is all there is.—WILL."

Now, the question I had written was addressed to a very dear friend who is now dead, and read as follows:

"WILL J——: In regard to the medium, Mrs. Piper, of whom we conversed on your last visit, I would ask if she be genuine, and if the tests she gave Professor Hyslop and others were genuine. Give me a test."

This was all nicely done, and I am sure would have greatly impressed nearly everyone. Being a performer myself, I could of course follow the performance in minute detail, and I am thus enabled to give to the readers of this paper a detailed account of the method used by the doctor. I will state that since that time I have very successfully operated this same test, minus the bowl of water and flame of fire; and that I can assure all that it is very practicable and that it is very deceptive.

HOW THE TRICKS SUCCEEDED

When the medium picked up the envelope in which to place my paper, there was within it a duplicate piece of paper folded the same, and of the same size (one inch and a quarter by two inches) as the one I had folded. He kept the face of this envelope opposite me so I could not see that side of it. On the face of it was a horizontal slit cut with a knife. This slit was about two inches long and was situated about halfway down the face of the envelope. The duplicate folded paper was placed vertically in the envelope at its center, so that its center was located against the slit. This piece of paper was held in position by a touch of paste at a point opposite the slit, which caused it to adhere to the inside of the back of the envelope.

When he picked up this prepared envelope with his left hand, he did so with the slit side or face in his palm next to the fingers of his left hand. This envelope lay slit side down before he picked it up; so that I did not see the face of the envelope at all, and he kept that side of the envelope from me during the entire trick. The paper within the envelope had been placed far enough down so that its top part was not exposed to my view. The envelope thus appeared perfectly natural, as an ordinary one with nothing in it.

He thus held the envelope in his left hand, flap open wide, with the back side of the envelope later to be sealed, facing me. Now he really inserted my paper in this envelope with his right hand as he took it from me; but in fact, he pushed it down just behind the hidden slip of paper within the envelope. I mean that he inserted it between the concealed slip and the face or slit side of the envelope; and as he did this he caused the lower end of my slip of paper to pass through the slit in the center of the front of the envelope. The lower portion of my slip was thus out of the envelope on its rear side, between the front of the envelope and the fingers of his left hand; although I could see nothing of this. He pushed it down so that the top still remained in view with the bent corner exposed, and then sealed the flap over it.

Holding the envelope toward the window, he called to my notice the fact that my paper was within, and that I could see it plainly. I could see the shadow of the two papers, which appeared as one, and thus his statement seemed correct. Of course he did not show me the rear side OR FACE of the envelope, with my paper protruding, which was immediately behind the duplicate, so that the shadow of it was also the shadow of the duplicate.

This shadow also hid from my view the shadow of the slit. The envelope was sealed fairly.

Now with his right hand he moved a small vessel on the table toward himself. Then taking the envelope in his right hand, slit side downward, he held it close to this vessel; at the same time with his left hand he took a match from his pocket and proceeded to burn the envelope. This move concealed the trick; and it was very deceiving and cleverly done. As he took the envelope from his left hand with his right hand, he, with his left fingers touching the protruding portion of my slip, caused it to remain in his left hand and to be drawn entirely out of the slit. His eyes followed the envelope as his right hand took it; which naturally caused my eyes to follow it, as his attention seemed centered on the envelope and it appeared to occupy the stage of action. This move was executed in a moment, not requiring any time worth mentioning, although it takes so long to describe it on paper intelligibly. Now while his eyes (and of course mine) followed the envelope, without pause his left hand went into his left pocket in a natural manner to get the match. He, of course, left my slip in his pocket with his surplus matches; and when he retired for the drink of water, he read my question.

As to the slate trick, all was fair until he picked up the top slate, wrote an automatic message, apparently read it aloud to me, and then upon my informing him that the message did not answer my question, he seemed dissatisfied, apparently erased the message, and replaced the large slate on top of the stack of slates. What he really did was to pick up the large top slate, bottom side toward himself, and at the same time to carry with it a small slate pressed tightly against its under side. He held the large slate with its under side tilted from me, so I could not see this small slate. There being so many small slates in the stack, the temporary absence of one from the stack attracted no notice.

He kept this small slate next to him out of my view, and really wrote the message on the small slate which was next to him, and which was concealed from my view by the larger slate. He did not read aloud what he had actually written, but merely pretended to do so, repeating something entirely foreign to the subject instead. What he had written really answered my question fully. When he appeared to erase the message, his movements were but a pretense; and he did not erase it at all. When he replaced the large slate on the stack of slates, he, of course, replaced the small one which was concealed under it, message side down.

It must be remembered that the operator, at the beginning of the slate trick, first took up and examined the large slate a time or so for a message; and finding none, seemed disappointed, and finally wrote the automatic message; then on being informed that it did not apply to the case, he seemed dissatisfied and appeared to erase it.

After the message was written and the slates replaced, he examined the top slate a time or so, and even lifted off a few small slates looking for writing, but did not turn them over; then seeing nothing, he scattered the slates around on the table, leaving their same sides downward; and handing me the cover, he requested me to cover them and place my hands on them.

The trick was now practically done. As the slates had been examined so many times and nothing found on them, even after the automatic writing, the majority of persons would testify that there was positively nothing on the slates when the medium left the table. The majority of persons would never remember that he at one time wrote on the large slate and erased it. The message being on a small slate, and these being spread around, few would have known that this message really appeared on the particular small slate that was originally next the top of the stack.

Most people would have certified that they cleaned all of the slates themselves, that the medium never touched any of the small ones, and that he only laid his hands on top of the stack a few times. Some would even forget that the medium handled their writing at all before burning it.

I am sure that the nickeled tube that carried the dripping water into the space over the glass bowl, had a second tube within it; through which his assistant from the adjoining room either blew, or sent by some mechanism, the chemicals (probably potassium) that would take fire and burn on striking the water.

. . . . .

When I perform the slate trick described above, after writing the "automatic" message, apparently erasing it, and replacing the slates, I do not scatter the slates around on the table as this medium did. Instead, I proceed as I will now describe.

We place our palms on the stack, and after a time examine the large slate for a message, but find none. I may incidentally remark that this last examination unconsciously verifies in the sitter's mind the fact that I actually erased what I wrote "automatically."

I now look on some of the smaller slates for a message, but find none. When I do this I do not turn these slates over and look on their under sides, but merely take off the top slate to see if there be a message on the upper surface of the one under it. I merely remark, "Well, there is nothing on that slate," indicating the second one from the top; and at the same time I drop the top slate (now in my hand) on the table beside the stack. I immediately take off the second slate and repeat this same performance, dropping it on top of the first one. I keep on with this performance until I have removed four or five of the slates, and have them stacked in a second stack beside the first one. Then seeming to grow discouraged, I remark, "I guess there is no message"; and I replace the second stack on the first stack. This places the message slate four or five slates down in the stack; as the bottom slate of the second stack, being the top slate of the original stack, is now the message slate.

I next up-edge the small slates and place a rubber band around them placing them in the sitter's lap. I, of course, place what was the top of the stack downward when I do so. As the stack is on the side edges of the slates when I first up-edge them, I next bring them upon the end edges, while I put the band in place. It is now easy to place the stack of slates upon the sitter's lap with the top slate down and to attract no notice to this fact. This is because the position has been changed a time or so in placing the band on; and I then take the stack in my hands by the edges of the slates, and simply place what was the top side of the stack in the beginning, at the bottom.

In due time I tell the subject to make an examination for a message, and of course four or five slates down he finds a message on the upper surface of one of the slates.

This seems very miraculous, as the slates have been so repeatedly examined and nothing found. Finding the message on the upper surface of a middle slate, where but a moment before there was nothing, seems to be truly a marvel. The subject having cleaned and stacked these slates himself, and having seen them examined so many times, naturally feels impressed that the message comes by some superhuman power.

THE NAME OF THE DEAD

In the book entitled Psychics: Facts and Theories, by Rev. Minot J.

Savage, at page 15, the following account will be found:

"Soon I began to hear raps, apparently on the floor, and then in different parts of the room. On this, the lady remarked, simply: 'Evidently there is some one here who wishes to communicate with you. Let us go into the front parlor, where it will be quieter.' This we did, the raps following us, or rather beginning again as soon as we were seated. At her suggestion I then took pencil and paper (which I happened to have in my bag), and sat at one side of a marble-top table, while she sat at the other side in a rocker and some distance away. Then she said: 'As one way of getting at the matter, suppose you do this: You know what friends you have in the spirit world. Write now a list of names—any names you please, real or fictitious, only among them somewhere include the names of some friends in the spirit world who, you think, might like to communicate with you, if such a thing were possible.' I then began. I held a paper so that she could not possibly have seen what I wrote, even though she had not been so far away. I took special pains that no movement or facial expression should betray me. Meantime she sat quietly rocking and talking. As I wrote, perhaps at the eighth or tenth name, I began to write the name of a lady friend who had not been long dead. I had hardly written the first letter before there came three loud distinct raps. Then my hostess said, 'This friend of yours, of course, knows where she died. Write now a list of places, including in it the place of her death, and see if she will recognize it.' This I did, beginning with Vienna, and so on with any that occurred to me. Again I had hardly begun to write the real name, when once more came three raps. And so on, concerning other matters. I speak of these only as specimens.

"Now, I cannot say that in this particular case the raps were not caused by the toe joints of the lady. The thing that puzzles me in this theory, is as to how the toe joints happened to know the name of my friend, where she died, etc., which facts the lady herself did not know, and never had known."

It has been the writer's good fortune to witness practically this same experiment, performed by a very expert medium, Dr. Schlossenger, who was traveling over the country a few years ago.

I was residing at that time in Falls City, Neb., a place of a few thousand population. For two winters I had traveled some as a magician, so when the medium came to town, and began to perform his miracles, certain members of the community suggested having me witness one of his seances, thinking I would be able to discover whether his tests were genuine, or whether they were performed by the aid of trickery. Accordingly, one evening, a prominent physician invited me, with certain relatives and friends, to attend a seance given in his parlors.

When we arrived I was introduced to the medium, an elderly gentleman with a long white beard, and wearing glasses. He appeared to be slightly deaf, as he placed his hand to his ear and had my name repeated. He was introduced to the remainder of the company en masse, the names of the visitors not being given to him.

The medium soon announced that "his mission on this earth was to absolutely prove to humanity the immortality of the soul." He now offered to give some tests to those desiring it, and asked for a small table which was placed in an adjoining room. He invariably held his hand to his ear, to catch what was being said, being apparently quite deaf. He also used this same expedient when listening to the voices of the unseen spirits, and reporting their communications.

My father and another gentleman were selected for the first test, as they were considered very skeptical in such matters. As they retired to a closed room I did not see the experiment, but will give some parts of it as reported to me, farther on. In a short time they returned to the parlor, engaged in a discussion over the matter; and my father remarked, "I do not know how you got your information, but I feel certain it was not from my brother, or he would have given a certain point correctly." The medium then said, "If I will tell you where your father died, and the disease he died of, will you be convinced?" My father replied, "I suppose I will have to be, if you can do that."

They then retired, and the medium succeeded partially in the experiment; and would have certainly succeeded entirely, had my father followed his instructions. I will describe what was reported to me of this test, farther on.

I now offered myself for a test. I retired to the room with the medium, and incidentally offered him one dollar and fifty cents, the same my father had given him; but he refused the money, saying: "Your father is not convinced, and I will not take any more money."

He now took a sheet of paper from a tablet, and drew five straight lines across it, spacing the sheet into six spaces about equal. Next taking my hand, and looking earnestly into my face, he said: "Promise me that if I succeed, you will not make light of this. Promise me, for this is very sacred to me." I did so. He now directed me to write names in the spaces on the sheet, any names I pleased, writing but one name in each space. All the names were to be of living or fictitious persons except one, this one to be the name of some one I had known who was then dead. He said, "Be fair with me, and I will scratch out the dead person's name." These were his exact words, therefore I in no way tried to hide my writing from him, although he stood at a distance and did not appear to watch me. I took a pencil and began writing the names; being unprepared I had to think of the names I wished to write. I desired to select names of persons living at a distance, so that he could in no possible manner know them. While I was writing he talked incessantly, which in spite of myself divided my attention. At the same time he kept urging me to write, and immediately after urging me, would begin talking rapidly on some spiritualistic subject. I remember saying, "You must give me time to think." I thought I used great care, so as to write each name with the same precision, and tried to betray no emotion when writing the dead person's name. I selected the name "Cora Holt" for the dead person's name. This was the name of an aunt who had died in another State.

As soon as I had written the names he asked me to cut them apart into slips, having one name on each slip. Now here I do not remember whether he folded them himself, or had me help, as I was not expecting them to be folded. However, we folded each one into a billet with the writing inside.

He now directed me to place them in a hat, and to hold the hat under the table, take out the billets one at a time, and throw them on the table top. This I did while he stood with his right arm extended toward the table and about one foot above it. After I had thrown a few billets on the table, as I threw the next one, I heard three loud distinct raps. He said, "There, that's the one that is dead. Open it and see if I am right, but do not let me see it. Fold it up again and place it in your pocket." I opened the billet. I did not know what the name would be, as I had mixed them under the table; yet I had a feeling that it was correct. I opened it and sure enough the name was "Cora Holt." I refolded it, placing it in my pocket. I must confess that I felt a momentary creepy feeling pass over me, as my emotions were wrought up to such a pitch by the intense manner in which I had watched all the details of the experiment. I informed him that he was right, but did not tell him the name. He now took my hand in his, and leading me into the parlor, had me state to the company what had just occurred. Now placing his hand on my head, he said: "I will endeavor to give you the name." Closing his eyes, his body trembled or shuddered with a kind of paroxysm, and apparently with a great effort he pronounced the name "Cora Holt." This effort seemed to greatly exhaust him, and coming out of his temporary trance he begged us to excuse him, saying that there were opposing spirits present and he could do no more that night; that he had done all for us that lay within his power. He now took his leave.

This was all very impressive to me at the time, except the raps. It was only afterwards that I thought out the explanation, which I will give farther on. As to the raps, they had the sound as of a pencil tapping loudly on a thin strip of wood, or a ruler, and not the sound of tapping on a table. I had previously known of the mechanical and electrical rappers, supplied by certain conjuring depots, and worn on the person of the medium, or attached to a table. My impression was at the time that possibly he had a rapper in the sleeve of the arm extended over the table, and by directing the attention to the table the sound would appear to come from there. As I was sitting right against the table, I will say that the sound did not appear to me to come from the table, but more nearly from his person.

Referring again to the test given my father, the medium first announced his prices, which he would accept if satisfactory. This was agreed to and paid. He then had my father write names on paper in a manner similar to the way I have described, except he did not request my father to write a dead person's name; instead, he requested him to write, among other names, his mother's maiden name, his wife's maiden name, his father's name, also the names of certain members of his family and of some of his friends, some of whom should be dead. This my father did.

Among the names written by my father was his mother's maiden name, viz., "Celestina Redexilana Phelps," a name certainly out of the ordinary. He also wrote his wife's maiden name, his father's name, his brother's name, and several other names—six or eight altogether.

When the medium had the billets taken out of the hat he said, "You have there the name of your mother; the name is something like 'Celestia (not Celestina) Roxalena (not Redexilana) Phelps,'" thus giving wrong pronunciations to the first two names. However, when my father opened it, sure enough it was his mother's maiden name. My father now took another billet which had written thereon his father's name. This the medium gave correctly, stating that this was his father's name. The next billet had written thereon the name of my father's brother; the name was James Asahel Abbott." The medium then said: "Your brother James is here, and he says to tell you that he is happy and that you are making a great mistake not to believe."

Now this brother had always been called by his second name and not by the name of James. My father said, "If you are my brother, give me your full name." The medium replied, "James Ash-a-bell Abbott," giving an entirely wrong pronunciation of the second name. This it was, with some other error, that led to the discussion they had on returning to the parlor, and in which my father remarked, "If you get your information from the dead, they should be able to pronounce their own names correctly."

My father, not being familiar with the methods of trickery, could not with exactness give all the minute details of the test as I would have wished; and as I never had an opportunity to see this experiment myself, I can only surmise the means employed in its production.

The second experiment with my father had been an effort to tell the disease of which my grandfather died, also the place where he died. The medium required my father to write on the usual ruled paper, a name of a disease and also a name of a place, in each space, that is, one disease and one place in each space. He remarked in giving directions, "Like New York measles, Philadelphia smallpox, etc." He required, however, that my father write IN THE SAME SPACE the correct disease, and also the correct place of his father's death. The remainder of the spaces were to contain the names of any disease or any place he might choose.

This my father did, writing in one space "Sacramento dysentery." This was the correct disease, but the city was the place of my grandfather's burial, and not the place of his death, the latter being a village called "Hangtown." The medium quickly gave dysentery as the disease, and

Sacramento as the place of my grandfather's death. It was plain that had my father written the village where his father died, instead of his burial place, the medium would have succeeded.

This, however, proved beyond a doubt that the medium obtained his information FROM THE WRITING, and not from the spirits of the dead.

. . . . .

After thinking the matter over, I decided that, while I was uncertain as to the manner in which Dr. Schlossenger had performed all of these experiments, I could reproduce two of them with certainty as often as he did. I immediately made the trial and found I could succeed fully nine times out of ten on an average. I might state that the doctor also failed about one time in ten on an average; nevertheless, the people of the community were greatly excited, talking of his miracles, in groups on the streets, for some days. The medium was coining money, yet I found a few cases where he failed totally. The failures were seldom mentioned; it was the successes that excited the people.

The method I use in reproducing the first test given me, is to so direct the attention of the subjects before the writing, by my discourse, as to cause them to select unconsciously the name of the dead person in advance. This is easily managed with a little practice in talking, and still they will never guess that it is done on purpose.

Now, as they begin to write, they will naturally pause before writing each name, to think of a name to write. The pause may be but slight, yet there is some pause. Of course, when they write the selected name, no pause will be necessary; and if hurried properly at that time they will make none. This is the object of the incessant talking during the experiment. If left to themselves, the subjects will, in about one half of the cases, write the selected name in the third space from the top. In about half of the remaining cases the selected name will be written in the fourth space from the top. This is especially true if in your instructions you direct the subject to "mix the dead person's name somewhere in among the others where you cannot know where it is." In the remaining cases the subjects are liable to write the selected name anywhere, generally first or last. Now my object is to so manipulate my subjects as to cause them to write the selected name when I want them to do so. This is done by continuous talking, and distracting their attention until the proper moment. I choose the third space, since this, being the one they are most liable to choose of their own accord, is the easiest to force. Just as they begin to write the first name, before they make a mark, I say suddenly, "Now be sure and select names of living persons that I could not possibly know." This is almost certain to insure a pause, and the name of a living person to be written first. I continue my talking in a natural manner, taking the attention to a great extent from the writing, and nearly always observing another pause just before writing the second name. When the second name is almost finished I exclaim suddenly, "Now write as rapidly as possible!" If the subjects have been properly impressed with the seriousness of the experiment, they will almost invariably, on finishing the second name (in obedience to my command "to be as rapid as possible," and in their desire to please me), hurry into the name already in their minds, thus writing the selected name in the third place. If such is the case they will now most surely pause to think of a fourth name. If so, I am certain that I now know the selected name. However, if they should rapidly pass into the fourth name, it is then uncertain whether the selected name is in the third or fourth space. This, however, seldom happens if worked in an expert manner.

In rare cases the subject cannot be manipulated by the performer, in which case it is purely guesswork; even in such cases, however, I stand one chance in six of succeeding; and if I make a second trial on failing (not uncommon with mediums), I stand one chance in three of succeeding.

It is hardly worth while to say that as I fold the billets, I fold the third one slightly different from the rest, so that while it will not attract attention, I can see at a glance what it is when thrown on the table. I memorize the name; also, if in doubt, I fold a second choice in a still different manner for a second trial. Frequently I memorize more of the names, folding so I can pick them out. Then, after giving the dead person's name with proper effect, I pick up the others, hold them to my head and call out the names. The effect of this on a subject is very impressive.

With a little practice the above test can be given with very small chance of failure; and in the event of making a failure it can be explained by the statement that "there are opposing spirits present," or some similar excuse. If one has other tests at his command, it is well, in the event of failure, to announce that he will try something else, and then give another test. As these experiments are always tried alone with one or, at most, two subjects, a failure attracts little notice.

Now I cannot say positively that Dr. Schlossenger performed this experiment in exactly this same manner; but I do have a recollection of his hurrying me along in my writing at some stage of its progress. I also know that I can succeed as often as he did. I will add further that a few days later I prepared six names in advance, and, with my wife, had a sitting with the medium; this time, although I paid him, he failed utterly. He tried in every way and had me write additional names. This time I guarded the points in the above explanation, yet no matter how he tried, he made an utter failure. All tricks require certain conditions, and this is why it is not safe to repeat the same trick for the same person. There is too much danger that the subject may notice the sameness of the modus operandi.

Referring to the second test which was given by the medium to my father, I will state that when the subjects are writing the cities and diseases, they will naturally pause after writing the city, to think of a disease to go with it. Of course, when writing the correct ones, which are already in mind, no pause will be necessary. Also advantage may be taken of the fact that a small per cent of persons die of smallpox or measles. If in giving the directions one says, "Write like this: 'Philadelphia smallpox, New York measles,'" and the subject writes smallpox or measles in the list, it is safe to eliminate that from the case. This is especially true if written in connection with some large city, the name of which occurs readily to the mind. It is safe also to eliminate Philadelphia or New York if these should be written, providing you mentioned these names in the directions, and that the test is not being given in their section of the country. A small per cent of the people of a country die in any two places of prominence. Yet these places will be written readily by most subjects if they are suggested, or at least other places of equal prominence will be written. If an unusual place or disease should be written, it is almost certain these are the ones.

It can readily be seen how expert one can become at this by continuous practice, such as a medium has many times a day; how one can learn to take advantage of every little point, and use it with telling effect on unsuspecting strangers, who do not know what is going to happen, or what to look for.

I have been told that Dr. Schlossenger had a very sharp eye, although wearing glasses; and that the glasses were probably to make the subject think it impossible for him to read writing when they were moved out of position and placed on the forehead, as they were during the tests. It has also been suggested that his poor hearing was feigned, to enable him to hear remarks made about himself in his presence. I have suspected that his memory had become trained to a high degree of accuracy, enabling him to give his tests with such marvelous success, as he did with nearly all wherever he went. That he does not use one set of principles only in his tricks, I am certain, but has many more at his command which he uses continually. However, I can only vaguely guess at them from having seen his tests but once.

Now, I do not say that this was the method employed by the lady with Rev. Savage, given in the account at the beginning of this chapter. But as the experiments are practically the same, it is safe to conclude that the methods used are the same, or nearly so. If the test were genuine in the case of the lady mentioned, it was probably genuine in the case of Dr. Schlossenger. On the other hand, if it were trickery in one case, it probably was in both.

MIND READING IN PUBLIC

Not long ago I received a letter from an old-time friend, in which he urgently requested me to make a journey to his city. In bygone days he and I had spent many hours together, discussing the mysteries of existence, the hidden powers which nature manifests to us, and the origin and destiny of the human soul. My friend is a physician, and what is more, an earnest student; and he is also an investigator of that strange phenomenon in nature which manifests itself in organized beings subjectively, as thought, feeling and things spiritual.

Many times had we discussed the possibility and also the probability of an existence of the spiritual part of man after death. Many times had he reported to me cases of strange phenomena that tended to prove the indestructibility of spirit.

When I received this missive, it stated to me that the writer most earnestly desired my presence in his city, that I might assist in investigating a very strange and marvelous case of psychic phenomena. The case was that of a certain traveling spirit medium, who claimed the power to summon from the realms of the invisible the shades of our departed friends and loved ones. He gave most marvelous exhibitions to prove his strange and miraculous power. My friend stated that he thought he had at last found a person with at least some queer psychical gift, if not even possessing the power that he claimed. He had watched the exhibition most carefully, and had even served on a committee on the psychic's stage; and he could find no evidence of trickery of any kind. He was inclined to believe that this strange being really possessed the power of vision without the use of human eyes as he certainly read sealed missives, of which he could in no secret manner have obtained knowledge.

Accordingly, on Saturday evening, I journeyed to a city one hundred miles away to witness the work of this modern sorcerer. On my arrival I suggested to my friend a number of ways by which such things could be performed by trickery, but he informed me that none of my explanations seemed to elucidate this strange work. The secret did not consist in the use of odorless alcohol, for the reason that the medium never touched the sealed envelopes at all. In fact he was never nearer to them than ten feet. This also made it impossible for him to use the principle on which the trick is based, which is known to the profession as "Washington Irving Bishop's Sealed Letter Reading."

He informed me that sheets of paper or cards were passed to the spectators in the audience, and at the same time envelopes in which to seal their questions were furnished for them; that the spectators wrote questions as directed, many times signing their own names to them. He was certain that many persons folded their written questions before sealing them, and that the operator himself did not even collect the envelopes on many occasions. He informed me that the best evidence of the genuineness of the performance lay in the fact that the medium seemed to have no fixed conditions for his experiments; but seemed to perform them in a different manner on each occasion. The conditions were different in every case, yet he always read the questions with the most marvelous certainty.

I thought the matter over after this, but could in no way think of any plausible means of accomplishing his work by trickery. I finally decided to wait and see the performance first, and to figure afterwards on the method employed.

Accordingly, at eight o'clock that evening I was seated in the hall with my friend, and shortly afterwards the "Seer" made his appearance, taking his seat on the stage. He was a very slender personage, with long hair and a particularly ghostly look. He took his seat quietly on the stage. In a short time his manager appeared and made an opening address, which I will not repeat, and then asked some boy in the audience to pass cards around to the spectators on which they were to write questions. Envelopes were also distributed, in which to seal the cards. When the writing was finished, the manager asked any boy to take a hat which he held in his hand, and collect the sealed envelopes. After the boy, whom everyone knew to be a local resident, kindly volunteered for this service and executed it, a committee was invited to the stage to properly blindfold the medium. This was done in a satisfactory manner, and the committee then returned to the audience. The manager now led the blindfolded medium to the rear of the stage, where he was seated somewhat behind a table, on which were some flowers, a music box, etc. However, the medium was in view plainly; and he never removed the bandage from his eyes or in any manner molested it.

When the boy came on the stage directly from the front with the hat full of sealed envelopes, the manager placed a handkerchief over the hat and asked the boy to take a seat near the front of the stage facing the audience. He was also directed to hold the hat in his lap, and to deliver the envelopes to the manager, one at a time, as he should call for them.

The operator now delivered a lecture, lasting some ten or fifteen minutes, explaining the strange powers of the blindfolded medium, who sat at the rear of the stage in full view; while the boy still maintained the seat at the front of the stage, and held the hat of envelopes in sight of all.

After the lecture, the manager requested the boy to give him one of the envelopes, which the boy did. The manager did not look toward it in any manner; but took it in the tips of his right fingers, held it in the air, and asked the medium to give the writer of this question a test. The medium shivered a few times, allowed his frame to convulse slightly, and thus began:

"I feel the influence of one who was a brother. I get the name of Clarence. Will the one who wrote this question identify it as his?" There was no response from the spectators, and the medium asked again that the writer speak out. Still silence greeted his request; when suddenly he pointed his bony finger into the crowd, while his blinded face confronted them, and exclaimed: "Mr. John H——, why do you not respond to your test?" A gentleman in the audience then acknowledged the test as his. The medium then continued: "Clarence was drowned. I sense the cold chilly water as it envelopes his form." At this the lady sitting with the gentleman began to cry. The medium continued: "The drowning was wholly an accident. There was no foul play. Now, Mr. H——, have I answered your question, and are you satisfied with your test?" The gentleman, a well-known citizen, acknowledged that he was perfectly satisfied.

The manager then laid the envelope on a small table and asked the boy for another one. The boy gave him another from the hat when the blindfolded medium, ten feet or more distant, gave the second test.

He shivered again and began: "I feel the influence of a young lady who died suddenly. She says, 'Sister Mary, I am very happy, and death was not so hard to endure. I want you to consult a good honorable attorney, and take his advice in the lawsuit you ask me about.'" The medium then continued, " Miss L——, your sister regards you with a look of great tenderness and love. Are you satisfied with your test?" A lady then replied that she certainly was entirely convinced.

The manager now laid this sealed envelope beside the other one and again called for another. This was continued until all of the envelopes in the hat were removed and the questions answered. None of the envelopes were opened. In some instances the medium first read the questions, word for word, before answering them; and when he did so, he described the writing minutely, even the formation of the strokes of the letters.

After all of these tests were given, the medium removed the blindfold and seemed much exhausted. Then the tables were removed to one side of the stage, and a cabinet erected; after which some cabinet manifestations that were very interesting were given. When these were over, the manager collected the sealed envelopes from the table, and placed them on the front of the stage, inviting the writers to call, should they so desire, and get their questions. Some availed themselves of this opportunity and tore open a number of the envelopes until they found their own questions. The audience seemed greatly impressed with this exhibition, and the next day it was the talk of the town.

. . . . .

On the next evening I again repaired to the public hall to witness and, if possible, fathom this performance. This time, however, I found that an entirely different method was employed. Envelopes and slips of paper were distributed; and after the questions were written and sealed the manager went about the room, gathering them up in a small black bag with a drawstring around its top. As he gathered up each one, and while the writer still held it, he gave to that person a number which was to serve as that particular person's number during the tests. At the same time the manager marked the number on the subject's envelope, while the subject held it, drawing a circle around the figure, after which the subject dropped the envelope into the sack.

When all were collected, the operator took the sack in the tips of his fingers, and holding it aloft, walked up the runway to the stage where a cord hung from a screw-eye fastened in the ceiling above. The other end of the cord was attached to a piece of furniture on the stage. The manager now attached the black bag containing the envelopes to the end of this string, and then taking the other end, drew the bag up to the ceiling near the screw-eye, where it remained in full view during the tests.

While the manager was doing all this, the ghost-like medium had been walking about the stage, reading in a large Bible. He now laid the Bible on a table and advanced to the front of the stage, while the manager delivered a lecture on spiritual philosophy and also on the strange power of the medium. After this the manager announced that the medium would hold a Bible service, during which time he would give the tests.

The medium now took his Bible, and seating himself in a chair facing the audience, began by reading a verse. After this he closed his eyes for a time, and then gave the first test. He began: "I will give these tests in the order in which the manager gave you your numbers, commencing with number one. Now, Mrs. Clara S——, I see standing near you an elderly lady, somewhat stooped; but I cannot see her face plainly. She seems to be your mother. She says to tell you that your son is doing well where he is, and for you not to worry, for he will return to you in time. Are you satisfied?" A lady in the audience was visibly affected, and acknowledged that the medium had answered her question correctly. The medium read another verse in the Bible, after which he gave the second test in a manner similar to the way in which he had given the first one. After this he read another verse, and so continued until all the questions in the sack were answered. The manager now lowered the sack, and emptying the envelopes into a small basket distributed them unopened to their writers.

The effect of this exhibition was fully as great as was that of the former one, and the medium continued to be the wonder of the town.

. . . . .

On the next evening I again attended the meeting. On this occasion questions were written and sealed as on the former occasions. This time the medium was dressed as a "Mahatma," wearing a large turban. As soon as the questions were written, the manager collected them in a small wicker basket, and emptied them on a table on the stage. He only talked for a moment, describing what the medium would do. During all this time the medium was seated near the front of the stage. The medium now tapped a little bell he held in his hand, as if summoning the spirits, and began giving the tests in the most marvelous manner. He seemed somewhat nervous, and finally arose and walked across the stage, stopped a moment and then continued his walk. Meanwhile he kept giving the tests. Occasionally he would walk about nervously, and sometimes he would seat himself in the chair for a time; but he kept right on giving test after test, with perfect accuracy, while the sealed envelopes remained in full view on the table. During this time, and in fact during the time the audience was writing the questions, neither the medium nor the manager had ever left the sight of the spectators for even an instant.

After all the tests were given, the medium, very much exhausted, fell on a couch on the stage; while the manager scooped the envelopes back into the basket, and then distributed them to their writers in an unopened condition.

I will now explain how this "occultist" gave these various billet tests.

We will first refer to the tests given the first evening. A boy from the audience gathered up the sealed envelopes in a hat, and brought them to the stage, sitting with them in his lap; while he delivered one at a time to the manager, who held it aloft, during which time the blindfolded medium in the rear gave the test.

There was a simple little move that escaped the eyes of the spectators in this instance. The spectators did not know what was to happen, neither did the boy. The move was executed as follows: Just as the boy came on the stage with the hat the manager received the hat in his right hand and in a natural manner. Nothing was thought of this, as there was nothing suspicious in the act. Meanwhile the manager directed the boy to take a chair that sat to the left of the front of the stage, and to place it to the right side in front, facing the audience, and to take his seat thereon. Now, this conversation with the boy naturally occupied the attention of the spectators; and while the boy was executing the directions the manager turned to the table, which was somewhat back on the stage, and apparently took a large handkerchief from it, and with the hat still apparently in his hand, he stepped to the boy, giving him the hat of envelopes and the handkerchief, at the same time instructing him how to cover the hat, and how to deliver the envelopes one at a time. All of this maneuvering seemed so natural that the audience thought nothing whatever of it.

Now, as the manager turned to the table to get the handkerchief, and while most eyes were on the boy as he placed his chair and took his seat, the manager deftly exchanged the hat in his right hand for another hat just like it, that was filled with "dummy" envelopes and which was behind the flowers, music box, etc., on the table. As he immediately turned with the hat apparently still in his hand, but with a large handkerchief in his other hand, everything seemed natural and the audience thought nothing of the incident.

The manager now, after giving the boy the hat and handkerchief, invited a committee to come forward and blindfold the medium who had been seated at the left of the stage. The committee first placed a lady's glove on the eyes of the medium as an additional precaution, and then placed a handkerchief over this and tied it behind his head. This method of blindfolding is the one usually employed by most mediums. If the face of the medium be properly formed, he can easily shift such a bandage with his eyebrows, sufficiently to see directly under his eyes, by looking down alongside his nose. The committee now retired to the audience, and the performer led the medium to a seat behind the table.

Now, while the manager delivered the lengthy lecture, the medium quietly tilted over the hat of envelopes behind the objects on the table; and then taking one at a time, opened the envelopes and removed the cards, arranging the cards on top of each other like a pack of playing cards. The lecture lasted long enough for the medium to complete this task; and as he held the cards in his left hand, he could now move slightly to the right so that he was pretty well in view of the spectators. However, his left hand did not come into view.

By the time the lecture was completed, the spectators had entirely forgotten the fact that the manager ever received the hat from the boy at all. In fact, next day I noticed from the talk of the spectators, that they invariably asserted that the hat never left the boy's hands or their sight.

Now, while the manager held each envelope aloft, the medium had but to read the top card in his left hand and give the tests in a dramatic manner. After the tests, when the tables were set to one side and a cabinet erected, an assistant out of view received the cards from the medium's left hand; and then while behind the scenes, replaced them in envelopes, sealed them, and then exchanged these for the "dummy" envelopes on the small table. After the entertainment the manager placed the originals (now again sealed) near the front of the stage for the writers to take and keep as souvenirs if they should so desire.

It is evident that this method could be varied a little. For instance, when the manager holds the envelope aloft, the medium could first read it and carefully describe the writing. He could then ask for the envelope, so as to become en rapport with the writer, in order that he may give the correct answer. In this case he could leave the surplus cards on the back of the table behind the music box, and have in his left palm only the single card he is reading. When he receives the envelope he should place it in his left hand directly over the card and tear off the end of the envelope. He should then apparently take out the card from the envelope, but in reality take the original card from the rear of the envelope with his right hand. He should then with his right hand press this card on top of his head and give the answer, while his left hand lays the opened envelope on the table or music box. In this case, as soon as he answers the question, he should return the card to the manager with his right hand and ask the manager to have some boy run with it to its writer. After it is returned to its writer, the manager can hold aloft another envelope and the medium continue with the tests. After the tests, the manager should remove the torn envelopes, as they contain "dummy" cards.

I will now explain the method pursued on the second evening. After the questions were written and sealed, the manager went among the spectators collecting the envelopes in a cloth bag. He first numbered the envelopes, at the same time instructing each spectator to remember his number, after which the envelopes were dropped into the bag. When all the envelopes were collected, the manager lifted the bag in the tips of his fingers and ascended to the stage with it in plain view. He quickly attached it to the cord and drew it up to the ceiling. So far all was fair; but just at this moment a person in the rear of the hall made the statement that he desired to place his envelope in the bag also. The performer asked a gentleman on the floor to take the bag, which he now lowered and detached, and to kindly go to the gentleman and get his envelope. While he was doing this the manager held the audience by his discourse. The two gentlemen were, of course, paid confederates; and when they met behind the spectators, they merely exchanged the first bag for a duplicate under the coat of the rear confederate, who then slipped around behind the stage with the original.

When the other confederate returned to the stage with the duplicate bag and handed it to the manager he ran this one up to the ceiling. This method can be varied by the manager making the exchange under his own coat in the first place when in the rear of the hall after collecting the envelopes.

Meanwhile an assistant behind the scenes opened and copied the questions neatly on a sheet of paper, and NUMBERED EACH ONE. As he did this he slipped each one into a duplicate envelope, which was also numbered by the manager with a ring drawn around the figure. This he sealed. As soon as all were copied this assistant carefully drew the medium's Bible just out of sight from the table near the flies where it rested, inserted the sheet containing the copied questions, and pushed it back into view again.

During this time the medium was walking slowly about at the front of the stage while the manager delivered his lecture. At the close of the lecture the medium stepped back to the table where he had laid his Bible a short time before, picked it up and came forward taking a seat facing the audience. He next opened the Bible and turned the leaves over slowly, passing the sheet of paper and reading and memorizing the first question quickly. He then turned the leaves beyond this sheet of paper and finally selected a verse and began reading it impressively. As he read this verse he allowed the Bible to tilt forward sufficiently for the spectators to see that there was nothing like a loose sheet in it, should such an idea occur to anyone.

As he had turned over other pages after secretly reading the question, the sheet was hidden from view. After reading the verse he allowed the Bible to close, and then closing his eyes gave the test for number one. After this he again opened the Bible and turned the leaves through it slowly, read the second question secretly, and finally found a second verse, which he proceeded to read in a solemn tone, he then gave a second test, and so continued until all the tests were given. He then lay down very much exhausted, and the manager lowered the cloth bag containing the dummy envelopes, and emptied them upon a small table near the front of the stage. He then stepped to the rear of the stage and picked up a little wicker basket, into which he scooped the dummy envelopes from the small table where they lay in full view. He now descended and rapidly returned the unopened envelopes to their respective writers.

The basket is what is known as a "Billet changing basket." It is lined with red satin and is a small affair with straight sloping sides. It has a handle which, when down, locks two flaps up against the sides of the basket. This is done by two little projections on the base ends of the handle. They are of wire and are bent into such shape that they project downward when the handle is down, and hold the two side flaps up against the sides. These flaps are of pasteboard, and are covered with red satin the same as the basket lining. There is a spring in each flap which

91

closes it upon the bottom of the basket when it is released by raising the handle. Envelopes in the bottom of the basket are thus hidden and retained, when the flaps are released, and the duplicates drop into the basket, from the sides where they were concealed by the flaps.

This basket can be supplied by the conjuring depots, or it can easily be made. The handle can be made of wire and wrapped with raffia grass which is on sale at the department stores. A pasteboard lining covered with red satin must first be sewed into the basket, and then two flaps of pasteboard should be hinged to a pasteboard bottom by pasting on a hinge of cloth. A suitable spring can be made of spring wire and sewed into position, after which this is all covered with red satin and placed in the basket. The basket should have sides about four inches high, and the bottom should measure about seven and one-half by ten inches. The sides and ends slope outward, and the basket is open wicker work. Suitable bows of ribbon on the ends of the handle and corners of the basket conceal the mechanism.

In the present instance, the assistant behind the scenes, after reading and placing the questions in duplicate envelopes which the manager had previously numbered, sealed them and placed them in the sides of the basket, bent up the flaps into position, and lowered the handle locking them in place. He now pushed this basket into view on a table at the rear of the stage; and when the manager was ready to return the envelopes, he scooped the dummy envelopes from the table (where they lay after the bag was emptied) into this basket. He then lifted the handle which released the flaps, covered up the dummy envelopes and dropped the originals into view. These he took down and quickly distributed to the writers. Being numbered, this could be quickly done.

. . . . .

I will now describe the method employed on the third evening. This time dummy envelopes were placed in the sides of the basket, and the handle left in a lowered position while the operator gathered up the envelopes. As the manager returned to the stage he took the basket by the handle. This released the dummy envelopes, and covered up the originals retaining them. He emptied the dummy envelopes upon the small table and then laid the basket on a table near the flies in the rear, and rather out of view. An assistant behind the scenes took out the original envelopes, opened them, and as he read the questions repeated them into a small telephone. The wires from this telephone ran under the stage carpet to a pair of metal plates with a tack in the center of each plate which pointed upward. These plates were located under certain spots in the carpet and directly in front of the medium's chair. There were also two other pairs of wires leading to two other positions on the stage. The medium was dressed as a "Mahatma" on this evening, wearing a large turban. A large tassel dangled by his left ear, completely concealing a small "watch-case receiver" which was attached to this ear. Two tiny wires led from this receiver, inside his collar, down his person, and were connected inside his shoes to other wires which penetrated the soles of his shoes. These latter wires were soldered to copper plates which were tacked into position on his shoe soles. He now took his position in the chair and placed his feet over the hidden tacks, which now contacted his shoe plates, completing the circuit, so that anything whispered into the telephone on the stage was repeated in his ear. He then gave a few tests, tapping his spirit bell, which was a signal for more information from the assistant.

He soon grew nervous and walked away giving a test as he walked. He now paused in a certain position for a moment, placing his hand to his head as if somewhat dazed and tapping his bell. In this position his feet were again over two concealed tacks, and he again secured information for another test, which he gave as he walked about. He now paused in a third position and gave another test, after which he returned to the chair, continuing his work. This maneuvering he kept up until all the tests were given; after which he fell upon a couch exhausted, but with his feet from the spectators.

The manager now stepped to the rear of the stage and took the basket, which was now in place containing the original (?) envelopes behind the flaps; and stepping to the small table he scooped in the dummy envelopes; then taking the basket by the handles, he stepped down the runway and rapidly returned the unopened (?) envelopes to their writers. The assistant had, of course, sealed the questions in duplicate envelopes previously numbered by the manager. He had placed these behind the flaps, and shoved the basket into view on a table at the rear of the stage.

I use a variation of these tricks in my double parlors. I have made a "billet changing basket" as above described, and have also made a similar basket except that it contains no mechanism.

I pass cards and envelopes to the spectators in the front parlor. When the questions are written and sealed in the envelopes, I gather them up in the mechanical basket; I step to a table in the rear parlor and apparently empty them upon it. In reality, I have just raised the handle so that the originals are retained, and the dummy envelopes are emptied on the table instead.

I now step to an adjoining room for an instant, to get a small decorated screen. I secretly leave the basket containing the original envelopes in this room and return with the other basket in my hand in its place. I place the small ornamental screen on the table back of the envelopes, but leave the envelopes in view and request the spectators to notice that I do not go near them until I get ready to give the tests. I now carelessly lay the non- mechanical basket on a table in the room where the spectators are and proceed with some other tricks.

Usually I give the series of experiments described in the chapter entitled "Mediumistic Reading of Sealed Writings." I state to the spectators that I will not give the tests for the sealed envelopes until later in the evening.

Meanwhile, should anyone think of such a thing, he can easily examine the little basket, which he thinks I have just used; as it still lies on the table in the front parlor with other discarded paraphernalia, including slates, etc. I use no assistant; so after a time has elapsed, and when by the performance of other sealed readings, suspicion has been diverted from the tests with the billets, my wife retires on some trifling errand. While out, she opens the envelopes in the basket, prepares the sheet of questions, and places it in the Bible; then she re-seals the questions in envelopes previously marked by me, places them in the sides of the basket, raises the flaps and lowers the handle. She then usually enters with some light refreshments for the spectators, which explains her absence with a word.

I continue with other experiments for ten or fifteen minutes after her return; then I gather up my surplus paraphernalia, including the dummy basket, and carry all to the room adjoining the back parlor, where I leave it. I return instantly with the mechanical basket which I place near my own table; and then I give another experiment of some kind.

I now pick up the basket and announce that I have decided to return to their writers the envelopes on the table in front of the screen before attempting to give the tests. I do this as if it were a later notion. I now scoop in the dummy envelopes, and raise the handle, which action covers them up and releases the originals (now sealed). I now distribute to the writers their envelopes, which I can do, as they are numbered as described earlier in this chapter. I request each sitter to hold his envelope until I shall give his test. Then I usually perform some other little experiment before giving the tests.

I now take up my Bible, which I will stake I brought into the room, unnoticed, when I returned with the last basket. I then seat myself and leisurely turn the leaves through the Bible, reading verses, and giving the tests as before described.

I always first read a question secretly, and then turn by the sheet of paper and begin reading a verse of Scripture. As I do this I permit the front of the Bible to lower enough for the spectators to see the printed pages. This prevents suspicion. Meanwhile, the spectators have forgotten that I ever stepped from the room at all with the basket, and even that my wife retired for some refreshments. Neither did they notice the Bible when I brought it in.

The effect on each person, as I call him by name and describe the "influence" of his "dear one," giving names and most marvelous information, is far superior to what it would be were I merely to read the questions literally, and give the answers.

SOME FAMOUS EXPOSURES

Probably the greatest swindle ever perpetrated in the name of spiritualism was recently brought to light in Stockton, California. The medium and his confederates materialized everything from frogs and small fish to a huge bowlder of gold quartz weighing several hundred pounds. This latter had to be brought from the mountains with a mule team.

The materializing was done through sliding panels in the walls, while the believers sat holding hands about the opposite side of a table, and loudly singing sacred hymns. They had the only door to the room locked and sealed, and never dreamed that the spirits who brought the quartz from the mine were mules.

Thousands of dollars were invested in this "spirit mine," the believers stacking their money on the quartz as it lay on the table at a dark seance, and receiving deeds in return for their money, which the spirits dematerialized.

The medium established, or had his spirits establish, a "Treasury of Heaven," for the faithful to deposit their money in, and on which they were to receive fifty per cent interest. This interest the believers continued to receive at dark seances from the spirits for a time. Each sitter's interest was found on the table stacked in front of him when the lights were lighted. When the spirit bank became insolvent and the chief medium disappeared, the believers were out about thirty-five thousand dollars.

No less a personage than a millionaire of Tacoma, Washington, is said to have contributed largely to this spirit fund. I had known of this case for some time before the exposure (conducted by a performer engaged for the purpose), and knew that certain interested persons were contemplating bringing it about, in order to rescue certain estimable persons from the clutches of these mediums. This was successful; and the confederates of the medium signed written confessions in the presence of one of the most devout of the believers, and a gentleman who is otherwise very intelligent. Upon this the gentleman was greatly crestfallen, but he still insists that there are certain mediums who are not impostors; and that certain mediums in Chicago who produce spirit portraits are genuine.

A full and very interesting account of this exposure is given in the San Francisco Examiner of March 3 and 4, 1907.

. . . . .

I could report enough cases of materialization to fill a volume. These I know of, from various sources, and in every case they were invariably fraudulent. I will give a short account of a materialization which a very expert medium, who is on friendly terms with me, witnessed. The gentleman was originally a minister, and afterwards began investigating spiritualism, as he was a believer in it. He hoped to become a medium; and at one time paid two lady mediums of some renown, who reside in Chicago, three dollars a sitting for three sittings a week. These sittings were conducted for the purpose of developing this gentleman in mediumship. He continued this for a long time, but he was no nearer to being a medium than he was in the beginning.

At one time he detected one of the sisters passing a slate to the other, and substituting another in its place. He saw the edge of one of the slates protruding from behind the dress of one of the sisters. They never knew they were discovered as he said nothing, but this "opened his eyes." After this he investigated everywhere, and at every opportunity, and grew to be a very expert medium himself.

Recently, when in Los Angeles, he visited a seance conducted by a medium who claimed to be a Buddhist priest. This medium was known under the name of "The Reverend Swami Mazzininanda." He had an altar in his home, constructed something like those in Roman Catholic churches. He had various candles and images on this altar, including an image of Buddha, and also a number of mystical figures. It was a great mixture of "fake" Buddhism, Roman Catholicism, and modern spiritualism. The medium also wore the costume of a Buddhist priest at his seances.

This "priest" held services here for the faithful. He conducted all in Hindoostani (?), his native tongue. He chanted, prayed to Buddha, etc., all in a queer-sounding "gibberish." Certain evenings of the week were devoted to "soul-travel," and certain evenings after the religious services a "Black Chapter" was held.

The gentleman whom I have mentioned attended one of these dark seances. He sat with other spectators around the room in perfect darkness. The spectators were not required to hold hands, so great was their faith. Finally, in the darkness, a queer-looking, vapory, luminous form floated around in the air and paused in front of the spectators. My friend slipped down quietly on his knees, and gradually worked closer and closer to the luminous form, until he could detect that the vapor was a kind of luminous "cheese cloth." He did not desire to expose this "priest," but he desired to have the "priest" know that some one had discovered him. My friend accordingly took hold of the gauze and gave it a very slight downward jerk. He then immediately returned quietly to his seat.

There was an immediate pause in the discourse of the "priest," who had really been floating this form on the end of a stick. Everyone knew that something had happened, but no one but my friend knew what it was. The "priest" then said in his slow, peculiar, eccentric and measured tones, "I have received a very great shock; and I will be unable to continue further this evening." The next day, when in conversation with some of the "faithful," this "priest" stated in his peculiar manner of speaking, and with intense earnestness, that which follows: "Last night I received a very great shock. I was just in the middle of the 'Dark Chapter' and the spirit of the Master, Krishna, was out. Having spent the greater portion of my life on the Himalayas, my right eye has become injured by the snows." Then pointing to his right eye, he added, "My right eye has a defect in it which you cannot see; but on account of that, I can only see in the dark with it. I immediately turned my right eye downward and I looked! I distinctly saw a lady's hand reached out toward my robe in the darkness, and this hand took hold of it and jerked it lightly just like this." The "Reverend Swami" here illustrated, by slightly jerking his coat downward. It was very amusing to hear him, in great seriousness, relate this in his low and measured accents to his faithful followers.

Shortly after this, when the Los Angeles Herald was conducting a crusade against the numerous mediums of that city, and when it had an exhibit in its windows of the confiscated material of some of them, this "Buddhist priest" was arrested and imprisoned for some of his practices.

Hereward Carrington

More Tricks of "Spiritualists"

"MATTER THROUGH MATTER"

There is one very clever "test" that is sometimes performed which would seem to show that something of this sort IS accomplished. It is, however, nothing more than an ingenious trick, and this might be a good time to explain its modus operandi. The general effect of the illusion is this: The medium requests some one to assist him in an experiment in which he is going to attempt to pass "matter through matter." As the test is one in which a confederate might easily be employed, he is very careful to choose some person who is well known, or whose character is above all suspicion. If this were not so, the entire effect of the test would be lost upon the investigators. Having secured his assistant, he hands him, for examination, a solid steel ring, just large enough to slip on and off the hand and arm easily. The ring is perfectly solid, and may be examined by anyone desirous of doing so. When this part of the performance is finished, the medium and his sitter then join or clasp their right hands (as in handshaking), and the sitter is instructed not to release the hand for a single instant. To "make assurance doubly sure," however, the hands are fastened together in any way the sitters may desire; the hands being tied together with tape, e. g., and the ends of this tape tied and the knots sealed. The tape connects the wrists and the hands of the medium and his sitter, and this tying may be made as secure as possible. A piece of thick cloth is now thrown over the two hands and the lower part of the arms, concealing them from view. With his disengaged hand the medium now takes the iron ring and passes it up under the cloth, so as to bring it in contact with his own arm. He holds it there for some time, but ultimately snatches off the covering cloth, and reveals to the eyes of the astonished audience the ring- -now encircling his own arm—in spite of the fact that the ties are still in statu quo, and the sitter never let go his hold for an instant. The ties and the ring may again be examined, if desired, before the hands are separated.

This is an exceedingly effective test, and has every appearance of being genuine—indeed, it is hard to see where trickery can come in. The trick is one of the simplest imaginable, however, and is performed in the following manner:

The medium has provided himself with TWO rings exactly alike; one of these the audience is free to examine, the other the medium is wearing on his right arm, under his coat. When the two hands are clasped together, therefore, it is a simple thing for the medium, under cover of the enveloping cloth, to slip the duplicate ring down his sleeve, and on to his own hand, and that part of the "miracle" is accomplished! It remains only to explain what becomes of the first ring. The cloth thrown over the arms is very thick and stiff, as stated, and the inner side of this contains a double partition, or sort of bag, into which the medium slips the duplicate ring. The cloth may now be shown on both sides, without disclosing the ring, and the medium makes away with it as soon as possible, in order to avoid detection.

DECEPTION EXPLAINED BY THE SCIENCE OF PSYCHOLOGY

The object [of this passage] is to enable the reader to see, more easily, how it is that the watchful observer is deceived into believing that a thing is so, when in reality it is not, and vice versa; and also to give an idea of the various methods employed by the medium in order to accomplish his results.

I must first of all call the reader's attention to one or two rules which every conjurer learns at the commencement of his study, and which he learns to apply so constantly that it becomes second nature to him. The first is: Never let the eyes rest on the hand that is performing the "sleight," but always on the other hand, or on some object on the table or elsewhere, as this will have a tendency to draw the eyes of the audience to that point also. The sitters or audience will always look at the point closely watched by the magician—their eyes have a tendency to follow his, and wherever he looks, there will the onlooker look also. Needless to say, the magician makes use of this fact, and many tricks and illusions are dependent upon it for their successful accomplishment. Whenever the magician or medium looks intently at one hand, therefore, the OTHER hand should be watched, as it is a sure sign that THAT is the hand which is performing the trick.

Another fundamental rule that is observed by all sleight-of-hand performers is: Never to let an audience know beforehand what is to be done; i. e., the nature of the trick that it is intended to perform. If the spectator knew what was forthcoming, he would be on the lookout for movements of the performer at certain critical times—just at the periods when close observation is least wanted— and would quite possibly detect the performer in the act of executing certain movements which would show how the trick was performed. But not knowing what is coming, the spectator is unable to watch closely at the critical moment—not knowing what that moment is—and so is unable to detect the trick, his attention being diverted by the performer, just before this movement is made, to some other object or movement.

The methods of diverting the spectator's attention are various. There is the use of the eyes, as before shown. Then there is the spoken word, the performer telling the onlookers to observe some certain object or action, and the effect is to cause them to watch it, as they are told. They follow the line of least resistance. The combined effect upon the spectator of the spoken word and the eyes together is generally irresistible.

Another important factor is this: A performer should always let any suggestion, right or wrong, soak well into the spectator's mind before attempting to change it. This is for two reasons. In the first place, if the suggestion is correct, if, e. g., the performer really DOES place an object in his left hand, and it is shortly found to have vanished from that hand, he is annoyed by hearing some one say that he was not really sure it was there in the first place, as "it was covered up so quickly." If, on the other hand, the suggestion given was a false one, if, e. g., the performer says he has placed an object in his left hand, when, in reality, he has not done so but has palmed it in the right, then it is still necessary to allow a certain time-interval to elapse between the performing of the action which apparently placed the object in the hand, and the showing of the hand empty, for this reason. If the hand into which the object is supposedly placed is IMMEDIATELY shown empty, the natural conclusion of the sitter is that the object was not in reality placed there at all, but was retained in the other hand, which would be the fact. If, however, the performer allowed some time to elapse, between the action of placing the object in that hand (supposedly) and the showing of the hand empty, he, meanwhile, keeping his eyes fixed on the hand, suggesting to the sitters that the object IS there, and in every way acting as if it WERE there, the idea will gradually gain a firm hold on the minds of the spectators that the object is there, in reality, and they are correspondingly surprised to find it ultimately vanished. It is just such a knowledge of "the way people's minds work," as a friend once said to me, which enables the conjurer to deceive the public; and it is precisely the same cast of mind that the medium possesses. He is, in fact, a good judge of human nature.

Another fact that must be borne in mind is that, when once a spectator has seen a movement made two or three times in the same manner, he frequently "sees" the performer make that movement on another occasion, when the performer had, in reality, only STARTED to make the movement, and suggested the rest. Thus, if the performer throws a ball up into the air two or three times in succession, and on the fourth occasion merely pretends to throw it up, really retaining it in the other hand, the great majority of the spectators will really "see" the ball ascend into the air on the fourth occasion, and will so state, on being asked. We here depend upon association and habit.[1]

[1] A very similar illusion is mentioned by Professor Hyslop, v. Borderland of Psychical Research, Pp. 228-9, in which pellets were apparently placed in a box, really being palmed in the medium's hand.

Professor Jastrow summed up this portion of the psychology of deception very well when he said:[1]

[1] Fact and Fable in Psychology, pp. 124-5.

"He (the conjurer) must dissociate the natural factors of his habits, actually attending to one thing while seemingly attending to another; at the same time his eyes and his gestures and his 'patter' misdirect the attention to what is apparently the essential field of operation, but really only a blind to distract attention away from the true scene of action. The conjurer directs your attention to what he does not do; he does not do what he pretends to do; and to what he actually does, he is careful neither to appear to direct his own attention nor to arouse yours."

Prof. Max Dessoir, in a very fine article on "The Psychology of Conjuring," writes as follows: "By awakening interest in some unimportant detail, the conjurer concentrates that attention on some false point, or negatively, diverts it from the main object, and we all know the senses of an inattentive person are pretty dull. . . . When causing the disappearance of some object, the conjurer counts one, two, three; the object must really disappear before three, not at three, because, the attention of the public being diverted to three, they do not notice what happens at one and two. . . . A specially successful method of diversion is founded on the human craze for imitation. . . . The conjurer counts on this in many cases. He always looks in the direction where he wants the attention of the public, and does everything himself which he wants the public to do. . . . If the trick is in the left hand, the conjurer turns sharply to the person to his right, presuming correctly that the spectators will make the same movement, and will not notice what is going on in the left hand. . . . Every sharp, short remark will, for a moment, at least, divert the eyes from the hands and direct them to the mouth, according to the above-mentioned law of imitation."

The successful conjurer has carefully studied beforehand every movement that is made— every word that is spoken—during a conjuring performance, and has seen that these all fit naturally into place, and help conceal the real workings of the trick. The right and left hands must be trained to operate independently, and without the need of looking at either. Many conjurers practice doing two separate things at the same time, one with either hand; and the ability to do this is essential. Above all, the performer must be full of conscious self-possession, and feel himself to be master of the situation, no less than to feel the ability to cope with any emergencies that may arise.

Turning, now, to a consideration of the seance, we find that many of these psychological rules still hold good, and their operation enables the medium to perform many actions which would otherwise be impossible. A certain suggestion is given to the sitters, and imagination and inference do the rest. "Our conclusions as to what we see or hear are always founded on a combination of observation and inference; but in daily life it is seldom necessary to distinguish between the two elements, since, when the object and its mode of presentation are familiar, our inferences are generally correct. But it is different when, owing to circumstances, such as a bad light, we have to infer more in proportion to what we perceive than usual; or when some one, e. g., a conjurer or a ventriloquist, is trying to deceive us by presenting one object under the familiar aspect of another, and suggesting false inferences. It is not uncommon to find people at seances encouraging each other in the belief that they see, say, a living human figure, when all that they actually SEE is something moving which is about the size of a human being; the rest is inference." How true these last remarks are is demonstrated by the statement, made in The Revelations of a Spirit Medium, that an old wire mask frequently used at materializing seances had been recognized "by dozens of persons as fathers, mothers, sisters, brothers, cousins, sweethearts, wives, husbands, and various other relatives and friends. None but the medium knew that it was only a fifty-cent wire mask, hence none but the medium could enjoy the humor of the occasion."

One of the most instructive incidents I know, in relation to this question of the psychology of deception, is the one given by Doctor Hodgson[1]—the case of the officer and the Hindu juggler. In this case, a trick was performed before an English officer and his wife, and Doctor Hodgson happened to overhear this officer telling some travelers of the experience at dinner that evening. "Referring to the movements of the coins, he said that he had taken a coin from his own pocket and placed it on the ground himself, yet that this coin had indulged in the same freaks as the other coins. His wife ventured to suggest that the juggler had taken the coin and placed it on the ground, but the officer was emphatic in repeating his statement, and appealed to me for confirmation. He was, however, mistaken. I had watched the transaction with special curiosity, as I knew what was necessary for the performance of the trick. The officer had apparently intended to place the coin upon the ground himself, but as he was doing so, the juggler leaned slightly forward, dexterously and in a most unobtrusive manner received the coin from the fingers of the officer, as the latter was stooping down, and laid it close to the others. If the juggler had not thus taken the coin, but had allowed the officer himself to place it on the ground, the trick, as actually performed, would have been frustrated.

[1] Proceedings Society for Psychical Research, Vol. IV., pp. 385-6.

"Now I think it highly improbable that the movement of the juggler entirely escaped the perception of the officer; highly improbable, that is to say, that the officer was absolutely unaware of the juggler's action at the moment of its happening; but I suppose that, although an impression was made on his consciousness, it was so slight as to be speedily effaced by the officer's IMAGINATION of himself as stooping and placing the coin upon the ground. The officer, I may say, had obtained no insight into the modus operandi of the trick, and his fundamental misrepresentation of the only patent occurrence that might have given him a clew to its performance debarred him completely from afterwards, on reflection, arriving at any explanation. Just similarly, many an honest witness may have described himself as having placed one slate upon another at a sitting with a medium, whereas it was the medium who did so, and who possibly effected at the same time one or two other operations altogether unnoticed by the witness."

In reading through descriptions of slate-writing seances, we very seldom find the statement made as to WHO placed the slates on the table, or under the table, etc., generally the account reading "the slates were then placed on the table," without any qualifying statement as to WHO placed them there. Accounts of this kind are absolutely worthless, from an evidential standpoint. We must at once ask ourselves: who placed the slates in that position? and if it was the medium— as it probably was in the vast majority of instances—then that test, in all probability, ceases to have any evidential weight. Anyone can read over a number of accounts of slate-writing performances, and verify these statements, if he chooses to do so. Frequently, the statement is made that the sitter did actually place the slate on the table, when in reality the medium did so. This error is quite unconscious on the sitter's part, of course, but the account is falsified, nevertheless. Mistakes of this kind are very common, the sitter thinking afterwards that he (the sitter) MUST have placed the slates on the table himself!

It will be seen from the above that there is a great difference between what ACTUALLY transpired, at any given seance, and what the accounts SAY transpired. The general public cannot get that all- important fact too strongly rooted in its mind: that the events which transpired at a seance may not be reported accurately, so that the report of the seance may be altogether wrong and erroneous, though the sitters, and those who drew up the report, may have been thoroughly honest in their belief that the report is accurate in every respect. The effect of all this is very great indeed. Many spiritualistic seances are quite inexplicable AS DE- SCRIBED, but the description is not a true report of what took place at the seance in question. The facts are distorted. Consequently, the person taking it upon himself to explain what took place at the seance is called upon to explain a number of things which, in reality, never took place at all. We must remember, in this connection, that a number of conjuring tricks, AS DESCRIBED, would be quite impossible to explain by any process of trickery. The description of the trick was not correct.

Let me make this still clearer, and at the same time illustrate the difference between what apparently occurs, and what actually happens, by the following example: A conjurer places a coin (say a quarter) in each hand, and closes his hands. Another quarter is now placed upon the fingers of each hand, so that there is now one quarter in each hand and one-quarter on the fingers of each. The magician announces that, by simply opening and closing his hands— which are held at some distance from each other—he will thereby transfer one of the coins from one hand to the other, so that there will be three coins in one of the hands, and only one left in the other.

Now, if the sitter were writing out an account of what happened, it would most certainly read as follows:

"The magician then tried the experiment—of opening and closing his hands rapidly, and causing the coin to be transferred, as promised— but failed in the attempt, the coins from the back of each hand falling on to the table in rather a clumsy manner. They were, however, again placed upon the backs of the magician's hands; the movement was repeated, and this time successfully. The coins disappeared from the backs of both hands, in one of which was now found three of the coins, while the other hand contained only one."

Such is precisely the description of the trick, as it would be given by the average person, on seeing it, and it would represent his honest opinion of what occurred; as it stands, it is quite inexplicable by trickery. Needless to say, the account is NOT a true statement of what actually occurred, as the following explanation will make clear:

The first time the coins were dropped on to the table, the movement was not so "clumsy" as might have been supposed. It was, in fact, intentional, being the principal factor in the accomplishment of the trick. What ACTUALLY transpired at that time was this: The magician, by a quick movement, dropped both coins from ONE hand on to the table, at the same time dexterously opening the other hand a trifle, and allowing the second coin, on that hand, to fall into the interior of the hand itself. Thus, while both hands are still seen to be closed, one is empty, and the other contains two coins. It is obvious, therefore, that, when a coin is placed upon each of the hands again, the magician has only to repeat the opening and closing movement, and there will be three coins in one of the hands, and only one in the other.

This trick illustrates, in a very simple and striking manner, the possibility of reporting a fact in an entirely erroneous manner, quite unconscious of the fact that this error in reporting has been committed. Just in this same manner, are many slate-writing and other phenomena misreported, and hence an explanation of the seance, AS REPORTED, is rendered impossible. The trouble is that the "report" does not REALLY report what actually occurred.

. . . . .

Many of my readers may feel somewhat insulted at this accusation that they cannot detect such obvious trickery when it exists, and that they are liable to make such mistakes in recording a seance as those here mentioned. They may comfort themselves with the thought, however, that it is no disgrace to make mistakes and errors of this kind; for, as Professor Jastrow pointed out:[1]

[1] Fact and Fable in Psychology, p. 148.

"The matter is in some aspects as much a technical acquisition as in the diagnosticating of a disease. It is not at all to the discredit of anyone's powers of observation or intellectual acumen to be deceived by the performances of a conjurer; and the same holds true of the professional part of mediumistic phenomena. Until this homely but salutary truth is impressed with all its importance upon all intending investigators, there is little hope of bringing about a proper attitude toward these and kindred phenomena."

These remarks will make it clear to us why many men of science have been deceived by very simple tricks and fraudulent devices, while investigating spiritualistic phenomena—their scientific culture is no guaranty that they are any more capable of detecting fraud than is the man-in-the-street—in fact their training has made them very much LESS capable of detecting fraud than the average person, who comes more in contact with the world, and is an acuter judge of character and human nature.

Anonymous

How Spirits Materialize

From "The Revelations of a Spirit Medium"—a book out of existence now, since the plates and all copies were bought up by "spiritualists" and destroyed. The following is given by courtesy of Mr. Hereward Carrington:

Reader, have you ever attended a "seance" for "full-form materialization?" Have you ever thought you had met your dead relative's spirit at these "seances"?

If you have never had the pleasure of attending a seance of this "phase" you have missed a rare treat. The writer has assisted at many a one and will relate to you some of the wonderful phenomena occurring at them and the means used to produce them. . . . There are hundreds of "materializing mediums" doing business in this country, who are swelling a good-sized bank account. Their business sometimes runs into the hundreds of dollars in a single week. This "phase" of mediumship is considered by the spiritual- ists as the highest possible attainable, and if you are a clever "full-form medium" your financial welfare is assured. . . . Many and various are the methods employed by the different "mediums" in producing this phase. It is in Boston, New York, and San Francisco that it is worked the finest. The full-form seances most often met with are very simply worked, and easy of performance by the medium. You are usually given a seat in a circle of chairs about the front of a "cabinet" made by hanging heavy curtains across the corner of the room. If you are a stranger or one who looks or acts as though he would "grab" the "spirits," you are seated at the farthest point from the cabinet; or, if there are two rows of seats, you will be given a seat in the back row. . . .

I made my way to the "materializing seance," at which my friends hoped to materialize. I was admitted to the seance room and found about twenty persons already assembled. I was seated in the front row of chairs. The cabinet used was a closet about six feet long and four feet wide. The ceiling of both the room and the cabinet was of wood. After a thorough examination had been made of the cabinet by all those who cared to do so, the sitters were rearranged to suit the medium. There were present now thirty-five persons. The seance room was very large. The door had been taken off the closet that served as a cabinet, and in its stead were hung heavy curtains. The floor of the room was carpeted with a dark carpet, as was the cabinet. The light was furnished by a lamp placed in a box that was fastened to the wall some eight feet from the floor. This box had a sliding lid in front, controlled by a cord passing into the cabinet. By this means the "spirits" could regulate the light to suit themselves, without any movement on the part of any of those in the seance room being necessary. When everything was in readiness the medium entered the cabinet, seated himself and was tied, and so secured to his chair that it was impossible that he could have any use of himself. He was most thoroughly secured to his chair, and his chair nailed fast to the floor by passing leather straps over the rounds in the side and nailing the ends to the floor. After it was shown to the sitters that he was utterly helpless, the curtain was drawn. The manager now placed an ordinary kitchen table in front of the door of the cabinet, so that it stood away from it about two feet. The table contained no drawer. On the table was laid writing materials, a guitar, and small bell. The manager seated himself close to one side of the cabinet entrance, and started a large Swiss music box. Before it had finished the first air the lamp was shut entirely off, making the room inky dark.

An illuminated hand and arm was now seen to come from behind the curtain, and played an accompaniment to the music box on the guitar. We could see plainly the movements of the hand, arm, and fingers, as it manipulated the strings of the instrument. It did not appear necessary to finger the strings on the keyboard, although the air was in a key that made it impossible to tune the guitar so that an accompaniment could be performed WITHOUT fingering. However, but one hand was visible, and it was picking the strings. After the tune was finished, the hand left the in- strument, and moved out into the room to the front of the table, and from the sound we knew it was writing on the tablet that had been placed there. The arm was of bluish light and appeared to end just above the elbow, and to have no connection with the body. It finished writing and seemed to float into the cabinet near the top.

The light was opened and the manager requested those who had tied the medium to examine his condition and see if the ropes had been tampered with. The examination was made and it was evident that the fastenings were undisturbed. The communication was read aloud to those present, and contained the following:

"We are pleased to meet so many seekers after light and truth here this evening, and, from the conditions, as we sense them, we will have a satisfactory and pleasant seance. The way to obtain the best results is for each person to maintain a passive condition and take what we have to give. You may rest assured that our best efforts will be put forth to give you entire satisfaction. The Control."

The writing was exactly on the ruled lines although written in absolute darkness. The hand and arm, although luminous, did not give out a particle of light. The arm had been at least five feet from the cabinet opening and seven feet from the medium. Surely, it was not he. The message read, the light was again shut down and the music again started.

Once more a hand appeared, and floating out to the table, again began writing. Of a sudden the hand disappeared, and, after a few seconds, I was astonished to feel a hand thrusting a paper into my top coat pocket. Now appeared two hands and they played an air on the guitar. Now came three, then four hands were visible, bright as the day. Two of them began writing again, and, when they had finished, two more sitters were the recipients of sheets of paper. Soon the light was opened for an inspection of the cabinet, which was made, with the conclusion that the medium had not moved. Those of us receiving communications were afforded an opportunity to read them. We found them nicely written, as before, and all contained "tests." . . .

After the light went out again, more hands were seen; the table was floated about over the heads of the circle, as was the music box, which weighed at least fifty pounds. Another examination of the cabinet was made and everything found satisfactory. This time the light was not put entirely out, but a very dim light was allowed.

The music box was again set playing, and, while yet it was playing the first tune, a tall figure, robed in creamy white, with gleaming sparks in her hair, and on her head a sort of crown, issued from the cabinet. She was recognized by a gentleman present, a spiritualist, whose spirit guide she was, and who addressed her as "my queen." She stood a few seconds behind the table and then stepped out in the open space between the sitters and the table. The gentleman now arose from his seat and, standing beside her, holding her hand, conversed in a whisper with her for some seconds.

This was most assuredly a lady, if appearances go for anything. Her hands were quite small, and were warm and lifelike, as several, including myself, can testify, having been permitted to shake hands with her. At last she started to the cabinet, and, as she went, appeared to grow shorter, until, as she disappeared between the curtains, she was not much taller than the table. The manager now explained that the spirit had remained out rather too long and came near dematerializing before she reached the cabinet. Now came the spirit of a young man, dressed in a light suit of clothes, who gave his name and said his mother was present. She was, and had a few words of conversation with him when he disappeared into the cabinet. The lady said that it was unmistakably her son; but there was SOMETHING that was not as he had been, but what it was she was unable to describe.

The next spirit to present itself was my son Eddie. He came out from the cabinet calling "Papa, papa." The manager asked "Who is your papa?" and he replied, "Mr. (Smith)." All this time he stood between the table and the cabinet, and only his head and shoulders could be seen. The manager told him to step out where he could be seen, when he came around to the front of the table.

It was rather dark, but I could swear it was my son. He was just the right size, with long flaxen hair and a very pale face. He wore a light-colored waist and darker knee-breeches and stockings, with a large black bow at his throat, Just as I remember seeing him last in health.

103

While Eddie was still standing in front of the table a large man came out and took him by the hand. Eddie spoke, saying:

"Must I go back, grandpa?" The form turned toward me, saying:

"My son, this is a great pleasure to us, but we must not long remain, as it is our first attempt at materializing." He turned to go when the manager said to him:

"If the gentleman is your son you ought to give him your name."

"The name of the child is Eddie, and my own is J. A. Smith," replied the form, as they vanished into the cabinet.

The manager suggested that it would be well to examine and see whether the medium had been out or not. The cabinet was examined and everything found satisfactory.

Spirit after spirit came from the cabinet, one or two at a time for an hour; some of them came to friends, and others were "controls" of the medium. Many of them were recognized by different ones of the sitters in the room. I, for one, could swear to the identity of my own son Eddie, while my father was plainly recognizable. . . .

The room was again made dark. Suddenly there appeared on the floor, in front of the table, a light about as large as a baseball. It moved about in a circle of perhaps a foot in diameter and grew larger. It soon lost the shape of a ball and appeared to be a luminous cloud. Seemingly we could see into and through it. In the course of thirty seconds it had become as large as a six-year- old child; still there was no definite shape, only a fleecy cloudlike mass, turning, twisting, and rolling. At the end of perhaps a minute it was the size and shape of an adult person. The face could not be seen, but light, luminous spots were visible as though the hair and ears were decorated with gems. The shape spoke and requested light. As the light was turned on the luminousness disappeared, and we beheld a beautiful young lady clothed in a dazzling white costume. Her arms and shoulders were bare, and about her neck there was a necklace of what appeared to be very brilliant diamonds. Her feet were encased in white slippers, with straps across the instep. In her ears and hair glistened and shimmered beautiful diamonds. Her face and arms were as alabaster, and altogether she was one of the most beautiful women I had ever beheld. She was recognized by a lady and gentleman present as their daughter. They had met her here before. They were from the East, and were wealthy. The spirit requested that they come to her, which they did, and were each kissed and embraced by it. They held a moment's conversation with her and resumed their seats, when the lamp was slowly turned down. As the light became dim the spirit became luminous. The face and arms disappeared and the body became as a cloud again, turning and twisting and growing smaller until it was nothing but a small light spot on the carpet, which of a sudden disappeared entirely.

Immediately after this manifestation an examination of the medium and cabinet was made, and it was certain the medium had not been away from his chair. The light was again turned out and the music box started, when TWO bright spots appeared on the carpet, one at either end of the table. These went through the same process of development until, when the light was turned on, there was another beautiful female spirit at one end of the table, and a child of perhaps eight years of age at the other. The child was recognized by a lady present as her daughter, while the adult spirit was recognized and rapturously greeted by a gentleman who sat near me on my left, as his "darling angel guardian." They had quite a long conversation, in which they made use of very endearing language, each to the other. I supposed it was the gentleman's wife. . . .

The spirits did not disappear as the first one had, but, when the light had been turned off, the luminous shape revolved a few times, and on two occasions assumed the garb and shape of men, and when the light was turned on again, there stood the men with beards and men's forms. After some eight or ten of these materializations and dematerializations, before our eyes, the last couple completely disappeared.

The light was again turned down and a luminous shape came from the cabinet, followed by others, until seven of them stood on the floor. The light was turned up until we could see the seven spirits. Five were females and two males. They were of different sizes. The curtain at the door of the cabinet was pulled aside and we could see the medium sitting in the chair in which he was bound. The forms now filed into the cabinet again, while the music box played. After they had disappeared the light was turned up, an investigation made of the cabinet, and the seance was over.

There, reader, is a truthful description of what can be witnessed at the seances of mediums who are artists. None of your bungling, amateur work here. The work of such a medium is always satisfactory for the reason that if a man feels SURE that the medium is a fraud, he has been so well entertained that he does not regret the money paid for the opportunity to witness it. This is the class of medium also who frequently succeed in getting large sums of money from wealthy persons they have converted to spiritualism.

Did the writer not give you the true explanation of the manner in which these things were produced, you would probably say it was conceived by a very fertile imagination. If you believed that he saw these things you would perhaps offer the preacher's explanation, by saying, "it is the work of the devil"; or that of the scientist, by asserting that "it is the mesmerist's power over your mind"; or "the operator has discovered an odd force in nature"; or go off on a long dissertation on hypnotism and fourth dimension of space problems. However, it is not the work of the devil, neither are there any but NATURAL laws necessary to its production.

The seance described actually occurred and was described in writing by Mr. Smith in the language used, although it was not printed, and the writer was one of those who assisted in its production. He will now proceed to explain this particular seance. . . .

It will be remembered that the room and cabinet were carpeted with a dark carpet, and that the ceilings were of wood. The ceilings were decorated by being put on in panels. The ceiling of the cabinet would not have been like that of the room had the closet been a part of the architect's plans of the house. It was not, but was made by the medium. He simply built a lath and plaster partition from the corner of a wide chimney to the wall, thus inclosing a space of six by four feet. The panel in the ceiling of the closet was twenty inches square. This panel was "doctored" and could be displaced, leaving an aperture large enough for the "spooks" to get through with perfect ease. A light ladder which reached within three feet of the floor of the cabinet was hooked fast above and furnished the means of getting down and up again. There were eight persons connected with the seance described by Mr. Smith, seven upstairs and the medium in the cabinet. Of course it was not necessary that the medium get out of his fastenings, and the facts are that he did NOT. The table was placed across the cabinet door, not to lay the instruments on, but to be very much in the way should anyone make a rush and "grab" for the materialized forms. In case this occurred, the "spooks" above would close the light, making the room perfectly dark, and the manager would do his utmost to turn the table on end, or side, with the legs out in the room. Before the "grabber" could get the lay of things and get past it, the spooks would have gone through the trap, closed it, pulled up the ladder, and the "grabber" would have found the medium writhing and groaning and bleeding from the mouth. The bleeding was for effect, and was caused by sucking very hard on his teeth or gums.

The table also served a convenient purpose in the materialization and dematerialization through the floor. You now know where the spooks came from, in this particular house, and how they got in and out. Now let us see how they managed the materializations, and the properties used to produce them. The trap and ladder were practically noiseless in their operations, but the music box made assurance doubly sure that the least sound from the cabinet should not he heard in the seance room.

When the box began its first air the trapdoor was opened and down the ladder came a young man clad in a suit of black tights. He was entirely covered with black with the exception of his right arm, which was bare to a point a little more than halfway from the elbow to his shoulder. The bare arm glowed with a luminous bluish light.

This condition of things was brought about by powdering his arm with pulverized luminous paint. If you are not told the method of transforming the sticky paint to powder, you will not be able to do it, and will conclude the writer was romancing in this case. The most essential thing to you will be to know where you can procure this paint. The writer has been unable to procure it anywhere, except of Devoe & Co., of New York City. It is put up in a package resembling six-ounce jelly glasses, and you will get six of them for five dollars. In order to reduce it to powder, thin the contents of one of the glasses with one pint of turpentine. When it is thoroughly cut and incorporated into the turpentine, soak strips of muslin in it and hang them out to dry. When thoroughly dry you can shake the powder from the cloth. In order to powder one of your arms, gather one of the cloths in your hands, and use it as a powder puff on your arm. You will not be able to get all the paint out, but the pieces will make luminous crowns, slippers, stars, and luminous decorations for your robes. You will be under the necessity of perfuming your robes each time they are used, for the odor of the turpentine will always remain to a greater or less degree. To illuminate a robe or costume (the mediums always say "robe") you proceed the same as in the powdering process, except that to the pint of paint you will add a wineglass full of Demar varnish, which will prevent its falling or being shaken off as powder. You are not to make the robe of muslin, but of white netting. Every lady will know what netting is. It is the lightest, thinnest material the writer ever saw sold in a dry goods store. Ten yards of it can be put into the vest pocket. Do not scrimp the material, but get as much of it into your robe as possible.

When he of the luminous arm steps from the cabinet into the dark room no part of him is visible save the arm. He picks the strings of the instrument with the illuminated hand and fingers the keyboard with the other. He makes a sound of writing on the tablet and tears off a leaf which he conceals, and, drawing a long black stocking over the luminous arm, places in the pocket of the sitter a communication that has been written upstairs in a good light. This accounts for the even, beautiful writing, supposed to have been done in the dark. He covers the luminous arm so that anyone so inclined could not locate it in order to "grab" when he is near enough. By mounting the table, that luminous hand and arm can be made to show as though it was floating about near the ceiling.

When four hands were visible there were two spooks at work with both arms illuminated. . . . You can readily understand the forces that floated the music box and table above the heads of the sitters, and an explanation is useless.

When the first female spirit appeared it was, in reality, a young woman, dressed in a gorgeous white costume without paint, hence the light was turned up instead of down, in order that she be visible. Rhinestones and Sumatra gems being cheap, she was plentifully supplied with "diamonds," although many of those who are the queens or spirit guides or "controls" of wealthy spiritualistic fanatics wear real diamonds, the gift of their wealthy charge, or "king" as they usually call him.

When she started for the cabinet she used her hands to keep her robe from under her feet, and as she went stooped lower and lower, until, as she disappeared in the cabinet, she went on her hands and knees. This is what caused the appearance of "dematerialization."

When Mr. Smith's son, Eddie, came from the cabinet, he was represented by a boy of about eight years of age, the son of one of the female "spooks" upstairs. He receives two dollars a night for his services, the same as the larger spooks. He was powdered until he was very white, a blond wig put over his own hair, and dressed as most boys are at the age Mr. Smith's son died. Mr. Smith recognized him by his size, his light complexion, and flaxen hair, and the fact that he called him "papa" and gave his correct name. His father was "made up" from the description given by the medium, and acknowledged by Mr. Smith as correct. Of course he knew his own name, for it was given him by the slate-writer. . . .

We now come to a part of the phenomena that all spiritualists who have witnessed it will swear by. What is referred to is the materializing and dematerializing of the spirit from the floor and before your eyes. In this you see first a small light, which grows larger and larger, until there stands before you a fully formed female or male spirit, as was described in Mr. Smith's experience.

In order to accomplish what he witnessed, the same spook who had before been recognized by a gentleman as "his queen," prepared herself in the following way: Divesting herself of all clothing she donned simply a long chemise that reached her shoe tops. She drew on a pair of white stockings, and over them a pair of white slippers. Into her hair and ears she put rhinestone diamonds, and around her neck a necklace of the same beautiful but valueless stones. On each ear lobe and around her neck were put small spots of the luminous powder to represent the diamonds while it was dark. Her face was powdered and her eyebrows and eyelashes darkened, while a dark line was drawn under each eye. She now took a black mask that covered her head, and her "robe" in her hands, and went down to the cabinet. Arriving there, she put the black mask over her head, to prevent the luminous diamonds being seen until the proper time. She carried her robe in a black bag. Crawling from between the curtains and under the table, she exposed on the floor a small part of her robe. This she shook and moved about, allowing it to escape from the bag until it was all out. She was now from under the table and on her knees, and it was time the head show on the form, so, getting close to the robe, she threw off and under the table the black mask. The shape was now the size of an adult; she adjusted the robe to her person, and rapped for light. As a matter of course, when any light was made the luminousness of the robe was drowned, and she appeared in simply a white costume. The necklace and eardrops could now be seen, but when the light was such as to reveal them, the luminous spots had disappeared, leaving the spectator to think the ones he now saw were the ones he had seen in the dark. The process of dematerialization will now be apparent, and a description will only tire the reader. One small spook was all that was required, as he could be made to represent boy or girl as was desired, by clothing him in the garments of either sex.

At the close of the seance, the full force of "spooks" came into the room. After disappearing, they shinned up the ladder, drew it after them, closed the panel and the trap in the floor above it, replaced the carpet and pushed over the place a heavy bedstead from which they took the castors. They now carried the ladder downstairs and concealed it in the coal house as they went through it on their way home. They will get their pay next day.

Should ever so close an examination of the cabinet be made, you would not find anything wrong. This particular medium has taken investigators into the cellar beneath the cabinet, and the room above it, scores of times, yet nothing was discovered.

You are not always to search for the trap in the ceiling, nor yet in the floor. A trap is not possible in the ceiling except a closet is used as "cabinet," and the ceiling is of wood. Where this condition of things does not exist, you must search elsewhere. The floor is a very likely place when it cannot be made in the ceiling. If you do not find it there, examine the base or mopboard. If it is in the mopboard you will find, upon examination, that there is a joint in it near the corner of the cabinet, but you will find it solidly nailed with about four nails each side of the joint. This appearance of extraordinary solidity will be absolute proof that it is NOT solid.

The nails are not what they appear, but are only pieces about one half inch in length, and do not even go through the board. The piece is fastened on the other side with a couple of bolts that hold it very firmly in place. There is a corresponding opening in the mopboard in the next room, although no attempt is made to so carefully conceal it, as no one is ever admitted to it. Through this trap the "spooks" enter the cabinet by crawling and wiggling. It is not a very desirable trap, for the mopboard is scarcely ever wide enough to permit of a trap that the spook could get through in a hurry; besides, they must assume their costumes after they get into the cabinet or tear them to pieces. You can see how this would make it very inconvenient.

If the room is wainscoted the spook will have all the sea room necessary in his trap, for it will extend from just below the molding on the top of the wainscoting to the floor behind the strip of quarter-round. . . .

It is next to an impossibility to detect these traps by examining in the cabinet. They were constructed to avoid discovery, and no pains spared to make them so absolutely perfect that not one chance in a million is taken. The proper place to seek for traps is in the adjoining room, upstairs, or in the cellar. One is foolish to undertake to find a trap by thumping the walls or floor; for, if you happen to thump one, the medium who is smart enough to make use of a trap is also sharp enough to make provision for its being thumped, and your sounding method goes for naught.[1] Bear in mind that when you are examining the cabinet, you are seeking at the very place that is prepared most effectually to withstand your investigations. . . . Do not forget the MANAGER in your search. He or she is never searched, or never has been up to date, which has been the cause of many a failure to find the "properties" of the medium when the seance was given in a room and cabinet furnished by a stranger and skeptic. Do not be deceived into a belief that all of the sitters are strangers to the medium. There may be from one to five persons present who pay their money the same as yourself, and who may appear to be the most skeptical of anyone in the room. They will generally be the recipients of some very elegant "tests," and weep copiously great grief-laden tears when they recognize the beloved features of some relative.

[1] It must be remembered that it is occasionally possible for the medium to do away with traps altogether, either by having a con- federate in the audience who produces all the phenomena—the medium sitting bound meanwhile—or by some such simple device as the following: Suppose the seance room is closed at one end by a pair of folding-doors; these doors are locked, the key kept by a member of the audience, while the keyhole is sealed, and strips of

gummed paper are also stretched across the crack between the doors, sealing them firmly together. Confederates enter the room, in this case, by merely pushing BOTH doors to one side, they being so constructed that this is possible. A small space is now left around the end of ONE door, through which the medium's confederate creeps!

They are the most careful of investigators, and, when the medium's trap is located in the door-jamb, will pound the walls, and insist on the carpet being taken up, when they will get upon their hands and knees and make a most searching examination of the floor. They are the closest and most critical of investigators, but they are very careful to examine everywhere EXCEPT WHERE THE DEFECT IS LOCATED. Because one or two men seem to be making such a critical investigation, do not allow that fact to prevent you making one on your own responsibility. Wait until they have finished and then examine not only where they did, but more particularly where they did NOT. Their examination is only for the purpose of misleading others. Their "tests" are received in a way to cause those about them to think they admit them very unwillingly, or because they were so undeniable that they could do nothing else.

A great many will probably deny that confederates are ever employed. They are not, by mediums who are not smooth enough to produce that which appears so wonderful as to make a good business for them. The writer would advise those mediums who give such rank seances to employ a few floor workers (they are easily obtained), and see what a difference it would make in the amount of business they will do. Get good ones, those who know human nature, and know when they have said all that is necessary. Most of them are inclined to say too much, thus causing the ordinary man to suspect that they are confederates.

Printed in the USA
CPSIA information can be obtained
at www.ICGtesting.com
LVHW091030031124
795564LV00008B/446

9 781522 951544